"DON'T YOU DARE WALK AWAY FROM ME!"

When he made no move in her direction, Darcy lifted her skirts and one foot. In the next instant, she slipped and landed on her bottom in the mud.

Jim glanced over his shoulder. A smile touched his lips. He went to her and bent to lend a hand. She smiled sweetly. Too sweetly. Suddenly she gave a yank. He fell face down with a splat.

He didn't know whether to be angry or amused. Suddenly he laughed. Laughed until his shoulders shook.

"I guess you just bring out the best in me," she said sarcastically.

Her words were cut off as his hand, dripping with mud, blazed a bold path from her neck to her breasts. He slowly lowered his head. "What a mess I've made," his mouth whispered against hers . . .

Heart of the Wild

DONNA STEPHENS

AVON BOOKS ◆ NEW YORK

HEART OF THE WILD is an original publication of Avon Books. This work has never before appeared in book form. This work is a novel. Any similarity to actual persons or events is purely coincidental.

AVON BOOKS
A division of
The Hearst Corporation
1350 Avenue of the Americas
New York, New York 10019

Copyright © 1993 by Donna Stephens
Inside cover author photograph by Martha Weaver
Published by arrangement with the author
Library of Congress Catalog Card Number: 92-90430
ISBN: 0-380-77014-8

First Avon Books Printing: January 1993

AVON TRADEMARK REG. U.S. PAT. OFF. AND IN OTHER COUNTRIES, MARCA REGISTRADA, HECHO EN U.S.A.

Printed in the U.S.A.

RA   10   9   8   7   6   5   4   3   2   1

To Tom, Leigh Anne, and Paul
for all their love and support

To my parents
who always believed

Heart of the Wild

Chapter 1

Hot, tired, and overwrought, Darcy McCall waited, feet primly together, for the foreman of Kopperella Station to meet her.

Perspiration trickled between her breasts, and her chest felt tight beneath her brown lawn dress. The high neck threatened to choke her, and the delicate lace at her chin and wrists lay limp and damp. How wrong she'd been to think the fine cotton would be cool enough for the heat of January 1890 in South Australia. The shade offered by the small inn's veranda brought that point home to her forcibly.

Three hours had passed since the mail buggy had delivered her to this way post. Three hours in which she'd regretted her impulsive decision of some four months past. At the time, the opportunity to become a station doctor had seemed a godsend, since no one back home wanted to employ a doctor fresh out of medical school. And a woman to boot. Now she recognized her decision, and the eagerness of the owners' agent to sign her on, for what it really

1

was—a ticket to what must surely be the most forsaken place on earth.

Whatever had possessed her to impulsively sign a year's contract with Messrs. Bell and Buchanan, Agents, of London? Had she really been so desperate that she would travel sight unseen to such a desolate country? Apparently so, for here she sat, frustration and dread running amok in her mind, waiting for the station boss, whose very tardiness proved his bad manners.

One of these days, Darcy McCall, you're going to get yourself in a fix you can't get out of, she said to herself. Hopefully, this wasn't that time.

Darcy relaxed her grip on the handle of her carpetbag. Her thick red hair drooped to the nape of her neck, and she secured the pins with one hand, an unconscious habit. Her large, thickly lashed green eyes scanned the vastness beyond the inn. Still no sign of her escort. Her annoyance soared like the midday temperature.

Flat crimson plains lengthened to the skyline, an occasional, solitary gnarled tree cutting into their expanse. With its gray-green herbage for a thin blanket, the scarlet earth slumbered, burnished and gleaming beneath the scorching sun. An inverted bowl of blue sky hung overhead. No cloud graced it; no breath of air stirred the hot, motionless land.

Darcy decided to go inside and have a drink. If she must suffer waiting for the lout to arrive, she might as well soothe her parched throat.

She rose, moved into the shadowed interior, and sat down at a small table near the door. The inn's proprietor, a bald, burly man, served her.

Curious, he plied her with questions. "What might you be doing way out 'ere? We don't get many visitors, especially ladies, this far into the Outback."

"I'm beginning to wonder myself," Darcy said beneath her breath.

"What?"

"Oh, nothing," she quickly replied. "It's just that this place is nothing like I expected."

The man chortled. "It never is. People never know what to make of the Outback."

He had that right, Darcy thought, sipping her drink. As for Australians, they were certainly a very straightforward people.

Just as she drained the last of her lemonade, a shadow fell across her. Darcy looked up at the man standing in the doorway.

Her first impression was one of rugged, almost crude masculinity. Brilliant sunlight, streaming in from behind, highlighted his figure, creating an intimidating silhouette.

His worn moleskin trousers clung to rippling calves and muscular, well-shaped thighs. Spurs were anchored to his dusty riding boots. His shirt, a sweat-strained blue homespun, hung carelessly open at the neck. A broad-brimmed hat dipped low, shadowing much of his face, but she felt uncomfortably aware of an almost defiant, clean-shaven square jaw.

He remained in the doorway for a moment,

staring at her. Finally, doffing his hat in her direction, he strode into the room. "G'day, John."

The innkeeper mopped up a spill on the bar. "Well, mate, I 'aven't seen you in these parts in quite some time. What brings you?"

"I came to collect the station's new doctor. He was supposed to have been on the mail buggy." The man moved closer to the bar and leaned casually against it. "I suppose I'll have myself a drink while I wait. Leave it to a Yank to be late."

The innkeeper's snort of agreement rankling, Darcy stood and came near. She cleared her throat. She instinctively knew that her announcement would unbalance this impertinent man and she relished the fact.

"If you're looking for Dr. Darcy McCall, I'm she. And I'm not late, you are."

His reaction didn't disappoint her. He whipped his head around and tipped his hat back from his forehead. The rakishly handsome brute paled slightly as his gaze passed over her. His jaw hardened.

"What the hell?" he drawled.

Darcy drew herself to her full unprepossessing height. "I said, I'm Dr. McCall."

"You!" He scowled. "You can't be. I'm expecting a man."

"Obviously you've been misinformed."

He turned his shoulder to her as if to dismiss her and faced the innkeeper. "Well, I'm not taking some female with me into the bush."

"I don't think you have a choice."

"You shouldn't deceive people. I'm sure the owners didn't know you were a woman."

"I've deceived no one. They were quite aware that I was a woman, so you can put that worry to rest."

He gave a disdainful snort. "I imagine my worries are only just starting where you're concerned."

He removed his hat and raked his fingers through his short blond hair, squinting his eyes as if he didn't trust his vision.

Whether he was handsome or not, she didn't take to his insult. Her voice rose on a swell of irritation and fatigue. "I assure you, I'm no more pleased about having to wait for over three hours than you are about my being a woman. But I suppose we'll just have to make the best of it, won't we?"

"Bloody hell!" was his soft but explosive response.

Darcy recoiled as if he had slapped her. Never in her twenty-two years had anyone spoken to her so indecently. His voice, like everything about him, sounded rugged and intense. There was something roguish about him, a virility that was unmistakable. From everything she'd heard, he embodied the perfect Australian bushman with his lean brown face and sun-bleached hair. His striking blue eyes were fanned by tiny wrinkles at each corner and even now slitted against the glaring Outback sun.

"Don't use that kind of language around me."

If she intended to put him in his place, she failed.

He wore a faintly menacing look, as if he was holding his aggravation in check. "If you can't stand my language, then I reckon you ought to find yourself a way back to Adelaide. In fact, if I were you, Yank, I'd get on the first boat back to America."

"I hardly care what you think. I've signed a year's contract with the company that owns Kopperella. I intend to honor that agreement."

"Well, don't think I'm going to play nurse-maid to you, because I'm not."

"Somehow I can't see you in a white cap and gown."

He ignored her remark and said, "You'll find out quick enough it's no picnic living and working in the bush. I bet you haven't got a fair notion what it's like at all."

Her face sour with dislike, Darcy uttered, "Just keep your opinions to yourself."

The innkeeper cleared his throat. "Looks like you've got a spry one on your hands, Jim. Wonder what the boys will think?"

"The same as me. That she's a bloody fool."

"I'll ask you not to talk about me as if I don't exist," she said coldly.

"How old are you?" the bushman asked abruptly.

"Old enough to know what I'm doing."

"You sure about that?" His eyes, openly bold, took in her dress and told her without words that she did *not* know what she was doing. "Your clothes, for a start. Who in their right mind would come to Australia during the middle of the summer dressed in long sleeves and lace?"

Every vile name Darcy knew rose in her throat, but she swallowed them back. "My apparel is no concern of yours."

"Let's get one thing straight. I'm the foreman of Kopperella, and what I say goes," the bushman said.

"You're insufferable," she answered through clenched teeth.

"I've been called worse." He returned his attention to his beer and downed the drink in one fluid motion. He then wiped his mouth on his sleeve.

She watched the foreman as his eyes returned to her. She realized how much she depended upon him since she didn't know the land, however unfair she thought his authority over her. But authority it was, and she had no choice but to endure. For the time being.

"I can well imagine," she said. "However, I'm sorry I don't meet with your approval, but I've never been here before. No one bothered to tell me what to expect. I had no idea how to dress except from what I'd read."

"No, I suppose you didn't." His voice had softened, she thought, from indifference.

Despite his irritation, Jim Burleson had to admit that he'd never seen so fetching a young woman. Her face was that of an angel, but her body belonged to a temptress—although he doubted she realized her effect upon men. He reckoned she probably spent all her time with her head in her medical books, with no thoughts of men except in a clinical sort of way. One plain fact presented itself: she was a high-spirited filly who didn't figure to be broken.

He was damn sure she didn't belong in the bush, yet he had no choice but to take her with him. After all, the bosses had signed a contract with her.

"The wagon's out front. I'll get your things," he groused.

Her shoulders sagging with relief, Darcy trailed after him into the bright sunshine.

"You could at least tell me your name," she said, trying to keep up with his long strides.

The foreman tossed over his shoulder, "Jim Burleson."

He came to a stop near a wagon parked out front. "Where's your gear?"

Darcy pointed behind her. "My trunks are on the veranda."

Burleson walked back to the porch, spurs jingling, and dragged her trunks in the dirt over to the wagon, leaving small furrows in the red dust behind him.

Muscles straining beneath his shirt, he lifted the larger piece of baggage onto the wagon bed. "It's heavy. What have you got in there?"

"My personal belongings. I didn't know what to bring, so I packed what I could."

"Well, it's too bloody much, I can tell you that," he said.

Darcy's hold on the handle of her carpetbag tightened. "You certainly take great pains to criticize me, Mr. Burleson. Tell me, are you always so friendly?"

"I'm not trying to win any personality contests, if that's what you mean."

She gave him a wry smile. "Congratulations, then, because you've certainly succeeded."

A muscle worked in his cheek.

Darcy's smile tightened. "Let me assure you that you don't have to be concerned for my well-being. I can take care of myself."

Burleson's eyes narrowed and his mouth tensed. "You haven't got the slightest notion how to survive out here."

"I may not at present, but you'll find I'm a quick learner. You need not give me constant instructions."

"Someone has to," he said.

She ground her teeth together. "Ohhh!" Lifting her chin, she walked toward the front of the wagon.

The man was insufferable. She could tell he relished giving orders. He'd find out soon enough she didn't take to them.

Burleson picked up the second, smaller trunk and hefted it upon a shoulder when Darcy called, "Be careful! Those are my medical supplies!"

Only his gaze, sweeping over her, revealed he'd heard her as he eased the container onto the wagon. He secured the trunks with a rope.

Darcy watched his hands moving with sure, swift motions. They were fascinating and sensual with their long, tapered fingers and thick, fleshy palms bronzed by the sun. How easily he could encircle her waist if he wished. . . .

Darcy's thoughts skittered to a halt. What was the matter with her? Had the Australian sun addled her brains? Here she stood fantasizing about a perfect stranger! And an arrogant one to boot. She wiped her brow in an attempt to restore reason.

Burleson then moved to her side. "I don't reckon you can manage a wagon by yourself, so I'll drive."

She couldn't dispute his logic, but she could refuse his assistance in climbing into the wagon. Fierce independence reared its head. "I may not be able to steer a team, but I'm not as helpless as you think." She tucked her carpetbag beneath the seat, squared her shoulders, and stared straight ahead.

Burleson chuckled and shook his head. "Excuse me if I don't take the time to argue the point."

Springs creaked as he hauled himself up. He laughed again as he released the brake and brought the reins down across the pair of horses with a snap. The harness jingled in the still air as the travelers pulled away.

Darcy didn't look back at what she was leaving behind, but she dared not consider what lay ahead either. An entire year of working with Jim Burleson was more than she could bear at the moment. Instead, she concentrated on the landscape.

She found the scenery fascinating. Heat danced across the flat plains; the land, in shim-

mering waves of green and brown, was bleached
by the sun.

This part of the country, the red center, was
beyond civilization, beyond anything she had
ever known. And they were heading for the
heart of South Australia, where the sun's fiery
breath scorched the land into a red-dust haze.
The Never Never.

After hours of travel, Darcy's fingers throbbed
from clutching the seat. Every bone in her body
ached. The mail buggy had been bad enough,
but this was torture. She felt certain her thighs
and legs would be black-and-blue from the
abuse, yet she wouldn't allow herself to utter a
complaint. She'd die before she'd let Jim
Burleson know of her distress.

Despite her weariness, her senses were tuned
to the man beside her, acutely aware of his
masculine scent. Occasionally she found him
looking at her out of the corner of his eye, but
she never acknowledged his curiosity. Instead,
she continued to stare straight ahead, seemingly watching the horses pick up one foot and
then another, monotonously making their way
north as tails and ears swished, keeping flies at
bay.

Sometime later, they came to a small creek
and halted. Gum trees lined the bank, and only
the lone sound of a galah disturbed the peace.
The parrot soon flew away. Gum leaves cast a
lacy pattern across the water, creating a serenity
that helped to smooth the rough edges of Darcy's nerves. While Jim Burleson was busy with

the horses, she surreptitiously removed her boots and stockings. Then, putting her hat aside, she slid down the bank and waded into the water. She inhaled and allowed the breeze to cool her. The water's gentle motion restored sensation to her partially numb legs. Bending over, she cupped her hands and brought the cool liquid to her sunburned face. Gingerly she ran one finger over her small upturned nose and winced from the pain.

What a sight she must be. She'd have to take better precautions for her skin to avoid damage.

Darcy waded out of the water and onto the bank. Her bladder hurt and she knew she must relieve herself. But where? She glanced over her shoulder at Burleson, who was watering the horses. If she was lucky, she could slip off before he noticed.

She'd begun walking toward a clump of low-lying brush when Burleson's voice stopped her. "And where do you fancy you're going?"

Darcy spun on her heels. Her mouth dropped open and then she clamped it shut, all the while blushing to the roots of her red hair.

Her embarrassment answered his question. He inclined his head and had the audacity to wink at her. Darcy's crimson hue deepened, but she continued onward.

She stretched her cramped leg muscles as she moved. Darcy kept to her course until she felt she had put enough distance between herself and Burleson. Thick brush gave her a measure of privacy.

She hadn't taken five steps to return to the

wagon when she felt the fine hairs rise on the back of her neck. Not ten feet from her stood a mangy-looking beast that resembled a stray dog. The animal's mouth opened and a slender pink tongue slid across sharp teeth. The beast took a step toward her and growled.

Darcy's heart thumped against her ribs. She slowly raised trembling hands to her face and wiped away the perspiration that stung her eyes.

Think! she told herself.

She took several deep breaths to calm her erratic pulse. Slowly, she began walking to one side of the wild dog, her eyes never leaving the creature. If she went slowly enough, perhaps the animal would lose interest and leave.

With each step she gained more self-confidence. The dog wasn't following her. Darcy thought she might just make it back to the wagon without being devoured.

Suddenly, from out of the brush, she heard Burleson's voice over her pounding heart. "Yank, everything all right?"

The startled animal bounded away, and relief rolled over her. Darcy ran until she collided with Burleson at the edge of the brush. He caught her as she rebounded off the muscular wall of his chest.

"What the bloody hell!" he grunted.

Her mouth worked as she gasped for breath, but no words came out. She only managed to point breathlessly in the opposite direction.

Burleson released her and stalked into the dense growth. Darcy sat on the ground. Her body shook as she contemplated what could have happened to her.

Burleson returned and knelt beside her. "By the tracks, I'd say it was a dingo that frightened you."

"Dingo?"

"Yeah, a wild dog. But you're safe now."

Her head began to spin. Hugging her calves and cradling her head atop her knees, she fought to exercise some control over her quivering body. She felt so helpless. And she didn't like that feeling one bit. She had always prided herself on her independence and her ability to manage for herself. Well, she thought, in the span of the past eight hours she had allowed herself to be browbeaten by a man and nearly consumed by a wild animal. So much for taking care of herself!

Evening was fast approaching when they came upon a river crossing. After passing over flat plains where only stunted bush grew on a limitless horizon, the sight provided sweet succor to Darcy's tired eyes.

A line of timber appeared, the first real trees she'd seen since leaving the Australian coast. An abundance of wildlife flocked to the water. Pink-breasted galahs rose from every tree, white cockatoos with red crests flapped shrieking from bank to bank, and clouds of finches filled the air. The place was alive with exotic birds: igeons and wild ducks, plovers, ibis, and egrets.

Darcy watched, entranced. A single word rose

in her mind—*beautiful*. Even the picture books she'd seen could not do this spot justice.

Burleson jumped down from the wagon. "We've got to spell the horses now and hobble them out, so we'll stay the night here. I've brought an extra swag, or you can sleep in the back of the wagon."

He held out his hand to help her, but she ignored it and climbed down under her own power. Her legs felt like butter from the ride, yet she managed to remain standing. She removed her small hat and pushed a renegade strand of hair from her eyes, patting it back into place.

A large, fallen tree trunk provided a bench for Darcy to sit on. While Burleson went about his chores, she looked skyward. The sun was setting in a haze of red and orange. Far off a dingo howled, an eerie, forlorn sound. She wrapped her arms around herself as a rush of wind flapped over the darkening plains like the sweep of a great bird's wings.

In no time at all, Burleson had the horses staked out and a fire going. Shortly, he had food prepared and handed Darcy a plate.

The hot, crusty damper baked in the ashes, the slices of corned beef, and the sweet black tea boiled in the billy tasted wonderful to Darcy. Under normal circumstances she'd have turned up her nose at the lumpy bread and salty meat, but not tonight. Tonight it was food fit for a king, or at least for one tired, sleepy young woman from Boston.

As the minutes passed, Darcy brooded while observing Burleson over the tips of the flames.

He certainly was an enigma. She didn't understand what about him sparked her interest.

Burleson glanced at her. He openly appraised
her, and she wondered if he could read her
mind. Her pulse accelerated slightly.

Finished with his own meal, Burleson rose
and stepped over to Darcy.

"There's no fancy tucker out in the bush, but
it's food all the same." He extended his hand for
her plate. "I'll take that, if you're finished."

"I have to admit it did taste good, although a
little strange."

"You'll get used to it."

"I hope so."

Their fingertips brushed when she gave him
her plate. She raised her eyes and stared wordlessly. Her heart began to pound as his blue
eyes caught and held hers. She jerked her hand
away, telling herself her nervousness stemmed
from the animosity between them.

She stood. "I'm going to bathe, if it's all right
with you," she said pointedly, diverting her unwanted feelings into sarcasm.

"Fine." He smiled rakishly. "Don't worry, I'll
be close by."

Darcy wanted nothing more than to wipe that
smirk from his handsome face, but she refrained
and walked to the wagon. She retrieved her carpetbag from beneath the seat and selected a few
items before setting out for the river.

From behind, she heard, "Remember, just call
if you need help, Yank."

She clutched her soap until she thought it
would snap in two. Oh, the absolute, unequivo-

cal gall of the man! At every turn he reminded her of her dependence on him. When the day came to put him in his place, she would relish every minute of it.

Stripping off her clothes, except for her chemise, Darcy waded into the stream cautiously, her feet feeling the mucky, slippery bottom for any sudden drops. The cool water felt heavenly against her hot, grimy skin. With water lapping about her waist, she ducked her head below the refreshing pool. Surfacing, she sighed with satisfaction and ran her fingers through her hair, rubbing her scalp to loosen all the accumulated dirt and dust. Thirty minutes later, she emerged reluctantly from the stream, her chemise clinging closely to her body.

Sitting on a flat rock near the water's edge, Darcy began toweling her hair dry.

"Need any help?" asked Burleson, a smirk on his face.

Frightened, Darcy scrambled to her feet and slipped on the wet rock, tumbling backward into the water.

She broke the surface, spluttering and gasping for breath. With her hair blocking her vision, she felt her hand being grasped as she was pulled to her feet.

Humor tinged Burleson's voice. "Still reckon you can make out for yourself, Yank?"

Blinking water out of her eyes, Darcy was almost speechless with anger.

"Well?" He came into the water after her and caught her shoulders. "Cat got your tongue?"

"Better that than my fist on your jaw if you

don't let me go," she said between clenched teeth.

"Bossy, aren't you?"

She froze just as she was about to give him a piece of her mind, suddenly realizing how she must look, the way her chemise exposed her body.

Burleson stood a foot away. His eyes traveled slowly over her. Darcy flushed. Instinctively she placed an arm across her breasts and moved a hand to her womanhood.

"You've been watching me the whole time, haven't you?" she demanded.

"Yeah."

"You're despicable. Can't I have a moment to myself?"

"Someday, but seeing how you don't know anything about our snakes or lizards, I thought I'd best keep an eye on you."

"In a pig's eye I would've called, *mate*." She stressed the last word.

"Mate, is it? Does that mean we're on friendly terms?"

Burleson's gaze outlined the curves and hollows of her body betrayed under the thin chemise. Her nipples, hard and pointed, strained against the soft material, and he glimpsed the darker triangle where her legs met.

He felt himself grow rigid. Blasted Yank! He'd have to keep his mind on business instead of on her soft piece of womanhood. Because right now he'd like nothing better than to glide between those silky thighs. He reined in his desire. This was neither the time nor the place for such thoughts. It wasn't going to be easy working with her. As a matter of fact, it was going to be damned hard! In more ways than one.

Burleson watched the sway of her hips as she stormed past him and marched back to camp.

He walked beyond the flat rock where Darcy had dried her hair and kicked the still warm body of a snake. She hadn't realized one had crawled into her clothes, but he had seen it and quickly killed the reptile. Let her think he was a Peeping Tom. The idea would keep her angry at him. And her anger would provide a good defense against their becoming at ease with each other.

Yet as he followed her, an unsettled feeling overcame him. Jim felt entangled, nervous. He didn't care for it. He wanted nothing more than to be back at Kopperella, doing what he did best—tending horses and cattle. And he wanted to be as far from Darcy McCall as he could get. First thing he knew, being around her would feel natural, right. Feeling relaxed and comfortable was the way a man lost sight of himself. And it wouldn't be hard to get lost in those green eyes of hers. Here in the Outback, a man needed to keep his wits about him. Only a fool would get involved with a woman like her. A bloody damn fool! Besides, the Outback was no place for a soft woman like her.

Darcy hurriedly dressed behind the wagon and was less gracious in her assessment of Burleson. Every fiber of her being shouted indignation as a dozen scathing remarks came to mind. Her hand trembled with anger as she buttoned her blouse. Oh, how she longed to slap his arrogant face. Nothing would give her greater satisfaction. He'd better not touch her, or he might find himself less of a man!

Chapter 2

When Darcy awoke, she found the hue of the earth blazed with the living gold of morning. She sighed and lay still, savoring the strangeness of camping out in the open in the middle of nowhere with the Outback wrapped around her. Rubbing the sleep from her eyes, she inched her way clear of the traveling trunks she'd slept between and slipped out of the wagon. Stretching, she felt ready to challenge another day. She straightened her clothing and quickly combed and arranged her hair.

Stepping around the side of the wagon, Darcy found Burleson tending a small fire on which the quart-pot steamed. The top of the billy rattled as the liquid inside boiled and spewed.

He looked up from the flames and flashed her a grin. "G'day. Breakfast, Yank?"

He unearthed the damper that had been left to bake in the ashes the night before.

They ate as dawn heralded a new day across the windswept land. Sipping her tea, Darcy glanced toward the river. Smoky tendrils of heated water rose in the early morning air.

Soon they were on their way to Kopperella.

Burleson broke the silence as they passed a deserted hut swallowed by drifts of sand. "Out here, we're dependent on natural water holes. If they go dry or are silted up, a man doesn't have a choice but to move on. No water, no life."

Miles later, sand spilled across the road dotted with claypans of layered soil that is virtually impenetrable by vegetation. Infertile, the land remained barren and dusty. At this point, the hills twisted and occasionally blocked the road.

Burleson halted the team.

"Why are we stopping?" Darcy asked.

"I wanted to warn you."

"About what?"

"See those hills? Getting over them might be a bit hard, so hold on."

"Oh."

Although Burleson's voice sounded detached, something in his eyes belied his tone as he said, "I wouldn't want anything to happen to you."

It took Darcy a moment to digest his comment. Was he being sarcastic again? Yet something about his expression conveyed sincerity. She decided to trust him this time, and take his concern as authentic.

She smiled her thanks, then clutched the seat as the horses attacked the extended bank. The wagon groaned as they strained and churned through the sand.

Darcy was pushed to the back of the seat and braced herself against the front of the wagon. Her eyes darted to the mounds of sand around her, and she wondered what it would be like to be swallowed alive in those red drifts.

Suddenly the wagon reached the top, then started down the other side fast. Darcy lurched forward but quickly regained her balance. She snapped her eyes toward Burleson. He labored with the reins, fighting to keep the horses steady. The wagon would topple if the horses faltered. Burleson checked their quick descent with the brake.

The arduous ride frayed her nerves. She clung to the wagon seat with every ounce of strength. She couldn't relax or she'd be thrown over the side.

Over the wind, Burleson turned his head and said, "No worries, Yank. Could be worse. We could be making the steep side first."

Darcy looked ahead. Drifting sand looked like smoke rising across the red crests.

"Is it always like this?" she ventured. Her breath caught at the unexpected beauty of it all.

"Yeah. I reckon it's different from anything you've ever seen."

Darcy nodded.

They stopped at the next sandhill crossing.

"Do you think it would be all right to stretch my legs?" she asked.

"Yeah, but don't stray far." And then he grinned. "Wouldn't want to lose you after coming all this way."

Darcy smiled idly back. When he tried, he certainly had a way about him.

She climbed to the top of the hill, the red sand sucking greedily at her legs. Delicate flowers and tiny shrubs dotted the landscape. One plant in particular caught her eye and she bent to pluck its silver leaf. She took a small bite of the leaf. It had a salty tang but was surprisingly tasty.

At that moment the wagon came abreast of her, and Burleson extended a hand and hauled her onto the seat. From their vantage point atop the summit, they could see for miles around.

Burleson pointed to the ground. "See those footprints in the soft sand? Lizard. And those," he said, pointing farther away, "are from tiny marsupial mice—creatures that live in holes during the heat of the day and come out at night to feed."

They labored on. The next water hole was dry. The hot wind blew across Darcy's skin and the flat stretches of clay, swirling among the sandy hills. Only the bleached, clean bones of cattle dotted the plain. Darcy felt restless and eager to be on the way to the next water hole, which Burleson knew was all right. There they could drink and water the horses.

By the time they got there, she felt smothered beneath her clothing as the Australian sun continued to beat down on them. Perspiration trickled down her sides and between her breasts, leaving wet patches under her armpits and in a thin line dissecting her bodice. She lifted her arms and felt the sticky material pull away from her skin. Inwardly groaning, she thought of how wonderful it would be to have a moment of watery respite.

Burleson pulled the team to a halt near the water's edge.

Darcy dismounted, careful not to tangle her skirts in the wagon wheel. She stretched and twisted, trying to work the kinks out of her body.

In the meantime, Burleson unhooked the horses and led them to water.

"We'll be on our way as soon as the horses have had their fill," he said.

Darcy sat at the water's edge. "Don't worry about me. I'll be ready when you are."

She took her handkerchief and dipped it into the water. She dabbed the back of her neck first, then her forehead and cheeks. Her thirsty skin absorbed the moisture quickly.

Darcy wondered how long it would take her to adapt to this new land. She hoped it wouldn't be long, because she intuitively understood that one didn't have long to learn how to survive in the Outback. The Outback wasn't patient.

"Do you have a cup?" Darcy called to Burleson.

He gave her a crooked smile. "They're all packed up. You'll have to use your hands."

Darcy removed her gloves, then knelt beside the bluish-green water and dipped cupped hands into it. Never had anything tasted so sweet. It was nectar from the gods, or so it seemed to Darcy.

Finished, she drew her hand across her mouth and rocked back on her heels. She took a deep breath. Dry air filled her lungs.

Darcy looked in Burleson's direction. She had

questions that needed answers. "What are the men like on Kopperella?"

"Hard-working. The same as anywhere else."

"Yes, but how do you think they'll take to having a woman doctor?"

Burleson pulled the team back into position and began fastening the harness. "I reckon the same as me. Wondering what the hell you're doing here."

"Does a woman always need a reason for doing something?"

"When she's doing a man's job she does."

"Is it written somewhere in stone that all doctors have to be men?" she asked in a flustered tone.

"It is in the Outback."

"Perhaps I'll be able to change your mind."

"I doubt it," Burleson said evenly.

"Is it so narrow, then?"

"No, just made up." He came around to the near side of the wagon. "Ready, Yank?"

The travelers had crossed the border of Kopperella hours ago. The expanse of flat red land lay before them—the olive-green stitchery of coolabah, box, and mulga trees marking the course of dry creek beds. Occasionally small salt lakes and ponds appeared, scattered about like shining silver coins.

Darcy clung to the wagon seat, suffering each bump with gritted teeth. Her backside hurt and those infernal flies buzzed around her head. With each mile of ground she and Burleson navigated, the insects hovered like a plague, attacking her eyes and nostrils.

Praying for strength to endure, Darcy tilted her head back and rolled her eyes heavenward. The sun beat down upon her viciously. She felt her arms and legs grow warm and sticky from dry heat and perspiration.

Her companion didn't ease her discomfort. He hadn't spoken for miles. When he thought she wasn't looking, he silently watched her. She never knew what he was thinking. Yet despite his rudeness, she vowed that no matter how rudely or inconsiderately he behaved, she would be poised and polite and completely imperturbable.

The hours dragged by until they reached the heart of the station, and Darcy got her first wondering look at what was to be her home for the next year.

Kopperella was a compound. The main building, built in typical bush fashion, had walls of wooden whitewashed slabs and a roof of tree bark. It was surrounded by a plank fence to keep the stock out. Some feet away, and to the rear of this building, appeared two smaller structures identical in design. A huge horse paddock sat farther back.

Dust, thundering hooves, cracking stock whips, barking dogs, and men's voices rose in the air as five drovers herded a group of wild horses into the compound toward the paddock. The scene was a cloud of color as horses of every shade moved within a whirlwind of red dust.

Darcy noticed Aborigines gathering together on the fringes of the corral. She wondered how a diversified population such as Kopperella's lived together, and she looked forward to treating not only the drovers but the natives as well. She hoped to learn the ways of these proud people.

Burleson pulled the wagon to a halt in front of the central building. "Well, this is what you've traveled half the world for. I hope you'll think it was worth it."

Darcy cast him a dubious sideways look. "No doubt."

He gave her a crooked grin. "No doubt," he echoed.

She opened her mouth to say something further, when the drovers dismounted and walked toward them. Hats waved in greeting, but when the men caught sight of Darcy, silence fell.

Burleson leaned near her and whispered, "They're not a bad lot, although they'll most likely give you a fair amount of trouble. But they're the best stockriders in Australia."

"As if I haven't already had enough trouble," she responded. She felt self-conscious because his wry smile faded abruptly, and his manner once more turned detached and cool.

The drovers gathered near the wagon.

Wrapping the reins about the brake handle, Jim Burleson announced, "This is our new doctor." He then hopped to the ground and walked to the rear of the wagon.

Darcy stiffened. She had hoped for a better in-

troduction. Something—anything—to ease the
tension between her and the men. Instead,
Burleson had left her to fend for herself.

As Burleson lifted the trunks off the flatbed,
Darcy watched the men's eyes as they traversed
her figure. Their gazes reflected disbelief at seeing a woman, resentment, and astonishment.

She'd have to take the bull by the horns, or
rather the drovers, she decided. By the stern expressions on their faces, they weren't going to
make this easy. A sigh lifted her breasts beneath
her lawn dress and she fingered the lace-
trimmed collar to free it from her sticky skin.
She got down from the wagon and faced the
first man.

Trousers low on his lean hips and tucked inside his boots, broad-brimmed hat fastened
under his chin with a leather strap, he looked
every bit an Australian stockman. He must have
been nearly six feet, a couple of inches shorter
than Jim Burleson. His black hair hung untidily
about his collar, and his jaw showed a day's
growth of stubble. He was handsome in his own
way, but his green eyes spoke volumes—page
after page of hostility.

She swallowed and extended her hand. "My
name is Darcy McCall."

No response.

"And yours is?" she persisted.

The question hung in the air briefly before the
man gripped her hand hard, as if to reinforce
his resentment of her presence. Yet her own eyes
never left his. They spoke as clearly as any
words. She was here to stay.

"The name's Craig Newley. I'm second in charge of Kopperella."

He released her hand, and Darcy moved down the line to the next man.

This drover's attitude seemed more tempered, the expression in his large brown eyes closer to curiosity. He appeared younger than Newley, maybe no more than fifteen.

The lad kicked dirt with a booted toe. "Dave Patterson. Miss . . . er . . . Dr. McCall."

"Pleased to meet you, Mr. Patterson."

Darcy noted that the boy puffed his chest out at the way she'd addressed him.

She smiled before moving on to the third drover. Bearded, he was clearly older than the others, his face wreathed in wrinkles. He, too, wore his drover's hat, and sported a blue shirt and tight-fitting moleskin trousers. On his belt hung a pouch for tobacco and his knife.

Once more extending her hand, she said, "And your name?"

His fingers tugged the brim of his hat. "Tom Rivers."

Darcy pushed her shoulders back and addressed them all. "I hope we'll have a good working relationship. Should any of you need anything, I'll be here."

Two of the men merely nodded, but Craig Newley snorted his derision.

Darcy knew she shouldn't allow his reaction to affect her, but it did. When would she be accepted? She'd been harassed in medical school, then politely excluded from a practice back home. Now she was being treated like the plague. Darcy struggled to find composure.

Her thoughts were interrupted when a short Chinese man came to her side and bowed. Straightening, he announced, "My name Kim Loo. I cook here. You follow me, missy. You need cup of tea."

Darcy smiled. "How thoughtful. I'd like that. Thank you."

The Asian turned and trotted ahead of her toward one of the smaller buildings. She followed, watching his black pigtail swing down his white cotton-clad back.

Entering the kitchen, Darcy made several swipes at her dusty clothes before she sat at the large oblong table dominating the center of the room. A delicious aroma filled the air and she wondered at its source. Her stomach rumbled in response, making her realize how hungry she was. Something about this Australian Outback certainly gave her an appetite.

Kim Loo retrieved a kettle from the stove and poured Darcy a cup of steaming black tea. Resting her elbows on the table, she sipped the brew. Although hot, the sweet tea tasted good after the long ride.

She set her half-finished cup down. "Kim Loo, tell me, how long have you been here?"

The Chinaman gave a toothy grin. "Five year."

"And you've always worked on Kopperella?"

"Yes, missy. No other place for me to go. I like it here. Boss good to me."

Darcy leaned forward and cupped her chin within the palm of her hand. "What's it like?"

Kim Loo, up to his elbows in flour now, rolled out damper on a smaller table across the room. "Oh, missy, it be hard on woman like you."

She sighed wearily. "And just what kind of a woman is that?"

"Thin and, I think, maybe headstrong. Why else you be here?"

"You're right about one point at least. But I don't think my being slender is a bad thing."

"You just like the old boss's wife. She not last long."

"What happened?"

"She die of fever."

Darcy fingered the rim of her cup. "Tell me, Kim Loo, was Jim Burleson working at Kopperella then?"

"Old boss's wife his mother. You see, his father was foreman of station before him. That why young boss no like women in bush. He say they should live in town in decent house."

Darcy sat silently for a moment. She hadn't entertained the thought that Jim Burleson might have had family living out here. She began to understand his resentment of her presence.

Another thought darkened her mind. As attractive a man as Burleson was, surely there had been at least one woman in his life. "Has there been no woman here since that time?"

Kim Loo missed only a stroke in his kneading. "No."

"Why?"

"There one woman in boss's life, but she say

she no come to the Outback. No place for a woman to live. Too hard. Too many flies, too much heat, too many black fellas."

Her throat tightened. "So none of the men are married?" she asked, though she was really interested in only one man in particular.

"No again, missy."

A strange relief rolled over Darcy. She didn't know why it mattered. But it did.

"One more thing, Kim Loo. Where do you suppose I'm to sleep?"

"Don't know. There only one place drovers on Kopperella sleep."

Outside, Craig Newley removed his gear from his horse and slapped the animal's rear. The gelding kicked up its hooves and scampered into the corral, twisting its neck from side to side.

Craig leaned against the fence and folded his arms atop the railing. His green eyes squinted at the dying sunlight streaming through the gum trees. Reaching into his pocket, he retrieved a match and stuck it in his mouth.

He tipped his hat back and spoke to Dave Patterson, who was standing beside him. "I reckon that woman doctor is going to be nothing but trouble."

" 'Ow so?" asked young Patterson.

"For starters, she's a real looker. That spells trouble for sure. 'Ow's a man supposed to get on about 'is work with a woman like that around, knowing 'e can't touch 'er?"

Patterson turned and leaned back against the

fence, his elbows on the middle rail and a booted foot resting on the last one. "Yeah, she's pretty enough, all right. I wouldn't mind 'aving a piece of fluff like 'er. I wonder if the boss kept to 'imself on the trip back."

Craig thoughtfully chewed on the match. "Hmm. I wonder."

Patterson cocked his head to the side. His brown eyes widened and then he slowly gave a cheeky grin, exposing slightly yellowed teeth. "You don't think—"

"Nah. A fellow can tell she's not that kind. But things might get interesting around 'ere."

"I don't reckon I've ever known the boss to take on about a woman before. 'E's always too busy working the station."

" 'E did. Once. But that was a long time ago." Craig removed the match from his mouth and flicked it away.

" 'Ow do you know?"

"Trust me, I just do. We've been mates since we was boys." With that he pushed himself off the fence, straightened, and slapped Patterson on the shoulder. "Come on. Let's go 'ave ourselves some tucker."

Appalled and incredulous, Darcy stepped inside and stared at the men's quarters, which consisted of one sparsely furnished room. Surely there had to be some mistake. She couldn't be expected to sleep here. Not with the men!

She whirled and her gaze fell on Jim Burleson.

She flung her hands out in frustration. "Don't tell me—"

Jim leaned against the doorframe and shoved his hands into his pockets. "No place else to bed down? Afraid so. There's never been any reason to make special allowances for anyone before."

"But there is now."

He shrugged. "Why? You came of your own accord. The men didn't ask you. So you've got to accept things the way they are."

"I'm getting tired of you saying that." Her voice rose a notch in irritation. "That's your excuse for refusing to change at all."

"There's no reason for me or any of the others to change. You're the one who's going to have to adapt. Unless you've decided to go back from where you came."

Darcy screwed her face up. "Oh, you'd like that, wouldn't you? For me to just pack up and leave." She stomped her foot. "Well, I'm not going to do that. Do you hear? I'm here to stay."

"We'll see."

"You're the one who's going to see. I'm not about to break my contract just because things are inconvenient."

"Then you've nothing to complain about."

"You still don't get it, do you? But then, that doesn't surprise me. You haven't given me any indication you have any decency within you."

"Never said I did." Out of one corner of his mouth he said, "Of course, if you don't want to sleep here with the men, you could bunk with me."

Indignation filled Darcy. This was the last

straw! "There must be another solution to this problem."

"Not unless you want to sleep outside with the dingos. And I don't give up my quarters for anyone—man or woman. I'm no gentleman."

"So I've noticed," she said between gritted teeth.

Darcy refused to give Jim Burleson the satisfaction of making a spectacle of herself. She took a deep breath and counted to ten.

"If you're going to stay on, you've got to learn to handle things that come your way." His eyes darkened momentarily. "Whatever they are."

Darcy thoughtfully chewed her lip.

"It's your decision, Yank."

Darcy shuddered. Her slender fingers drifted to the high collar of her dress in an attempt to conceal her rapid pulse.

"What about observing the rules of propriety?"

"People in the bush don't have much use for the social graces. Not when you live day to day."

Despite her previous resolve, her temper flared. "Do you have so little regard for me?"

A muscle twitched in his jaw. "Look, I'm not the one who convinced you to come traipsing across Australia! As a matter of fact, I'm the one who told you to go home, remember? And it's not my fault there's no place for a woman." He pushed himself off the doorframe.

Exasperation overrode her common sense.

"Kim Loo told me your mother used to live here. Where did she sleep?"

Darcy feared she'd gone too far when Burleson's eyes narrowed to slits of blue. "The main house was torn down after she died, not that it's any of your business."

Darcy regretted her impulsive question, for behind his eyes long-repressed pain simmered. "I'm sorry—"

"I don't want your apology."

"I was only trying—"

Burleson came to stand in front of her. His face loomed near hers and she felt his breath fall softly across her face as he spoke. "I know what you were trying to do. Just stay the bloody hell out of my business. You got that?"

Instead of answering him, Darcy settled her gaze on his mouth, lingering on his sensual lips. Suddenly she could almost feel her body pressed against him in a passionate embrace, his strong arms holding her, his lips hard on hers. Oh, what sweet torture.

"Well, what's it going to be, Yank? Here or with me? I haven't got all day."

The rough impatience in his voice brought her out of her reverie. Retreating a step, she deliberated over her predicament. She knew for certain that she didn't trust Craig Newley, not after the way he'd looked at her. She'd seen the lust in his eyes. Yet what she contemplated doing held no less danger—possibly more. Her pulse thrummed wildly as she deliberated.

At last she mumbled, "I'll stay with you."

She would take a chance on Jim Burleson's sense of decency.

Alone for the first time in her makeshift quarters situated at the rear of the station store, Darcy set her carpetbag down and dropped disconsolately onto her rickety cot. Her throat constricted and her eyes suddenly stung. She gazed, eyes watering, at the blanket and length of rope which acted as a barrier, separating the two beds.

He's only one man. Only one egotistical bastard. I'm a certified doctor, and the agents in London saw fit to hire me. Shouldn't that mean more than his bigoted opinion?

Nonetheless, she hurt.

The memory of the expressions on the other drovers' faces only added to her pain. They obviously shared Jim Burleson's opinion. She had read censure in each weathered face.

She'd once imagined how relieved the men would be to have a doctor on the station again—female or otherwise. She had rehearsed in her head a thousand times how they would greet her and she them. Now all her expectations had curdled like soured milk. They were no different from the men back home.

Well, she'd show these Australians her true Yankee backbone. She'd show each and every one of them. Most especially, she'd show Jim Burleson.

She never knew when sleep claimed her.

Sometime later, Darcy awoke upon hearing Jim enter. She followed his movements in her groggy mind as his footsteps neared. Her breathing grew shallow when she heard him stop close to her bed. Her mind sharpened as she lay listening to him.

First a bed creaked from his weight. Then a pair of boots thudded to the floor. The rustle of material followed as his shirt slid free from his waistband before his belt jingled in the still night air.

Next he'd remove his pants, she imagined. Her mind's eye followed his movements as he undid the buttons.

One . . .

She licked her suddenly dry lips while she pictured the hair at his navel beneath his long underwear. Blond and wispy.

Two . . .

She tried to swallow the lump in her throat at the thought of a thatch of curling hair. Covering his thick masculinity.

Three . . .

Perspiration dotted her upper lip as she imagined his pants easing down his narrow hips.

Four . . .

Darcy pulled her pillow over her head.

Did he sleep in the nude, his muscled form highlighted by the brilliant moonlight streaming in from the window adjacent to his bed?

She threw the pillow off. Her palms grew sticky and she clutched the sheet. What was the matter with her? She swallowed painfully. Never before had she fantasized about a man. Why now? Why Jim Burleson? She pressed her hands to her aching head.

After what seemed like an interminably long time, she heard his even breathing in the stillness—slow and easy, long and somnolent.

Darcy eased up onto her side and prayed for sleep to claim her once more. Anything to chase the image of Jim Burleson out of her head.

Chapter 3

The next morning Darcy awoke early, ate breakfast, and then stepped out into the crisp dawn. The coolness felt good against her face and she breathed deeply. She knew that only too soon the glaring sun would be beating down upon her.

She stopped momentarily and looked out across the corral.

The drovers were busy working the wild horses. Above the heads of the brumbies Darcy could see Jim Burleson's virile figure atop his own mount, stock whip at his side, as he cut out certain animals from the pack.

Her thoughts of him last night flooded her. Her face reddened. Pressing a cool hand to her warm cheek, she turned away. She would have to control her foolish notions concerning the man if she was to maintain a professional air. After all, she was here to serve as a doctor, not behave like a wanton hussy.

Darcy kept on walking, her skirts snapping against her legs, toward the Aborigines' huts on the fringe of the compound.

From what she could tell, Aboriginal life was a poor one. Their homes, constructed of bits of bark and mud over a twig framework, and their lack of decent clothing testified to the fact.

She found Newley standing in the center of their encampment, talking to an old man who seemed to be someone of authority.

"You fellas work for white man. We give you flour, sugar, and tobacco," drilled Newley. "You fellas work in garden, work in men's quarters, work cattle. No work, no rations, eh?"

"More baccy."

"No work, no tucker," Newley shot back.

"More baccy," the elder insisted.

Newley's veins stood out along his neck as he hissed, "Look, you bloody savage, that's all you're going to get. Take it or leave it."

Darcy's sense of righteousness overcame her common sense. No human being deserved to be treated in such a manner. "I don't see that it's necessary to speak to him that way. You'll get better results if you show some kindness," she said indignantly.

Newley whirled on her. "Who told you to butt in, lady? You may be the station doctor, but that doesn't give you the right to interfere in men's work."

"Oh, men's work, is it?" She laughed shortly. "Since when does a man have the right to mistreat another?"

Newley took a menacing step toward her. "I'm telling you to mind your own business."

Darcy's own temper flared. This was the second time in as many days that one of the men had told her to stay out of things. She didn't intend to be ignored, or to meekly back down.

"Then I suggest you get back to yours and leave this man alone," she said evenly.

Just then Burleson came into Darcy's field of vision, over Newley's shoulder. He strode toward them, stopping a foot from her.

"What's going on?" he demanded.

"She's interfering, that's what," growled Newley.

Burleson's eyes bore down on Darcy. "I thought I told you to stay out of matters that don't concern you."

"And I'm sick to death of being told that. I'm a member of this station, too, or have you forgotten?"

"I wish the bloody hell I could!"

"And I wish I'd never laid eyes on you. But that doesn't change the situation. What are you going to do about this?"

"Nothing. Newley's in charge of supplies, and it's his job to take care of the natives."

"Since when is it another's job to bully others?"

"You don't know how to deal with Aborigines. We do." Burleson's words came like a crack of a drover's stock whip.

Darcy flinched.

They glared at each other. Neither was going to back down.

Suddenly a scream pierced the air. Both Burleson's and Darcy's heads jerked in the same direction. A second later, another scream came.

Darcy's eyes widened as she saw an Aboriginal man raising a club and striking a young woman.

Lifting her skirts, Darcy ran to the pair. "Stop it! Do you hear me, stop it!"

The man ignored Darcy and continued to rain blows across the woman's shoulders and head. The woman sagged to the ground and crossed her arms around her face in a protective gesture.

Seizing the club, Darcy tried to twist it away from the older man. The Aborigine appeared stunned momentarily. Then his eyes narrowed and he stuck a finger in Darcy's face, spouting in his native language, which Darcy didn't understand. She didn't need to. His expression spoke for him. He was furious.

Inwardly, Darcy cringed at the spate of heated words, but outwardly she stood her ground. "Now, you see here. You don't frighten me. You leave that woman alone."

The Aborigine hesitated for a moment before he jabbed Darcy's chest with the club and caused her to stumble back a step. "White fella's woman have no say." The man swung his club in the direction of the fallen girl. "That my woman. She not do what I tell her. I beat her."

"You can't," Darcy said, starting to move forward.

Suddenly a hand seized her arm, stopping her short. Her head whipped around. She blinked, trying to clear the red haze clouding her thoughts. Her gaze met Burleson's. His eyes burned blue with stark warning.

"Leave it alone, Yank." His fingers flexed about her arm. "Now!"

Darcy drew a ragged breath. "Take your hands off me!"

"Will you quit?"

She tried to extract herself from his grip, but it only tightened.

"I said, will you quit?"

"No."

"Then, by God, I'll have to make you."

All Darcy's frustration and anger came to the fore, overweighing common sense. She slapped his cheek with her free hand.

His expression made her gasp. Never had Darcy seen such fury in a man's eyes. Potent fury.

Before she could react, Darcy found herself steered toward the compound.

Thinking it wiser not to resist until they were away from the others, she suffered Burleson's manhandling as he pulled her to a halt on the far side of the station store.

Seizing her upper arms, Burleson hauled Darcy to him.

She wanted to speak, but no words came from her parched throat. Her anger heightened her senses. She was beyond rational thought. His fingers seemed to scorch her skin as his hold tightened. Yet it was the warmth and strength of his body that branded her senses.

A blush crept up her neck and spread to her face. The quickening of his breath and the flare of his nostrils gave evidence that he, too, was aware of how their bodies touched. Her trembling legs felt hot and liquid, and her hips burned against his. Her nipples ached and strained against the fabric of her blouse. She moistened her suddenly dry lips while his eyes tracked her movement. She squirmed against him, needing to put some distance between them, but he gave no quarter.

Overhead, the sky darkened and rumbled with an approaching storm. Neither Darcy nor Burleson noticed.

Think, Darcy told herself. Think. She didn't want to lower herself to his level, but she also couldn't afford to let him bully her.

She determined that her best defense was to attack. "Look here, *Mister* Burleson! You don't own me, so keep your hands off."

She swallowed as his body shifted against hers. She raised her chin to him, determined to remain cool.

Burleson released her and stepped back. He placed his hands on his hips. "Bloody stupid female! Do you know you could have gotten that girl killed? And you're talking about me grabbing you?"

Darcy's face lit with incredulity. "All I know is that he would've killed her if he'd kept on beating her."

"There's a lot you don't understand."

Her jaw clenched. "Oh, I'm beginning to understand, all right. Men think of themselves as gods, and women are nothing but dirt beneath their feet."

Burleson sighed heavily. "You don't know the first thing about us."

Red stained Darcy's cheeks. "Oh, don't I?"

"No. Aborigines have their own way of doing

things. You've got to learn to respect that," he said through clenched teeth.

Darcy hesitated. She knew he spoke the truth. Maybe she was tired of fighting with Jim Burleson. Maybe, just maybe, she was a little bit oversensitive about people telling her what to do. Nevertheless, her anger funneled toward Burleson.

"Listen to me," Darcy said. "The next time you reach for me, you're going to draw back a nub. You understand that?"

What courage she possessed, Jim thought. Even facing overwhelming odds, she never surrendered to doubt. The green fire of defiance in her eyes confirmed his opinion. She was remarkable. Only her soft exterior hid the steely determination that kept her backbone straight.

But however much he admired her, Jim couldn't show his weakness.

"Always the spitfire." He shook his head and hooked his thumbs into the waistband of his pants. "Does your tongue ever rest? I've met a lot of mettlesome females in my time, but you need a bridle."

"Coming from you, I'll take that as a compliment." She lifted her chin a notch higher. "But I'd appreciate it if you'd just leave me alone from now on."

Courageous defiance could bring a man—or a woman—low in the Outback. She had to learn when to back down, and for that reason, he fought her. Or so he told himself.

"And what am I supposed to do? Let you get yourself into something you don't know anything about? I thought as a doctor that you'd have a fair bit of intelligence. So far, I've seen little."

His words were like a red flag to a bull. "I don't give a tinker's damn what you think. Just don't you ever touch me again. Or—"

He gave her a wry smile. "Or what?"

"Don't try me." She didn't know if her tone sounded convincing. How could she be convincing when he stared at her that way—his eyes hard and glittering?

"I'd like to try and talk some sense into you!" Burleson snarled.

"Since when do you care?"

"Let's just say I don't want to have to pick up the pieces."

"Don't worry, I'm not about to fall apart," Darcy reassured him.

"Oh, I reckon you're tough enough. But are you smart enough to know when you're wrong?"

"Why don't you just let up?"

Burleson laughed. "And miss the way your cheeks get red when you're mad?"

"You're insufferable."

"Yeah, I suppose I am."

"Just leave me alone," Darcy cried.

"Well, Miss High Society from wherever the hell it is you come from, I wouldn't keep that nose of yours in the air too long. You might get it out of joint."

Darcy renewed her struggle. "Ohhh."

Although Burleson shrugged his shoulders, the tension in his face belied any indifference.

"Suit yourself. But let me give you this one last piece of advice." His eye pinned her. "No, a warning. Don't ever slap me again, or I'll take you across my knee and give you the spanking you deserve."

Darcy gasped. "You wouldn't dare!"

"If I were you, I wouldn't want to find out."

She marshaled her anger. "You don't scare me."

"I should." His words were softly but evenly spoken.

"Oh, so now we think we're such a rough man."

"If you're not careful, I'll show you just how rough I can be, or how much of a man I can be. It just might be more than you could handle."

Apprehension slithered down Darcy's spine. Somehow his threat was one she didn't have the nerve to test at that moment.

Lightning split the sky. Thunder boomed like bass drums as raindrops began to fall. Darcy paid no heed. She was aware of nothing save the man who stood before her.

And then he did the unspeakable. He turned his back on her and started to move away. No one did that to her. No one!

Rain pelted her face and she cupped her hands to shield her eyes. "Don't you dare walk away from me! Not until I'm through."

Burleson inclined his head and mockingly tipped his hat before striding onward.

Darcy tried to step forward but found her foot mired in the quickly developing mud. Rain fell in sheets now and the ground couldn't absorb the water fast enough. Mud, thick and oozing, crept up her ankles.

Her eyes narrowed and her nostrils flared. "You come back here," she shouted above the din.

When he made no move in her direction, she lifted her skirts and one foot. In the next instant she slipped. Arms flailing, Darcy yelped and landed on her bottom in the ooze.

Despite the driving rain, Burleson heard the commotion and glanced over his shoulder. A smile touched his lips.

Sitting, she flung away the mud from her hands and arms and glared mutinously at him.

Even in her present state, she was the loveliest woman he had ever seen. Loose strands of hair hung damply about her face, and the planes of her features were delineated, soft and beautiful. Water beads dotted her eyelashes as she blinked at him.

Jim went to her and bent to lend a hand. He grinned and she returned his smile sweetly. Too sweetly.

That should have been a clue.

Suddenly, she gave a yank. He fell facedown with a splat. Slowly he rolled onto his back and sat up.

Wiping the mud from his face, he looked at her. He could have sworn he saw a twinkle lurking in her eyes. He didn't know whether to be angry or amused. He should be mad because of her defiance and interference. But somehow the simple sight of her made him forget to be mad.

Darcy sat and waited for him to explode. She feared she'd gone too far this time. What would he do? Take her over his knee? She held her breath.

His face was expressionless. She wished to God she could tell what he was thinking. She swallowed painfully.

Suddenly he laughed. Laughed until his shoulders shook. Darcy looked perplexed. "Why are you laughing? Another man wouldn't find this so funny."

"I'm not another man. And no other woman but you would have dared to do what you just did."

"I guess you just bring out the best in me," she said sarcastically.

And then a wicked grin lifted his lips. Ever so slowly, he scooped up a handful of mud and reached out toward her.

"But—"

Her words were cut off as his hand, dripping with mud, blazed a bold path from her neck to her breasts. For a brief second it lingered against their fullness, burning her flesh.

"What a mess I've made." His eyes glittered. "Shall I wipe it away?"

"You'd just love that, wouldn't you?" she snapped. Breathing hard, Darcy struggled to rise.

Burleson stood also. He cocked his head at her and his smile broadened. "Now that's what I like about you, always a woman of action."

"I'll give you action, you pompous ass."

"There's nothing pompous about yours."

"Ohhh."

Her arm swung in an arc toward him, but she lost her footing and crashed into him. They went down in a heap with Darcy atop Burleson.

Darcy lost her breath as her mouth hovered inches from his. His sparkling blue eyes enveloped her. His body heat flowed through hers, and she felt hot and liquid inside. Except there was nothing soft about the feel of his muscles beneath her. They were hard and unyielding. Masculine and sensual. Any thought of protest fled. Even the driving rain was relegated to the back of her mind.

His breath, warm and light, whispered against her lips. "Hmm. You feel good."

"Do you always think with what's between your legs?" she snapped, then inwardly groaned at her impertinent tongue.

"Only when a beautiful woman is on it."

His rigidness beneath her gave credence to the fact. And for a second she wondered what it would be like to lie atop his body with no fabric between them.

With difficulty, she managed to recover her composure. "Would you please help me up now?"

"Certainly. First, just one thing to do—"

Jim smeared mud across her face.

Darcy was speechless. All he could see were the whites of her eyes contrasting with the red mud. But even dirty, she was beautiful. Too damned beautiful. To look at her face—graceful, alluring, and candid—nearly made him forget himself.

He sobered. He needed to get away from her. He didn't want to see all the passion and furor and loveliness that shadowed her eyes.

He didn't want to desire her.

But he did.

As if his arms had a will of their own, they reached for her. Jim couldn't stop himself. He pulled her to her feet and into his arms.

Even the weather seemed to do his bidding, for a furious thunderclap exploded, shaking the ground beneath them, and she instinctively pressed closer to him.

His fingers traced a lazy pattern down her cheeks, leaving tiny furrows through the mud, skimming to the base of her throat where he felt her pulse beating. His fingertips wiped away the grime from her lips. He slowly lowered his head, his mouth whispering against hers. His tongue eased into her mouth, caressing the insides. Desire burst upon him like the brilliant stars of the Southern Cross sparkling diamond-like across the heavens at night.

The pressure of his hand and the force of his mouth were too great for Darcy to resist. Their lips seemed to fuse. Her hands opened and closed on his shirtfront. Her blood, fast and heated, flowed through her veins, a molten current of desire.

Through sheer effort of will, she managed to pull away before insanity claimed her. She turned her head, not wanting him to see his effect on her, and she lifted a shaking hand to her still warm and trembling lips. She forced her irregular breathing to steady before she faced him again.

Her voice came as a whisper against the storm. "Burleson?"

Their eyes met.

"What?"

"Don't ever do that again."

"Darcy—" He stopped. It was the first time he had used her given name. "I'm—"

"Don't apologize. I don't like liars."

If she had taken the time to look, she would have recognized the flash of true emotion in his eyes. But instead, she turned on her heel and tried to stride away, discovering as she did what a singularly painful exercise it was to walk with dignity when covered with mud. Especially when she'd just been kissed by a man who elicited unwanted emotions in her.

But somehow she managed to step into the store and go to her quarters. She was grateful Burleson made no move to follow.

Not wanting to dirty her bed, she wearily sank to the floor and folded her hands in her lap. What was she to do now? She'd certainly made a mess of things today.

An even uglier thought crept into her mind. Had any of the men seen her unseemly behavior?

Outside, the storm had intensified. Rain battered the roof and thrashed against the side of the store. Like the storm within her, her emotions whirled in circles.

Moments later, Kim Loo arrived with two buckets of hot water.

Darcy stood, mud drying on her clothes and skin, and watched with longing as he poured the water into a hip bath, hidden behind a partition, located in the far corner of the room.

Steam rose lazily from the hot water. Darcy sighed. She imagined how heavenly the bath would feel. It would be like food to a starving man. She hadn't enjoyed a real bath since she'd left the States.

"Boss say this for you, missy," Kim Loo said with a wink. "I leave towels and soap on stool by bath. You enjoy."

At first Darcy was amazed at Burleson's goodwill gesture. But then she grew suspicious. She knew water in the Outback was a precious commodity. "Where is the boss?"

"He say he not bother you. He gone outside."

"Oh."

"Now get in water before grows cold," Kim Loo finished before shutting the door behind him.

Darcy stared at where Kim Loo had just stood. Clenching her fists, she doubled over and screamed, a furious and frustrated scream. Spontaneously, another clap of thunder boomed, masking her shriek.

She straightened and inhaled deeply. There, she'd done it. So why didn't she feel better? She felt as confused and upset as ever. Nothing had worked out the way she had anticipated since her arrival here. Nothing!

That evening a cleaned and refreshed Darcy went to Kim Loo's kitchen to have something to eat. She didn't want to dine with the men. Not after what had happened earlier in the day. She'd face them tomorrow.

She paused in the doorway at the sight of Jim Burleson sitting alone. He looked up from his food. Wariness lurked in his eyes.

Darcy summoned her good breeding, determined to be polite. "Oh, I'm sorry. I had no idea you were here."

"Or you wouldn't have come, right?" he said caustically.

His remark stung. Her thoughts flashed back to their shared laughter. The Jim Burleson of old had returned.

Darcy sighed. "Well, I can see your good mood has vanished. If you'll excuse me." She turned to leave.

"Don't go on my account. I'm nearly finished," he said.

Darcy walked to the cupboard and picked up a plate, utensils, and a glass of water before moving to the table. She sat opposite him.

"I'll try not to bother you," she said.

"A little late for that." His voice, masculine and full-bodied, flowed through her, down to her nerve endings. She reached for her glass and took a sip of water.

And as if her reaction to Burleson wasn't bad enough, she discovered him looking intently at her.

She attempted to make light conversation. Anything to relieve the anxiousness she felt. "This looks good."

"Yes, it does."

Something in the tone of his voice caused her to wonder if his words held some double meaning.

Darcy filled her plate with beef, succulently roasted with onions and herbs. Potatoes, bread, and cheese completed the course.

"Kim Loo is a good cook," she said between bites. "You're fortunate to have him."

Jim sopped up gravy with a piece of damper and popped it in his mouth. A drop of gravy trickled down his lip. He wiped the brown trace away with his tongue.

"Fortune changes all the time. Mine has," he said before slowly chewing another piece of meat.

Darcy realized she had been staring. Her eyes darted to her plate and she clutched the napkin in her lap.

Hell's bells! Did he always have to look at her that way? As if he knew what she looked like without her clothes on.

Flustered, Darcy abandoned all attempts at conversation.

An uncomfortable silence ensued, broken only by the sound of forks moving across plates.

Darcy tried to keep her eyes on her food, but soon discovered that her neck hurt from the strain of looking down and ignoring her company.

She looked up as Burleson raised his fork to his mouth. Ridiculous that she should notice how the white of his shirt contrasted with the golden richness of his skin. Or recall how full and sensual those lips had felt as she watched him take another bite of food. She nearly dropped her own fork.

What was the matter with her? He probably couldn't care less that I'm sitting here, she thought.

She couldn't have been farther from the truth.

Jim was all too aware of Darcy.

She wore her hair pulled back and tied simply with a ribbon. The red coils fell gently down her back. In the lantern glow, her hair appeared fiery and silky. It beckoned a man's touch. Jim refrained from the impulse to reach out.

Discerning the course of his thoughts, he knew he had to leave. He wouldn't sit there and torture himself with visions of Darcy McCall, willing and eager in his arms. Damn! He'd been without a woman too long.

It had been three years since his relationship with Cynthia had ended. He had thought he'd found the perfect woman until he had brought her to Kopperella. Cynthia had been aghast at what she had seen. Within minutes, she had been ready to leave.

What woman would want to live in the Outback when she could live in comfort in the city? she had asked.

What woman indeed?

He rose.

"Don't go yet." Darcy moistened her lips, not comprehending how seductive her innocent gesture appeared. "There's something I need to talk to you about."

Jim sat down again, straddling the chair, his arms crossed atop the back. "I'm listening."

"I think we both realize that my sharing accommodations with you doesn't work at all."

"If you think—"

"I'm not accusing you of anything."

"So what are you—"

She raised a hand to silence him. "Just listen to what I've got to say. Please." She breathed deeply. "I need a place of my own. Not only for privacy but for my practice. I've got nowhere to put my instruments and medicines. You can't expect me to work under these conditions."

"You knew what you were getting yourself into."

Darcy thought she had, but she hadn't been prepared for what she'd found. She wouldn't enlighten Mr. Burleson on that point. He'd use it as another stick to beat her with if she gave him the opportunity.

"But even doctors in the most primitive of places must have somewhere to work."

"You've got a point." Jim thoughtfully rubbed the side of his jaw with the back of his hand. "I see your problem."

"Good. Then I can depend on your cooperation?" Hope brightened her eyes. Hope and relief.

"I'll see what can be done." Jim rose. "I'd best be going now. There are things to be done before nightfall."

Darcy watched his broad shoulders disappear through the door. She rested her elbows on the table and cradled her cheek in the palm of one hand, musing. He actually seemed to be sorry for the way he'd behaved, and willing to listen to reason. She could hardly believe it. She sighed and shook her head. At least she could count on one thing—life on Kopperella would never be dull. Not if Jim Burleson had anything to do with it.

Chapter 4

A week later, Darcy observed her new home with pride. The men had worked diligently and produced a more-than-adequate dwelling.

It was a quaint little house, whitewashed, with a bark roof and the usual veranda hugging the four sides, set off from the compound. A fence, to keep out unwelcome visitors, enclosed a small yard. But best of all, it was hers.

A smile on her lips, she straightened her apron and set about scrubbing the floors. She picked up a bucket and went to the pump. She gave a hearty push—once, twice—until a steady stream poured into the metal container.

Kneeling, she lit into her chore with a cheerfulness that she hadn't believed possible in quite some time.

She dipped her brush into the bucket and brought the bristles away sudsy. Sliding the brush back and forth vigorously, leaving tiny tracks of white foam, she put her weight into the task and felt as though she was accomplishing something. Soon the men would have a place to come to for treatment, and her mission would be complete. At last she would be accepted as the doctor she was.

The afternoon drifted away as Darcy lost herself in her thoughts and plans.

It wasn't until she heard the sound of the front screen door opening and closing that she looked up from laying out her instruments on a table next to the wall in the front room.

Pushing loose strands of damp hair from her eyes, Darcy stared into the face of an Aborigine girl who, she guessed, was nearly eight years old. The youngster's eyes, large and dark, sparkled with inquisitiveness as she regarded Darcy from just inside the doorway. Her features were small and delicate, framed by a short, ragged line of hair which had been chopped off around the sides of her head. A faded red dress hung from her thin frame.

"Oh." Darcy said, then patted her hair into place and wiped her brow with the end of her apron.

The girl made as if to leave, but Darcy called to her, "Don't go."

The small visitor looked dubious. Darcy spoke reassuringly. "It's just that you scared me. I didn't expect anyone." She motioned for the girl to come closer. "I won't hurt you."

The child turned in profile, her back and shoulders straight. The sun streamed in from the open door and kissed her dark gold skin.

With a soft smile on her face, Darcy moved toward her. "What's your name?"

The girl glanced first at Darcy, then around the room, taking in Darcy's instruments and medicines. Darcy imagined that to the child they appeared wondrous and a bit mysterious.

Momentarily, her gaze resettled on Darcy. "Rosie."

"Rosie? Where'd you get the name?"

"Mother liked white name."

"Well, Rosie, what brings you here?" Darcy's heels scuffed softly across the wooden floor as she stepped closer to the little girl. "Do you want me to look at something? Are you hurt?" Her eyes scanned the small figure.

With all the innocence of a child, Rosie said, "No. I come to see you. Wanted to see what others talk about."

"You're welcome here."

"No come in white fella's house."

"This is my home and I say you may." Darcy spoke softly but firmly.

"I get in trouble."

"No, you won't." Darcy added thoughtfully, "Are you afraid of me?"

"No. I see lots of white men on station."

"If you're not afraid, then come in."

That seemed to please the girl, because she smiled. It was a smile of guilelessness and warmth.

"Would you like to look around? I promise not to hurt you."

Rosie moved about the room, examining first one thing and then another. She moved with a delightful natural grace, yet an aura of wildness surrounded her. She seemed a creature free and untamed.

What a wonderful uninhibited child she was,

Darcy thought. So unaware of any pretentiousness.

Then Darcy had an idea. Perhaps the girl was in need of help, but unable to ask for it. Even these people had pride. Darcy could offer that help. At least, nothing would be lost if she tried.

"Rosie, would you like to help me? I'll give you food."

Darcy touched the child's shoulder. How thin and fragile it felt. She made a mental note to give the girl an examination later, after she'd won her trust.

"Here in house?"

Darcy knelt to the child's level. "Yes, here in house."

"You want me to start now?"

Darcy touched the side of the child's face. Her cheek felt warm and soft. "If you want to."

"All right."

"Don't you have to tell your mother or something?"

"Mother and Father not here."

Darcy's brow knitted. "Who do you live with?"

"With others in village."

"But with whom?" Darcy persisted.

"Just others. Go to different ones."

"You're an orphan, then."

Rosie frowned. "What that?"

"Oh, never mind. It doesn't matter. Come on and I'll get you started." Darcy stood and took Rosie's hand.

Another thought struck Darcy. She wondered if the child had eaten today.

"But first, I was just about to have a bite to eat," she said inventively. "Are you hungry?"

Rosie's small dark head bobbed eagerly. "Yes."

"Good. Me, too."

Hand in hand, they started for Kim Loo's kitchen.

The sun had traveled its course and now sank low on the horizon. Shadows lengthened across the landscape as the pair continued walking.

Smoke from Kim Loo's kitchen eddied along the buildings, and clouds of mosquitoes and flies thickened as dusk approached. Then a breeze rustled and scattered both the smoke and the insects with wispy tendrils of air.

Across the compound fires burned brightly among the Aborigines' shelters. In the men's quarters a lantern glowed in the window. The sounds of the insects and frogs along the creek in the distance closed around them.

Another lantern, casting a yellow glow on the dusty ground, dimly illuminated Darcy and her companion as they neared their destination. Delicious aromas wafted from the kitchen as they stepped inside the door.

Craig Newley, Dave Patterson, and Tom Rivers were eating their evening meal. Conversation flowed freely, interspersed with occasional laughter.

Darcy spied Kim Loo in the corner tending to the stove. "Something smells wonderful. Would you have enough for me and a friend?"

At first Darcy failed to notice the sudden silence that dropped like a heavy curtain. But as she crossed the room, the tension gripped her. Something was wrong. Very wrong.

The hairs on the nape of her neck prickled as she steered Rosie to a spot at the table with a guiding hand on the child's back. Whatever the problem, she would face it squarely.

However, the hatred emanating from Craig Newley's eyes smote Darcy in her tracks. She instinctively pushed Rosie behind her.

"We don't allow their kind to eat in 'ere," Newley spat out at Darcy, lowering his fork.

A look of utter disbelief marred Darcy's face. "You can't possibly mean that. She's just a child."

Newley's hand clenched beside his plate. "The little bugger is worse than a rat, and I don't eat with the likes of 'er."

Darcy refused to be intimidated. The rightness of her cause firmed her determination. "I'm sorry you feel that way, but I brought her here and we're staying."

She turned to Kim Loo. "May I have two plates, please?"

There was the scrape of a chair leg against the floor and then the sound of menacing footsteps as Newley approached Darcy. They stood but inches apart.

Darcy braced herself against the imminent affront. "Kindly step aside."

"Maybe Dr. McCall doesn't 'ear so good," Newley tossed over his shoulder at the other two drovers.

"Or is it that you're too simple to understand?" she offered in rebuttal.

Tom Rivers looked up from his food. "Let it go, Newley. The boss wouldn't want no trouble."

"Trouble, is it? Well, the doctor 'ere should 'ave thought of that before she brought this nit around decent folk."

Anger exploded inside Darcy's head. "You don't have a decent bone in your body, Craig Newley! You're a poor excuse for a man."

A blast of foul breath struck her and she turned her head in disgust as Newley spoke. "Maybe I should show you just 'ow much of a man I am."

Her gaze snapped back to his. "You make me sick."

Newley snorted. "If you don't get 'er out of 'ere, I'm going to toss her out myself." He reached out for Rosie.

Knocking his hand away, Darcy drew herself up to her full height and retorted, "You can try. But you'll have to get through me first."

Newley stepped closer. Their bodies nearly touched. "If that's the way you want it."

The air bristled with tension. The two of them stood that way for a long moment, but then Tom Rivers jumped up and placed himself between the combatants. He faced Newley. "Leave it alone, mate."

"I'll not 'ave some fancy woman tell me what's right and wrong. She's got to learn 'er place."

"And just what is that?" came Burleson's voice.

All eyes fell on the doorway.

Darcy was outraged. How could these men call themselves civilized when they treated the less fortunate like the plague?

She steeled herself to do battle.

Tom Rivers stepped back. Darcy and Newley were left in the middle of the room, staring at each other.

An ominous silence wrapped around them. Darcy imagined she heard each ragged breath she drew. She braced her feet slightly apart. Her eyes never left Newley.

Behind her, Rosie squirmed under Darcy's hold, wanting to flee.

But Darcy wasn't going anywhere. Resentment stiffened her spine.

Burleson broke the impasse. "I suggest you men go along to your quarters."

Rivers and young Patterson started for the door, each tugging on his hat and nodding toward Darcy before disappearing into the night.

Burleson's gaze leveled upon Newley. "Get going."

"I'm not moving," Newley groused.

The authority in Burleson's voice brooked no argument. "Yes, you are, mate." His words were enforced with a visible tensing of his body. "Straightaway."

Tension rippled through Newley's body as his hand clenched at his sides. "You're the boss. That's the only reason I'm leaving." With that he grunted and brushed past Darcy, walking over to Burleson. "You mark my words. You're going to regret the day she set foot on Kopperella."

"The agents in London have the say on that, and you know it. The two of us just work here."

"You just going to let 'er run us?"

Jim's eyes narrowed. "Don't back me into a corner."

"She's nothing but trouble. I don't want 'er 'ere, and neither do the boys."

"You're the only one doing the talking."

"Cowards, the lot of them," Newley grumbled.

"I want nothing more said."

"It's a free country. I can say whatever I like."

"Not if you want to keep your job."

Newley's expression revealed his disbelief. "I'm the best drover you've got on this bleedin' station. You're not going to give me the sack because of 'er."

"I'll fire you if you don't follow orders."

Burleson's reply did nothing to sweeten Newley's mood. He stomped past Burleson into the night.

Burleson followed, striding to overtake him.

He caught up with Newley ten feet from the kitchen. "Let's get something straight right now. You're to do what I say. Understand?"

Newley whirled, his face cast in a play of light and night shadows. "Aren't we the big man?"

Jim ground out, "I said, do you understand?"

"All right. I reckon you mean to get the doctor to yourself and 'ave a fair go beneath her skirts."

Jim grabbed the front of Newley's shirt and hauled him close. Their noses nearly touched.

"Well, you reckoned wrong. You got that, mate?"

Newley knocked Jim's hands away and pulled back. "Yeah, I got it, all right. I got it perfectly clear."

Rearranging his shirt, he strode to the men's quarters, leaving Burleson behind.

Jim looked down at his feet. Anger, heavy and cold, coiled inside his stomach. He'd never come so close to striking one of the men. He didn't like the feeling. And it was all because of Darcy McCall.

He slammed his fist into the open palm of his other hand. The sound smacked into the night chorus of insects. Damn! Bloody well damn! His footsteps dragged as he went back to the kitchen. But when he saw her there with the little girl, he couldn't seem to hold on to his anger. He stood at the threshold watching her.

Darcy patted Rosie on the shoulder. "You sit down at the table." She spoke above the child's head to Kim Loo, who had stood silently during the heated exchange. "Will you get her something to eat?"

The cook nodded and set about filling a plate.

Darcy turned her attention to Burleson. He pulled out a chair and sat down opposite Rosie. His hair was wet, as if he'd recently washed it, and an appealing musky scent clung to him.

"Don't take offense to Newley. He doesn't know any other way." Burleson's voice traveled softly across the space separating them.

Darcy doubted his statement, but she didn't care to argue the point. Some feminine instinct told her that Newley would be her nemesis as long as she stayed.

Despite the apology, shadows lingered in the foreman's eyes, shadows that suddenly alarmed her. Jim Burleson could be appeasing when he chose to, yet she sensed something lurking beneath the surface, something that both fascinated and frightened her. She really knew so little about him.

Darcy settled herself next to Rosie. The way the child gobbled down her food, one would think she hadn't eaten all day.

Placing a hand on the child's shoulder, Darcy cautioned, "Slow down, little one, or you'll choke."

She tucked the girl's hair behind her ear. Rosie never looked up or slowed her chewing.

Burleson sipped the cup of tea Kim Loo had poured for him. Over the rim he studied the orphan. "What do you reckon to do with her?"

Darcy placed her elbow on the table and cradled the side of her face in her hand. "I don't know exactly. I did offer her work, though. And I thought I could learn from her. There's so much I don't know about these people."

Burleson set his cup down and fingered the handle. "What is it you want to know?"

"Everything. To me they're fascinating. They've survived on precious little where most people couldn't."

"Be careful."

Darcy's brow knitted. "Of what?"

"Don't get caught up in something you don't understand."

"Like?"

"Danger in losing your judgment."

"What's that supposed to mean?"

"It means you haven't got the slightest idea about them. One day they're here, working, doing what they're told. Then for no reason we can figure, they're gone. For weeks at a time on walkabout."

She frowned. "Walkabout?"

"Yeah, they wander off."

Darcy shook her head. "Rosie is too young for such. She won't do that."

"I'm telling you that she will. Just don't get too attached to her."

"You don't have to lecture me. After all, I'm a doctor and a grown woman."

Jim nearly groaned aloud. He, of all people, knew how grown she was. He tipped back in his chair and looked at her speculatively. "I can't help but wonder what brought you out here. I mean, a woman like you . . ."

Darcy blushed at the frank appreciativeness of his gaze. "Mr. Burleson, medicine means everything to me. It wasn't easy for me to get as far as I have. Even after I graduated from medical school, they made it almost impossible for me to practice—just because I'm a woman. So I signed the contract to work at Kopperella."

"You leave a lot of family behind?"

Darcy looked over his shoulder, then shrugged. "I lost my father while I was in school, and then Mother remarried."

Jim saw a cloud pass over her eyes, and for a moment he felt as if he could see behind the mystery of Dr. Darcy McCall. But then the cloud was gone. He changed the subject. "We go on muster tomorrow. Being the doctor, you'll need to come along."

"Muster?"

"That's where we round up the cattle, do our branding and the like."

"In the States we call that a roundup." Darcy's eyes lit with enthusiasm.

Burleson laughed. "You'll have to learn how to live with the insects and the rest. To sleep out in the open under a tent. And for the next week, you'll swat flies and eat dust."

"Sounds wonderful," Darcy said. "I'll be ready at sunrise."

Chapter 5

The following day Burleson's words came back with a vengeance as Darcy rode with Kim Loo. She sank into a dull stupor from the suffocating heat as the wagon trailed behind the drovers.

The drovers' route lay over country flat to the horizon's end, meandering through a maze of claypan channels edged with saltbush and gums. Red sand hills, beaten and laid bare by desert winds, serrated the skyline as the bushmen veered toward the nearest creek.

She was only dimly aware of the flurry of activity ahead, the exhilaration of the season's first muster gripping the men.

Darcy glimpsed Jim Burleson atop his mount through the billowing clouds of dust kicked up by the horses. He cut a virile figure with his hat pulled low and his stock whip at the ready.

Before noon, Kim Loo pulled on the traces and shouted at the horses as he stepped on the brake lever. The wagon rolled to a halt. He put the whip in the socket by the seat and wrapped the reins around it.

He glanced at Darcy before climbing down. Between breaths he spoke. "We stop here. Boss want men fed soon."

He disappeared around the back.

Darcy rolled her neck from side to side and hunched her shoulders. She felt as if she were still moving.

Gathering up her skirts, she stepped over the side of the wagon, placed her foot carefully on a wheel hub, then lifted the other foot and gained the ground. She removed her straw hat and tucked renegade strands of damp hair back into place. Pulling the perspiration-moistened material of her dress away from her neck, she vigorously fanned herself before she replaced her hat atop her head.

With the settling dust, the insects swarmed. Flies and mosquitoes gathered in a knitted ball of sound and movement. The flies congregated around the eyes and the mouth, and crawled into the nostrils. Darcy felt as if she would go mad. If she opened her mouth, one or two flies were sure to get in. The mosquitoes gathered in droning clouds, biting through clothes with a ferociousness, raising irritating bumps. The lotion she had applied did little to thwart the insects.

"Can I help with the cooking?" Darcy asked Kim Loo, who had returned.

"Oh, no."

"But I want to. Just tell me what's to be done."

She stood in abject misery and held the flies at bay by waving a hand near her face as Kim Loo unhitched the team from the wagon. He led the horses away and hobbled them among the kangaroo grass, where they began munching happily.

Kim Loo scuffled over to the tailgate and dropped it, chains rattling. He pulled out a bag of flour and lifted a couple of large pans, metal pinging, down from a hook on one of the bows supporting the canvas cover on the wagon. He then retrieved a smaller bag of salt before he picked up a bucket and went around to the side of the wagon to dip water out of the barrel.

"I make damper," Kim Loo explained.

"I really want to help. Show me," Darcy offered as she watched him ready his ingredients.

He dipped flour into a bowl, spooned salt into it, and poured in the water.

"You use hands," Kim Loo instructed.

"I see."

When Darcy began to wash her hands, Kim Loo said, "Boss no like wasting water."

She knew water was precious, but the habits of a doctor were hard to break. As far as she was concerned, the boss could be damned. Too many diseases were caused by uncleanliness.

Darcy plunged her hands into the cool, sticky dough. Soon it took on a lumpy shape with a thick consistency.

Flies and mosquitoes swarmed about her face. She tried to shrug them away with her shoulder, which proved nearly impossible.

Meanwhile, Kim Loo gathered wood and built a fire. He threw green boughs on the hotly burning fire. Thick smoke blanketed the wagon, making it difficult for Darcy to breathe and causing her eyes to water. Yet she was grateful because it drove away the maddening insects.

Darcy finished the damper. Kim Loo put the dough into the pans, placing them on the fire. He took the bucket used for making tea around to the barrel, filled it, and put the billy on the fire.

Burleson rode up and dismounted, removing his hat and fanning the flies away from his face. He looked at Darcy's hands and smiled impudently. "I see you're making yourself useful."

"At least Kim Loo isn't too proud to accept my help." She grabbed a towel and wiped away the dough.

"Actually, that's why I'm here. I need you to look at my eyes."

"Sit down." Darcy motioned toward a tree stump nearby.

Sitting, Burleson raked his fingers through his hair, pulling it away from his forehead. "Damned dust. Gets into everything out here."

Placing a hand on his brow, Darcy gently pushed Burleson's head back so she could get a better look at his red and inflamed eyes.

Her gaze strayed to his mouth. Lips, framed by deep lines cut by the weather, beckoned to her. Lips that tugged at her sensuality. She forced her thoughts back to her job. For heaven's sake, she was a doctor and must behave like one.

"I have some drops. You should be feeling better in no time."

She applied two drops to each eye. "Now blink so the medicine will spread evenly."

She observed how small beads of moisture coated his eyelashes. Ridiculous that she should notice how long they were. And then he looked at her with those startling blue eyes.

Her mouth tightened in annoyance at the wild thudding of her heart.

He stood, his figure rimmed by the faint rays of the setting sun, and suddenly his eyes were looking into hers, their blue reflecting the leaping firelight.

His voice spun a silken cocoon around her. "Thank you."

"You're welcome." Unconsciously, her tongue moistened her lips.

She should move, but her body refused to obey. Somehow his closeness mesmerized her. His scent bathed her heightened senses, and her vision filled with the lean, whisker-stubbled planes of his face. He was an enigma she could not fathom. Still, she had the crazy impulse to lean into him and wrap her arms around him.

"The others will be coming in soon," Burleson said crisply, breaking the spell.

"You wouldn't want to be caught talking to the enemy, would you?"

His eyes crinkled in amusement. "Never at a loss for words, are you?"

Only when you're near, she thought.

Aloud, she said, "Not often."

He turned as if to leave. Suddenly the thought of him leaving distressed her. But why?

She'd already spent more than a few sleepless nights mulling over her reaction to him. It was ridiculous that she should feel anything at all for him—let alone attraction. They had been at odds with each other from the beginning. What she should feel was professional detachment. In medical school she had been told never to become personally involved with any of her patients.

But Darcy had never been able to follow her teachers' advice. She cared for all those she treated during her training, no matter their race or circumstance. They were all people. And in the case of Jim Burleson, it was somehow especially hard to be detached.

The next morning the sun rode low on the horizon, casting its golden mantle over the landscape. The rising temperature toasted the flora and dispelled the lingering night chill.

Darcy sat atop the mount Jim had provided and watched the men work the cattle. She batted away the flies and groaned. Blast the infernal creatures! They were almost as intolerable as the men on this station.

Darcy dismounted and sat in the shade of a gum, its ghostly white bark reflecting the rising sun's light. She removed her hat and fanned herself. Loose tendrils of hair whispered across her neck and face with each flutter of her wrist. She sighed.

In the distance, cattle bellowed as the drovers gathered them. The smell of manure permeated the air and fine dust particles floated about.

Tom Rivers and Dave Patterson rode in close pursuit of a heifer. Thundering hooves echoed across the land; dirt and bits of dried grass swirled in their wake.

Eventually the drovers got close enough, and Patterson leaned over his horse to twist the animal's tail, yanking the creature to a halt. The heifer dropped to the ground, and Tom Rivers bounded off his horse and tied the animal with a length of rope. In a matter of minutes the men had the cow marked and branded.

Suddenly a bull crashed out of the brush. It stopped some twenty feet from Darcy and eyed her. Snorts of rushing air streamed from the bull's nostrils.

Her eyes widened and her face paled beneath a sheen of perspiration. Her nostrils flared with the scent of danger. Darcy was numb with fright.

Nearby, her mount twisted its head in a frenzy to be free. The horse lunged backward, muscles bunching and sweat rolling down its sleek sides. The reins pulled away from the branch where Darcy had loosely tied them, allowing the mare, with ears laid back and eyes rolling, to race away.

Suddenly Jim shouted at her, "For the love of God, woman, get up!"

His voice pierced her paralysis. She scrambled to her feet and braced herself against the tree, the bark biting into her back. Her shaking hands reached around the trunk and her icy palms rested against the wood.

To keep herself from screaming, Darcy bit her lip until she tasted blood. Dear Lord, please don't let me die!

The bull pawed the ground. Dust and small rocks showered the air. Darcy imagined its fiery breath as the beast snorted again and flung its head from side to side.

"Darcy—the tree. Move your ass!" Jim shouted as he reined his horse in a sharper angle toward her.

A single word throbbed through her—*Survive!*

She became a whirlwind of motion. Facing the gum, she tried frantically to scramble up it. Her skirts hampered her and her boots slipped on the bark as she jumped up and clung to a low branch.

She heard the angry bull bellowing. She heard the pounding of her heart.

Her hold was tremulous and her fingers ached unbearably. One by one, they grew numb and uncurled from the tree limb. Slowly she slid to the ground.

She felt tears threaten as she pressed her forehead to the bark. She took a deep, shuddering breath, then snapped her head around as she sought an avenue of escape. A stand of trees came into focus. If she could just reach them . . .

But she didn't even have time to turn and run, for suddenly Jim drew near. His charging horse dwarfed her as it came abreast.

Leaning to the right, ducking branches, he reached down and caught Darcy within the solid circle of his arm. With a low grunt, he hauled her in front of him.

The tree of the saddle bit into her thigh, but

discomfort was quickly forgotten as his arms held her tightly. Never had she felt so secure.

With her face inches from his, she saw his eyes reflect his concern and relief.

"You all right?" he breathed in a raspy rush.

"Just scared."

Taking his eye off the bull proved to be Jim's mistake. A snort sounded dangerously close, and his mount was bumped.

Darcy cried out as the bull's horn slashed an angry gash in her calf. She gritted her teeth and turned her face into Jim's chest.

The bull changed direction and Tom Rivers turned his mare into the morning sun, his long whip snaking out to cut the bull's flank. The angry beast turned, head down, to charge, but Rivers, his gun already drawn, shot the bull between the eyes before it could attack again.

The body, gripped in the throes of death, twitched until it relaxed and went still. Crimson stained the rusty earth as the powdery sands quickly absorbed the blood.

Satisfied that they were out of danger, Jim bent his head as a tremor passed through Darcy's body. "What's the matter?"

Darcy clutched the front of his shirt with one hand. "My leg . . ."

Jim reined his horse next to the wagon. He dismounted, sweeping his leg over the rump of his mount, and pulled Darcy into his arms. He walked two steps, spurs jingling, and gingerly sat her down on the ground. He knelt on one knee beside her.

Worry etched deep lines about his mouth. "Are you hurt bad?"

"I don't ... know." Tiny gasps of pain punctuated her voice.

She leaned against the wagon wheel. A light film of perspiration covered her forehead as she lifted her skirts with trembling fingers. Blood trickled from a large tear in her stocking. Moistening her dry lips, she probed the wound gently with her fingertips.

Darcy knew in an instant the wound was deep. Infection would set in if it wasn't properly cleaned and sutured.

"Get my bag."

Jim got the bag from the wagon and handed it to her. Their fingers touched briefly and their eyes met.

"Do you need any help?" he asked.

"I think I can manage."

Darcy reached inside the bag and retrieved a pair of scissors and began to cut away her hose. In spite of her careful, slow movements, threads of skin clung to the stocking. She sucked in her breath.

"Could you get me some disinfectant?" she rasped.

Jim poked inside. "Right."

He quickly uncorked the small bottle and poured a trickle of the liquid across the wound.

Darcy's body trembled at the contact, but she didn't utter a word.

"You always manage to be in the wrong place at the wrong time." Jim's voice sounded teasing and light, but his face appeared solemn.

Darcy gave him a tentative smile. "You don't have to talk for my sake."

Pulling out a roll of gauze, Darcy cut off a section and dabbed at the wound, trying to staunch the flow of blood. She then brought out a needle and some catgut.

Jim's voice revealed his admiration. "You going to sew yourself up?"

Darcy sat forward. "Well, I'm the doctor, aren't I?"

"And a strong one," Jim murmured.

Darcy didn't falter, although his words caressed her as if he'd touched her physically.

She moistened her lips. "Pour the disinfectant over my hands and the needle, please."

Jim did so.

She threaded the needle and began. But when the point pierced her flesh, Darcy hissed. She broke out in a cold sweat and her face grew white. Her hand fell to her side and she leaned back against the wagon wheel.

"Here, let me do that." Jim's hand closed over hers and slowly removed her fingers from around the needle.

Darcy feebly shook her head and shut her eyes.

"Don't you want anything for the pain?"

"I can't. My body doesn't tolerate laudanum."

"I'll try not to hurt you."

"Just get on with it."

Stoically, she remained still as Jim set about his grim task after he had disinfected his hands.

With each pass of the needle, Darcy ground

her teeth. She forced her mind to a far and distant place. A place where pain didn't exist.

Her eyes fluttered and she fainted.

Jim picked her up and carried her to her swag, where he lay her down.

The faint scent of roses from her perfume, carried on her warm skin, invaded his senses.

He touched her pale cheek, then traced the soft column of her graceful neck, so delicately etched with faint blue veins.

Jim grimaced as he tried to staunch the tender feelings flowing through him.

Feelings that always came when she was near.

Feelings he couldn't afford to let live.

Chapter 6

Darcy awoke the next morning to a throbbing leg. She raised herself on her pallet and gingerly stretched out the injured limb. Lifting her skirts, she inspected the gash. She breathed a sigh of relief at the lack of redness or puffiness. It would heal properly.

If it hadn't been for Jim's steady hand, she wasn't so sure she could have stitched and dressed the wound. Again he had come to her rescue.

Thoughts buzzed in her mind like swarming bees.

She realized she owed him her gratitude. So why did she resent his help? Because she didn't want to acknowledge her limitations? She'd striven to be independent of men. For what? To be reduced to a bundle of nerves by a stampeding bull? Or was her resentment due to the fact that, despite herself, she was becoming accustomed to his company and looking forward to being with him? Was he becoming important to her?

He was a complication she didn't need. She pressed a hand to her aching head.

Kim Loo's voice broke into her thoughts. "Missy, you wake?"

Darcy lowered her skirts. "Yes, Kim Loo. Come in."

The swag's flap jerked open and he entered, holding a steaming cup of tea. "Thought you like this."

"Thank you. I could use something to drink."

She accepted his offering. After taking a couple of sips, she inquired. "Where is everyone?"

"With cattle, missy."

"Why didn't someone wake me sooner?"

"Boss, he say no bother you."

"Oh, because I'm a woman. If I were a man, the boss would've expected me to be up before dawn with the drovers. Well, I can assure him that I'm perfectly capable of resuming my duties. They might need my help."

Kim Loo grinned. "Glad you better. I worry."

His concern touched her. "That's very kind of you. I'm all right, really."

"I go now. Much to do before noon meal." With that Kim Loo disappeared through the tent's entrance.

Darcy finished her tea before she attended to her thick hair, arranging it on top of her head. She then brushed her teeth, using only a handful of water to rinse.

Feeling groomed and invigorated, she left her swag and walked toward Kim Loo's wagon. Her steps were slow, since her calf hurt, but the twinges were bearable.

Darcy shielded her eyes against the morning glare with a slender hand and looked out across the land. A faint breeze wrapped her skirts around her willowy legs.

Beyond the wagon, she saw a sea of red-brown backs and tossing horns moving toward a temporary holding pen. Whips circling above their heads, the drovers coaxed their horses to surround the herd.

A lone figure cut away from the group and rode toward her. Jim Burleson stopped his horse at the back of the wagon and looked down at Darcy, his blue eyes piercing beneath the brim of his hat. "I see you're all right."

Her heart beat a nervous tattoo. She felt like a schoolgirl instead of a twenty-two-year-old woman. Her hand dropped and she squinted at him. "Yes, thank you."

"Good. Think it would hurt your leg to ride?"

Despite the pain, Darcy wanted to be with Jim—even though she couldn't explain her attraction to him. "I believe it'll be all right."

"I've got strays to round up and thought you might like to come along. We'll make a slow go of it."

Darcy's stomach fluttered with unnamed emotions. When she replied, it was as if her voice had become a living presence separate from her body. "That would be nice."

Shortly, Jim had her horse saddled and they headed south.

Her mount, a chestnut mare, was wiry and quick. Darcy had learned that Australian horses were different from American ones. Overall, they were smaller in stature and narrower in the chest. These animals were ideally built for the land they served. Australia demanded horses that drank less and endured more.

Darcy rode sidesaddle, one shapely leg hooked securely around the rest, the other booted foot in the stirrup. She pondered where he had gotten the saddle. Just as swiftly another thought popped into her head, and she made a mental note to inquire about purchasing a pair of men's trousers. Riding sidesaddle was ladylike, but not practical. She grinned. What would Jim say?

The hard red earth echoed with the rhythmic thud of hooves as Darcy moved with the cantering of her mount, matching Burleson's pace. He rode his horse with the graceful ease of a man born in the saddle.

The ride brought a glow to Darcy's smooth cheeks. To be alive was a wonderful thing, she thought. She cherished life. That was why she'd become a doctor in the first place.

"It's lovely in the morning ... while it's still cool." Her tongue tripped over the words because she felt slightly winded from the pace.

"There's a special quality about Australia." Burleson checked his horse to a walk. Darcy followed suit. "She's like a high-spirited horse. You always need a firm hand and never take her for granted. Treated right, she'll serve you well."

Darcy's pulse jumped at the softening of his features when he spoke. She found him even more handsome when his expression wasn't guarded.

"You love it here, don't you?"

"I've never known anything else."

"I don't think that would make any difference."

"No, I suppose not. It's in my blood."

Darcy reached over to pat the sleek neck of her mare. "Tell me something about yourself."

He squinted into the sun. "What do you want to know?"

Burleson wasn't going to make this easy on her. Like everything else. "Tell me about your boyhood. What did you do for fun?"

"My mates and me used to race kangaroos, if we weren't taking target practice at rabbits." He turned the tables on her. "What about you?"

She paused, surprised and pleased at Jim's interest. "Well, I grew up in Boston. Quite a hoyden early in life, to the despair of my mother. I rebelled against being taught only social graces and the like. I wanted to read the classics, speak foreign languages."

Her laugh was pleasing and light. "By the time I reached eighteen, my mother gave up trying to make me into a marriageable, proper lady. It was then that I decided to go to the London School of Medicine for Women. I had to prove something to myself. I never accepted that women were meant to be subservient. Fortunately, my father was on my side." Regret eclipsed her gaze. "I miss him."

Breathing deeply, Darcy brightened, hugging

happy memories close to her heart. "But we had good times while I was growing up in Boston. He took me skating, and to his office sometimes. He owned an import company."

"Family had money, then."

She shrugged. "Papa never said we were rich. But we were comfortable."

"That's why you're used to getting your way." His voice conveyed a mixture of gravity and amusement.

"I wouldn't call it getting my way. Rather, being stubbornly determined."

"I'll give you that."

They rode along in silence for a while, though Darcy still found herself curious about Jim. "Any sisters or brothers?" she finally asked.

"A brother, but he died when he was young."

"I'm sorry—"

Jim cut her off. "Don't be."

"I was going to say that I was sorry my parents never had more children. I was an only child." Her horse dipped its neck and Darcy adjusted the reins. "You haven't said anything about your parents."

"Dad was the station boss. I was raised on Kopperella."

"And your mother?"

Tenderness glowed in his eyes. "She was a gem. Nothing ever got her down." His voice grew distant, and the light dimmed in his gaze. "Except the fever. Dad didn't last long after that. Said life wasn't worth living without her."

"We have two things in common, then. We

both come from loving families." Wistfulness played in her voice like soft music. "And we're both alone."

"Yeah."

Had she imagined a trace of vulnerability in his answer?

The question she had long wanted to ask burned on the tip of her tongue. "Why do you resent women in the Outback?" Darcy caught his eye with a candid gaze. "Or is it just me you resent?"

She drew a long breath, then expelled it slowly as she awaited his answer. And in that same breath, she chided herself for caring what he thought at all.

"I've got my reasons."

"That's taking the easy way out."

"Maybe."

"What are you afraid of?"

"You want the straight of it? All right. If you're not hard, this land will kill you off quick enough. Women who come from the city, with all their pampered ways, have no business out here."

"I wouldn't say I've led a pampered life. And certainly not lately. I've had to fight for my education and my place in the world."

"Whatever that place is, it's not here."

"You don't know that," Darcy said firmly.

"I have a fair notion."

"You have an opinion, and it's wrong."

"We'll see about that."

Darcy heard the irritation in his voice. She

fell silent, failing to notice Jim's appraisal of her.

He had to admit he admired her courage, spirit, and compassion. He forced his eyes away from her, reminding himself of the reasons that she shouldn't be there. He'd cared deeply for his mother, but then he'd lost her to the Outback. He wasn't about to care for another woman, only to lose her again. He didn't need another Cynthia.

Several hours later, Darcy noticed Jim staring toward the northeast. She strained her thickly lashed eyes, seeing only a few swirls of sand. But in just a matter of minutes, the color of the sky changed to a sickly reddish yellow.

"What is it?" she asked.

"Storm's coming." The wind caught Jim's voice and cast it at Darcy. "We've got to find cover. There's an abandoned drover's shack not far from here."

Darcy opened her mouth to reply when a gust snatched her hat. She watched helplessly as it soared heavenward.

Jim whirled his horse in the opposite direction. Darcy wasted no time in following.

Bending low over her mare's neck, its mane whipping her face, Darcy used every bit of riding skill she had to keep up with Burleson.

She couldn't tell if it was the pounding of hooves or the thudding of her heart that nearly deafened her.

Soon a weathered hut appeared on the horizon. Pepper trees swayed wildly around it.

When they reached it they halted and dismounted. Jim took Darcy's reins and hobbled the horses at the rear of the structure.

Meanwhile, Darcy ducked her head and started for the door. The wind lashed at her with such force that she was hurled off her feet, all but swallowed by the whirling dust.

At last she gained the entrance and shoved the rickety door open. Jim rushed in behind her. He shouldered the door closed and dropped the latch into place, then cast his gaze about until it settled on a corner littered with discarded clothing. "Grab some of these," he instructed as he went to gather up rags in both arms. "We'll have to stuff every crack."

Darcy needed no further encouragement. She scooped up several torn shirts. Ignoring her throbbing leg, she hurried about, cramming fabric into every nook and cranny she found.

Finished, she straightened. Stifling heat and dust filled the hut. Outside, the monstrous wind howled and beat at the walls and roof with giant fists of dust.

Uneasiness closed about Darcy. She licked her dry lips. She tasted and felt the dust in the air. And she smelled her fear. "Burleson?" she asked nervously.

"Jim."

"All right—Jim. How long will this last?"

He removed his hat and hung it on a wall peg. Dust caked the lines and hollows of his face. The upper half of his forehead appeared white where his hat had shielded it.

"Hard to tell. Several hours at least."

"Well, now what?"

"We wait."

Jim settled into a chair at the small table. Darcy sat opposite him, closer to the door.

Minutes passed filled with only the darkness, the wind, the dust, and the pounding. Darcy didn't know if she could stand it. She twisted her slender hands in her lap, looking at the door every few moments.

Storms had always frightened her. But this one was more terrifying because of its strangeness.

Her mind ran amok with torturous thoughts. Would they be buried alive? Would they suffocate? The air was stale and her lungs labored for breath. The walls seemed to close in. Looming panic outpaced common sense. She stood and limped toward the door. "I can't stand this."

Jim came after her. "Don't be a fool. There's nowhere to go."

Darcy's control unraveled. Perhaps it was the repeated dangers, or the endless tension between her and the men, or the strain of having to prove herself every single day.

She touched the wooden latch. "I've got to get out of here."

Firm yet gentle hands anchored her slight shoulders. "Listen to me. Nothing's going to harm you."

She tried to shrug off his hold. "Let go of me."

"Darcy, look at me." He shook her when her

eyes didn't focus. "You're not making sense. Calm down," he coaxed.

She began to claw at his hands. "Don't you see? We've got to leave, or we'll be buried alive!"

"If either one of us walks through that door, we'll never make camp. It's too far. We've got to wait the storm out."

"No—"

Gently, Jim cupped her heart-shaped face between his callused hands and held her head immobile. "You're safe. I won't let anything happen to you."

In the dimness, he saw her eyes widen like a child's and brim with unshed tears.

His own gaze warmed with compassion.

Never had he wanted to kiss her more. There was no stopping it.

His thumbs outlined her full lips, and then he lowered his head to claim her soft mouth.

She struggled in his arms. "The storm ... I can't. . . ."

Tenderness threaded his voice. "Shh. There's nothing to be frightened of. I promise to take care of you."

Even though her fear began to subside, she kept her hands wedged between them. "You don't understand. I can't. We mustn't ..."

But then she stopped in mid-sentence. There was something different about the Jim Burleson who stood before her now, something lurking in those compelling blue eyes.

She could contend with his verbal onslaughts,

his insistence on her leaving, even his anger, but she was powerless against this softer side of him—his vanquishing gentleness and patience.

These qualities were her undoing, stripping away her resolve.

"There's nothing wrong with a man showing his interest in a woman."

"There is when it's you ... and me." Darcy's voice quavered, his blue eyes mesmerizing her.

"There are no rules when it comes to you and me."

A shudder rippled through Darcy. His persistence wove a subtle spell around her. "I can't think when you're near."

"You're not supposed to." His mouth lifted in a singularly masculine smile. "I can't either. I'm not even going to try."

She studied those chiseled lips. How she longed to feel them against hers. A strange warmth spread through her. "But I'm not that kind of woman. This isn't right." Her words sounded hollow even to her ears.

"I know exactly what kind of woman you are. Soft, warm. It couldn't be more right, Darcy, for me to love you." His voice was a soft entreaty. His mouth drifted close to hers once more. "Relax and let me show you."

Darcy trembled as his candid words were underscored by an even more candid look. Her quickening pulse reverberated in the pit of her stomach.

His fingers floated down her arm, to her fingertips. He lifted her hand to his mouth and lightly licked the tip of each delicate finger in turn.

He kissed her full on the mouth then.

"Stop, Jim," she gasped.

"I can't. I'm only a man. Don't ask the impossible," he groaned as his lips moved over hers.

Instinctively, her slim arms circled his strong neck. She opened her mouth fully and met his tongue with hers. He drew hers slowly into his mouth. Her soft moan escaped in a breathy, feathery exhalation.

For Darcy, all other thoughts and emotions were dispersed by Jim's nearness. There was only him. And the need to be with him.

Jim raised his head. His gaze fell to her delicate cheekbones and slender upturned nose before it settled on her lush mouth, still open and wet from his kiss. She felt so small and fragile in his arms, and a fierce sense of possession engulfed him.

He should release her, but the thought of it opened a strange void inside him. Nothing had prepared him for the way it felt to have Darcy in his arms, soft and trusting.

Noble intentions and desire battled within him. Never, at any time in his life, had he wanted any woman more than he wanted Darcy.

He watched the play of emotions across her face, saw the sensuality infusing it. Her eyes fluttered open and she gazed at him, openly, honestly.

The crippling need to be with her overruled his conscience.

He kissed her again. "You know I want you," he murmured against the lushness of her mouth. "Here and now—" He nibbled at her bottom lip.

As if he were picking some precious fruit, he removed each hairpin to free her wealth of red hair. He combed the lush strands with his fingers, letting them drape around her dainty shoulders.

Moving his hand to her blouse, he opened one button. "You don't know how long I've thought about doing this." His fingers slid under the cotton and passed the thin barrier of her chemise to stroke the gentle swell of one soft breast.

Darcy moistened her lips to answer, but when his thumb and forefinger touched her nipple through the lacy fabric, all words scattered like petals on the wind. Agonizingly, slowly, he coaxed her body to respond to his touch. She had never known such sweet torture. Her breathing grew raspy. She closed her eyes, her lashes forming crescents against her creamy skin.

He dispatched the remaining buttons and eased her blouse over her shoulders, down her arms. Only her thin chemise remained between Jim and what he desired.

Lowering himself, he pressed his face against her and, taking lace and silk into his mouth, suckled one breast, then the other. He hardened with need.

He rose and gripped her arms, crushing her

to him. His lips blazed a fiery trail up the slender column of her neck and across her mouth.

His hands skimmed down her spine, resting upon the small of her back. He pressed her closer, her curvaceous body molding to his, his desire flagrant against her flat stomach.

Darcy gasped. She knew she needed to stop this now, before it went too far. But it was hard, so hard.

"Please don't touch me like that," she entreated.

"I can't help myself. Your body was made for a man's touch."

"But I'm not that kind of woman."

"I hear you say that, but you don't mean it. I can feel it in the way you kiss."

Darcy fought to find her voice. "Jim ... please." She pushed at his shoulders. "We will regret this. I'll regret it. I've worked too hard to become a doctor to let myself be compromised like this. You've got to understand."

His body stiffened as he pulled away; his breathing slowed.

Silent, he regarded Darcy. Despite the fact that at this moment he wanted nothing more than to kiss her and make love to her until she cried out, he had to admire her for stopping him. She had fight and determination. He knew of no other woman who could have overcome the odds stacked against her to become a doctor. Hers was a fiery disposition and a will of iron, and he'd wager a month's salary that she would never admit defeat.

But he'd also wager she would be beyond his

wildest dreams in bed. Within her gaze blazed a zest for life, a spark that couldn't, or wouldn't, be extinguished. He wanted her to set him afire with that spark. And that was what made her so dangerous to him.

Chapter 7

⟨~～♦♦～～⟩

Four days into the muster, the men set about the task of building a larger paddock. The sounds of chopping and sawing filled the morning.

Darcy sat on a prone tree trunk and watched them at their work. Lately she'd spent a good deal of time thinking about Jim Burleson, avoiding him when their paths crossed, looking away from him when his eyes met hers over the campfire at night. It was as though the very air between them was charged with palpable tension, but if the men suspected anything, they were at least keeping it to themselves.

That afternoon in the drover's shack, they'd ruined any chance of finding a way to coexist peacefully. The memory of what had taken place was burned inside her head. After all, she had nearly surrendered to the man.

He didn't understand why she'd stopped him, that she couldn't let herself become vulnerable. She couldn't disregard years of training, hardship, and tribulations to gamble on Jim when he only wanted to take. The taking felt like nothing she'd ever imagined. Looking out over the red plains, she could still feel his lips and hands on her. But she had to be a doctor first.

Tom Rivers startled her when he approached. "Sorry to bother you, but my 'and needs seeing to."

Darcy masked her surprise. This was the first time any of the men, except Jim, had asked her for help. She felt no small measure of elation.

"Certainly." She stood and pointed to the tree trunk. "Sit down and let me have a look."

She cradled his hand in her smooth palm and carefully unwrapped the blood-soaked handkerchief. A two-inch gash bisected his palm, halfway between his thumb and forefinger.

Rivers grimaced and flinched when she gently probed around the edges, blood covering her fingertips.

Her brow knitted. "What happened?"

The old drover looked sheepish. "Patterson tossed me an ax and I caught the wrong end. Split me open like a bleedin' boar."

"When are you men going to start being more careful?" she said, noting that the blade had narrowly missed a tendon. Rivers was a lucky man. Or a stupid one. At that moment, Darcy couldn't decide which.

"It's the way we live," he said defensively.

The pained expression on his face made Darcy regret her remark. He was paying for his lack of judgment. He didn't need her tongue as further punishment.

"It'll need stitches." She settled his hand on his lap. "I'll get my medicine bag."

Rivers watched her go. His hand throbbed painfully and he gritted his teeth. Yet despite his discomfort, he couldn't help but admire what a fine woman the doctor was. She was pleasing to the eye. And her touch was that of an angel.

Like the others, he had first resented her presence. He'd been in the Outback for a long time, and he'd sure never come across a lady doctor. But now he'd grown used to having her around. Newley could stay sour, but not him. He liked her.

He shifted in his seat, jarring his hand. Another stab of pain traveled up his arm. Damn thing! Made a fellow wonder if he was getting too old for this kind of work.

Darcy returned and cleaned the wound thoroughly.

"I'm going to give you something for the pain." She picked up a syringe and a vial from her bag.

Rivers shook his head. "Just get on with it."

Darcy sighed. "All right. Suit yourself."

Never once could these men allow themselves to show weakness, she thought. At least he'd come to her.

She put the syringe and the vial away. She found the proper needle, cleaned it with carbolic acid, and threaded it with catgut.

Darcy could have sworn that Rivers grew a shade paler as he watched. Sitting beside him, she sutured the wound with practiced hands, the needle flashing silver against his skin.

A light film of perspiration broke across his skin, but only a quick inhalation came from Rivers.

She tied off the stitches, then cleaned the gash again and applied a thick bandage.

Finished, Darcy commented, "There'll be a faint scar, but you'll have full use of your hand. I don't want you doing any more work today."

Rivers nodded.

Darcy thought her patient could use some color in his face. "Would you like something to drink?"

"I'll just get Kim Loo to—" He made as if to rise and then quickly sat down, cradling his injured hand on his midsection.

"Nonsense. I don't want you on your feet yet. Your body has just been through a shock. I don't want you fainting on me." When his lips tightened, she quickly amended that. "Although I'm sure you wouldn't." A smile dimpled her cheek.

His expression softened. "I don't suppose it would 'urt anything to sit 'ere a spell."

"I'll get you some tea."

"Tea?"

"After what you've just been through, you can't possibly drink any alcohol. You might go into shock." With her slender hands on her hips, she added in a motherly fashion, "And there'll be no further discussion. Doctor's orders."

" 'Ow can I argue with that?"

Her eyes twinkled. "You can't."

"Should 'ave known, you being a Yank and all."

"Why, thank you." His teasing boded well, she thought. Maybe they could become friends.

Darcy went to Kim Loo's wagon and returned with a white enamel cup. Quickly, she turned her back on Rivers, then gave him the cup of sweet black tea. Tucking her skirts beneath her, she settled beside him.

He raised the cup in a mock toast. "Tea, God bless it."

Darcy smiled, wondering if he'd taste the laudanum. If he were too proud to ask for it, she'd save him the trouble. She understood pride all too well.

Searching for something to say, she seized upon the first thing that came to mind. "What exactly are the others doing?"

Rivers grinned, white teeth flashing beneath his graying beard, obviously pleased to be asked. "First thing you do is pick a good, straight tree, one with stringy bark. Then you take a small ax and cut a ring around the bottom. But you've got to be careful and cut only the bark, not into the wood. About seven or so feet above the first cut, you ring it again. Then on the south side of the tree you join the two rings with a cut going up and down." Making a vertical motion with his good hand, he illustrated his point.

Darcy kept the conversation flowing, knowing if he talked about something familiar, he'd relax and the medicine could work. "Why the south side?"

" 'Cause that's where the bark's the thickest.

You see, 'ere in Australia the south side gets the least bit of sun."

"Oh, I see. But don't stop."

"Well, after you makes the split, you take your ax and pry the bark away from the trunk until it comes loose all 'round. That way a fella can pull it off."

"Let me guess. And then you use those big saws."

"Right-oh. You're catching on." He drained the last of his drink and rose. "I reckon, since I'm under orders, I'll go lie under that tree. All of a sudden I've got the urge to rest."

Rivers took two steps and turned. "Thank you, Doctor." He touched the wide brim of his hat.

A rainbow of happiness glowed inside Darcy. "You're welcome."

Later that afternoon, Darcy made the rounds with water for the laborers. She had offered her assistance to break the boredom. Anything to keep her from thinking about Jim. He made her feel things that she didn't want to acknowledge.

Her strategy worked until she came near him splitting rails for the paddock fence.

He had laid his shirt aside and wore only his tan pants. Each time he raised the ax over his head, muscles rippled beneath his skin. The breadth of his shoulders and the remembered strength of his arms caused Darcy to tremble despite the heat.

His rib cage arched gracefully over his stomach, which dipped into a slightly concave curve

with each lift of the ax. Glistening sweat outlined and defined the well-knit muscles of his
back, highlighting his bronzed skin.

Her breath stuck in her throat. A single
thought flashed through her mind—to touch
him. Her long fingers flexed with the need. Oh,
to run her hands down the sinewy length of
him. She clutched the cup handle to still her
shaking.

Where had reckless passion led her? She'd
nearly lost her virginity. With regret pressing on
her, Darcy forced her eyes away. She pivoted,
determined not to look at him again.

But she could feel him.

She walked to where Dave Patterson worked.
"Here, I thought you might like something to
drink."

Setting down his ax, he wiped away the perspiration from his face with the end of his neck-
erchief before accepting the cup. "Thank you
kindly. I could sure us it."

"I suppose you get used to this heat."

"Yeah, I suppose. But it's 'ard. Never an easy
life out 'ere."

Darcy didn't want to be alone. "Mind if I sit
down?"

"No. Just be careful not to get yourself any
splinters."

He leaned against the ax handle and sipped
his water, then poured the remainder down his
neck.

"How'd you come to be on Kopperella?"

"I 'ired on after my dad died."

Suddenly Darcy felt as if she were prying. She bit her lower lip. "I shouldn't have asked."

"I don't mind talking about 'im. Dad lived life the way 'e wanted. 'E never was one for taking orders."

"I'm sure he was a good man."

"Dad was always one for giving advice. 'E used to say, Why stand when you can sit? And why sit when you can lie down? And why walk when you can ride?"

Darcy laughed. "Sounds like a practical man to me."

"I thought a lot of 'im."

Suddenly her own father's image rose in her mind. "Do you miss yours as much as I do mine?" Her voice caught on the last word.

"Yeah. 'E raised me, 'cause my mom died when I was born." Moisture gathered in his eyes and he wiped it with the back of his hand. Lamely, he said, "Too 'ot."

Glad of the change in subject, she replied, "Yes, it is."

"Reckon I'd best be getting back to work."

Darcy sighed and turned her face upward. Sunlight filtering through the leaves of the blue gum trees danced across her face.

Maybe it would be best if she didn't ask the men personal questions. Those questions only served to reinforce how desperately she missed her father.

Yet she needed the companionship of the drovers to ease the loneliness.

She gave a shuddering sigh.

Pounding hooves and reins slapping on

horseflesh alerted Darcy to the approaching rider. Pumpkin, one of the young Aborigine drovers, or ringers, galloped into the stand of trees. The lad was off his horse and striding toward Burleson before the animal had come to full stop.

"Boss, found dead cattle by dry creek."

Burleson looked up. "What's this, Pumpkin?" He buried his ax in a thick stump.

"Cattle by creek. Been dead one hour, maybe two."

Jim shrugged into his shirt and tugged on his hat. He spoke to Newley and Patterson. "I reckon someone's been paddy dodging."

Newley, a bland expression on his face, replied, "Who'd be stupid enough to steal cattle off Kopperella?"

Jim strode toward his horse. "Don't know, but we're going to find out."

The others quit their tasks and followed.

Darcy sprang into action, suddenly realizing she was about to be left behind. "Wait, I'm coming, too." Lifting her skirts, she ran after Jim, puffs of dust kicked up by her laced shoes.

She nearly collided with him as he stopped suddenly and pivoted. "No, you're not. You're to stay here."

Defiance flowed through her. "I'll do no such thing. You might need me."

Their eyes met and held.

Only a second passed before Jim said curtly, "Then stay out of the way."

Stung by his gruff tone, she cocked her chin.

"Just don't you get in *my* way" she called back, then hurried to get her mare.

Darcy wasn't prepared for what they found. Her stomach lurched and she pressed a hand to her mouth. There on the dusty banks lay the mutilated corpses of two heifers. She bowed her head and closed her eyes against the nausea. How could anyone inflict such a horrible death on any living creature?

She could stomach what had to be done in the course of her practice. But senseless cruelty was a sin against man and nature. She abhorred such brutality.

The creaking of saddle leather and the jingling of spurs caused Darcy to look up. The men dismounted to examine the bodies.

Jim slowly walked around the carcasses. His keen eyes missed nothing. A muscle bunched along his jaw. "Pumpkin, Aborigines did this, didn't they?"

Pumpkin shrugged. "Yes, boss."

Newley snorted and tossed his head in Pumpkin's direction. "Bloody buggers. Told you that you can't trust 'em." He stood with his thumbs hooked in the waistband of his pants. "First one I see gets a bullet between the eyes."

"No one gets off any shots unless I say so," Jim told Newley before turning back to Pumpkin. "How much of a head start do they have?"

"Two hours. Maybe more."

"Then we'd best get going." His boots crunched against the dust and rocks as he headed for his horse.

Exactly how far or long they traveled, Darcy didn't know. But at every checkpoint the signs indicated they hadn't gained any ground on the Aborigines. She had already regretted her decision to come along.

The muscles in her legs and back were cramped from the sidesaddle position. The cotton of her dress was damp with perspiration. Wisps of hair stuck to the sides of her face.

With no other means at hand, Darcy raised her arm and used the sleeve of her dress to blot at the moisture beading on her upper lip. Her mouth and throat were parched from the choking dust.

Unable to stand the torture any longer, she urged her horse alongside Burleson. "Could I please have some water?"

"We should come upon some soon." He raised himself in his stirrups and called to Pumpkin, who traveled ahead. "Where's that watering hole?"

The Aborigine only grunted in answer.

Newley came abreast of Jim and Darcy. " 'E's not going to tell you anything."

Darcy's beautifully arched brow bespoke her incredulity. "He helps you with the cattle. Why won't he show you where the water is?"

Jim eased back in his saddle. "He knows that someday we might be hunting him. If there's a watering hole we don't know about, it makes a good hiding place. Very cunning."

"I don't know about cunning. Sounds like common sense to me."

Jim cut her a sideways glance. "Depends on your point of view."

"Obviously we don't share the same opinion of the Aborigines."

"You would if you knew them."

"You keep saying that. What makes you think you're right?"

"Because out here, there's a certain way of doing things. Always has been. Always will be. If you want to stay, you'll have to accept that."

Darcy's hands tightened on her reins in irritation. Men and their single-mindedness!

"Backward thinking, if you ask me," she said between gritted teeth.

Jim snapped his head toward her. "I don't remember asking you."

She knew she should exercise restraint, but her patience had grown thin. "You didn't. But I just can't stand such narrow-mindedness." Devilment gleamed in her eyes. "Of course, one has to have the ability to think before one can be considered narrow-minded. So you and Mr. Newley probably don't have to worry."

"You do enough thinking for all of us."

Newley, listening to the exchange, laughed in agreement with Burleson. His horse began straining forward, fighting the bit.

Still chuckling, Newley said, "My 'orse smells water. We'll let 'im do our thinking." He laid the ends of his reins to the horse's flanks. The bay spurted ahead. "Just follow me," he called over his shoulder.

Darcy bit her tongue to keep quiet as she

glared at Newley's back. Lord grant me tolerance, she prayed as her horse moved out.

Half an hour later they topped an almost imperceptible rise, and there in the earth's indention stretched water. Saltbush, bullockbush, and clumps of grass fringed its edges.

Newley patted his horse's neck. "Never known an animal to be wrong when it comes to sniffing water."

Darcy slid off her horse. When her feet touched the ground, her legs sagged from numbness. She grabbed the stirrup of her saddle to steady herself. Presently the blood returned to her legs and she could stand on her own.

She walked stiffly to the water's edge, dropped to her knees, and brought small handfuls to her mouth. The liquid felt refreshingly cool as it slid down her parched throat.

Everyone milled around, allowing the horses to drink, then themselves.

Feeling refreshed, Darcy rose. She dabbed at the corners of her mouth. Lifting her skirts, she walked back to her horse. Sighing, she stroked its velvety muzzle when something caught her eye.

She pointed across the way. "Look."

"Bloody hell!" Jim's words exploded into the air when he saw the thin plume of smoke hanging on the horizon. Within minutes the whole company had remounted and was headed over the hills. But the smoke only proved to mark the site of a recently abandoned fire. Jim whirled on Pumpkin. "How'd they know we were coming?"

"They just know, boss."

He glared accusingly at the Aborigine. "You remembered that water hole, didn't you?"

Pumpkin gave his usual answer—a shrug.

Suddenly there was a flurry of motion from Newley as he drew back and slammed his fist into the side of the Aborigine's face. The ringer crumpled to his knees.

Darcy gasped. White-hot anger burned inside her. Acting instinctively, she came to the man's aid and placed herself between him and his attacker. "Is violence always your answer, Mr. Newley?"

"Get out of my way so I can finish what I started."

His eyes told Darcy that he would like nothing better than to strike her, too. His body sang with tension, ready to fit deed to thought.

Outrage rose in her chest. "I'm afraid I can't do that."

"Why do you always defend those 'eathens? And that's what they are—bloody 'eathens."

"They're God's creatures, the same as we are."

" 'E didn't tell us about 'is friends. 'E'd 'elp them before 'e would us."

Newley's stupidity was beyond comprehension. "And why not? They're his people, and this is their land."

"Their land? What makes it their land? When I came 'ere this land was empty."

"Except for the Aborigines."

"What 'ave they done? We're the ones who've stocked it, worked it."

"That's no reason to mistreat them."

"Well, they're worthless. You can't teach them anything."

"Instead of trying to teach them, why don't you learn from them?"

"Them? You're crazy. That's what you are." Newley pivoted and walked away.

Darcy released her breath. Newley would never change. And that meant trouble.

She knelt beside Pumpkin. "Are you all right?"

He nodded.

Jim cast a shadow across her. "Well, that's it. There's no catching them now that they know we're after them." He gave an exasperated sigh. "We'll camp here for the night and head back tomorrow."

The men began leading their horses toward a stand of trees. Pumpkin slowly came to his feet and retreated.

Darcy stood and faced Jim squarely. "Why didn't you do anything to stop that?"

"Leave it."

"Leave it? How can you expect me to ignore such behavior? Newley ought to be fired."

"You don't run Kopperella. I do. Newley is one of the best drovers this station has ever had."

So much for honor. So much for justice. Darcy glared at him mutinously. "No wonder the Aborigines distrust the whites."

The campfire was a brush stroke of light against a canvas of black. Overhead, the stars held court in a heavenly palace. The breeze rose, carrying the smells of horses and sweat to the people bordering the fire.

After a simple meal of dried beef and hard biscuits, they sat around the comforting heat and light.

With her knees drawn to her chest, Darcy hugged her calves in an attempt to keep warm. Her gaze strayed across the fire.

Catching Jim's eyes, Darcy's instinct told her where his thoughts dwelled. Indignation flooded her. How could she have allowed him to take such liberties? It had been a serious mistake. He was nothing but a conscienceless rogue.

She watched him clamp his teeth together and slowly flex his hands. Darcy rested her cheek atop her knees and looked to the side.

With a cigarette hanging from the corner of his mouth, Newley sat drawing his initials in the dirt with a stick. Patterson reclined against his saddle and looked through a book, its pages yellowed and dog-eared.

Newley stopped his sketching and thoughtfully observed what he had traced. He took the cigarette out of his mouth and held it between his thumb and forefinger, the tip glowing soft red in the night. "Dave, which way does C go?"

"Don't you know, Craig?"

"Now, if I did, would I be asking you?"

Patterson glanced at Newley's feet. "I'm not sure, but I think you've got it backward."

"Certain letters is 'ard for me. Never can remember."

Darcy welcomed the diversion and asked, "Didn't they teach you in school?"

Newley said, "I've learned a few things in my time. Reading never taught me none of them."

"Yeah." Patterson continued to leaf through the book.

The way Patterson had sighed his reply gave Darcy insight. "Don't you read either, Dave?"

His manly pride apparently stung, he shot back, "Of course I do." Then, more truthfully and on a softer note, he added, "A bit. Still practicing."

"I'd be glad to help you, if you like," Darcy said, smiling.

Patterson glanced at Newley. The muscles in Newley's jawline were tight with disapproval.

Patterson then answered, "I reckon I'm doing all right. Thanks anyway."

A cold lump settled in Darcy's chest. Their rejection hurt her. She stood and drew a deep breath—a breath filled with the scents of tobacco and woodsmoke.

She walked away from the men and toward a group of gum trees. She couldn't remain, for tears brimmed in her eyes, and her fierce pride demanded that she hide them.

Frustration, anger, and hurt swelled in her heart, pushing everything else away. She had thought she'd encountered every form of prejudice and rebuff during her studies, but Craig Newley proved her wrong. Why was he always hostile? Why wouldn't he accept her?

Darcy was so preoccupied that she never heard Jim's approach.

His rich, masculine voice broke into her thoughts. "We need to talk."

She whirled and her hand touched her throat. "I didn't know you were there."

"Sorry if I frightened you."

"I wasn't expecting anyone."

"Newley upset you."

His words were a statement, not a question, and Darcy knew it would be useless to argue. "If you're here to find out if it's going to affect my ability as doctor, you've wasted your time. I'll maintain my professionalism."

Brilliant moonlight illuminated his figure as he stepped closer. "What we need to talk about is us."

Tension clasped the nape of her neck in a steel grip. Well, at last it would be out in the open. "I'll be the first to say that whatever amount of intimacy we had was a mistake."

"The mistake was your coming to Kopperella."

She retreated until the trunk of a large gum blocked her way. "What are you saying?"

Jim drew near. So near that Darcy could feel the warmth of his breath on the bridge of her slightly upturned nose. The hard, lean length of his body sent primitive signals to the softness of hers as he imprisoned her by bracing himself against the tree, one hand on each side of her.

"It's trouble, your being here."

An earthy essence emanated from his skin. "Why?"

His face hovered close to hers. "You're getting in the way."

"You don't like me arguing with you," she said breathlessly.

His gaze skimmed her eyes, her shoulders, then her breasts. He almost slid his hand from her arm to her waist, but then he stopped himself and stood back. "No sense in arguing now. I've decided it won't work."

The arrogance in his voice sharpened her senses. Sick of his high-handedness, she snapped, "You've decided? On what basis?"

"My common sense."

"When did you find some?"

"You're right. It all left the day I laid eyes on you." His features hardened. "You should resign." He paused. "Or I could sack you."

"You've forgotten one thing: you don't have the authority to dismiss me. Only the agents in London can."

"I believe your contract says that you must be of good moral character. . . ."

Darcy had never been so angry. How dare he! "Then you'll have to report me, because I have no intention of leaving. I have an obligation and I intend to see it through. I don't give up without a fight."

Darcy turned on her heel and strode toward camp. Jim stood absolutely still, watching her. He felt as if his heart were being torn from his chest. He could not let her go like this. In seconds he'd covered the distance between them, seized her shoulders, and pulled her around.

"I can't let you go on believing what I said." Remorse tightened his voice.

She felt the raw energy radiating from his

eyes. Her mind raced with thoughts that had little to do with blame, and everything to do with forgiveness.

How easy it would be to forget what he had said. . . .

But anger spoke louder than her bruised self-respect.

She fixed him with an accusing glare. "And why shouldn't I believe you? I'm sure that a great many people would consider me a whore for what happened between us. Thank you for reminding me of my transgression. I can't explain my actions, but I assure you I won't repeat them."

"Hold on. I never called you a whore."

"It was implied."

"You don't understand."

"To the contrary, I understand very well. You've made it perfectly clear from the beginning that you resent me and don't want me here. I'll learn to live with that."

"Can you teach me how to live with the fact that I hurt you?"

For the space of a heartbeat her eyes betrayed her desire to believe him. "What a cool liar you are."

"All right. The truth is that I wanted you to hate me."

"Oh, please!" Darcy expelled her breath in a rush of frustrated impatience and anger. "Do you honestly expect me to believe that?"

"I'm telling you straight."

"And I'm telling you that you can go straight to hell for all I care."

"I can't blame you—"

The contrite note that she thought she heard in his voice was like oil on a fire. She clutched a fold in her skirt until her knuckles turned white.

"That's a funny word for you to use. Considering you blame me for something with your every other breath."

"I *am* telling you straight. For your sake, and mine, it'd be best if you left Kopperella."

"Leave? So you'd feel better about what happened?" She rushed on, denying Jim a reply. "You don't give a damn about anyone else's needs. Or feelings. You're very good at looking after number one, and to hell with everyone else."

Jim gritted his teeth. "Hold on—"

Her words bubbled with pain. "What did I do to deserve this?"

"Nothing except be the most desirable woman I've ever known." His brow puckered and his eyes narrowed. He shared her pain. "Don't you see? There's no future for us. I didn't want either of us to wish for something that could never be."

Darcy's bruised heart and stung pride demanded that she refute him. "Don't flatter yourself. I'm not about to pine away because of you."

She gasped when he hauled her against him, her fingers laced tightly through his and held taut at the small of her back.

Frustration roughened his voice. "Don't do this."

She couldn't bear his touch. She despised her vulnerability. She hated the shivers that seized her and the way her blood flowed thin and hot through her veins.

Tears sparkled in her thick, sooty lashes. "You want me to forgive you just like that? You hurt me, but I swear you'll never do it again."

For a timeless moment they studied each other, two prideful, independent wills locked in silent combat.

A muscle constricted in his jaw, then relaxed again. He released his hold and stepped back.

With quiet dignity, Darcy walked away.

Chapter 8

Two days later, the drovers headed the herd toward the home paddock. The cattle plodded along, hooves raising dust and swishing tails keeping flies at bay. Their lowing filled the air.

Again Darcy rode with Kim Loo in the wagon.

She sat, holding a handkerchief to her nose to ward off the dust and the smell of cattle and horses, and stared beyond. Ahead sprawled limitless stretches of dessicated brush and brown, dry grass, interspersed by occasional stands of trees.

But Darcy didn't view it as the same wasteland she had first encountered. She now knew that behind the desolate facade lay a country brimming with life—albeit different from what she was used to, but life nevertheless. And life was a precious commodity in the Outback.

She also had come to admire the tenacity of those who pioneered this land. How well she knew what iron will supported and drove these people. She was beginning to understand the men and what compelled them; the same fierce determination was taking hold of her. No one was going to run her off. Especially not Jim Burleson.

Through a cloud of fine dust she descried Jim, a distant figure at the head of the moving group, standing in his stirrups motioning with his arm. The drovers continued to encourage the cattle forward.

Even as his single-mindedness repelled her, his undeniable strength drew her. Never had she met a man like him. Never had she felt so helpless.

Her careening emotions were maddening. She wanted his companionship despite his treatment of her. She wanted his arms around her once more. She wanted his kiss upon her lips again. She wanted him.

The realization jolted Darcy.

She must have appeared pale, for Kim Loo asked, "Missy, you sick?"

"I feel fine, Kim Loo. It must be the heat." She made a show of dabbing at the back of her neck with her lace handkerchief and looking up at the sun.

Today did feel hotter than usual, if that were possible. The air seemed to sizzle with energy, as if it were about to unleash some terrible force upon the moving group of men, horses, and cattle.

What had been pocket-size clouds began developing into towering white cumulus billows with black underbellies. Soon the sky turned ashen, and then the bottom dropped out. Lightning zigzagged through the black clouds, followed instantly by a deafening thunderclap. The bolt struck a huge gum. A shower of ruddy chips flew through the air.

Darcy nearly lost her seat when the team of horses panicked. Eyes rolled back, they reared, twisting their necks and slicing the air with their hooves. The leather harness strained but held fast.

Darcy's heart pounded. Her mouth went dry. She gripped the edge of the seat, her knuckles whitening, bracing herself with her feet. Kim Loo maintained control.

Cannon blasts of thunder boomed across the sky, causing watery fists of wind-driven rain to follow and pound the group.

In a matter of seconds, Darcy was drenched to the skin. She blinked her eyes rapidly in order to see.

Kim Loo shouted above the din, "We move, missy. I get down. You stay here. Help with brake."

Darcy scooted over and occupied Kim Loo's vacated seat as he climbed to the ground. Head bent against the driving rain, he made his way to the horses and grabbed the harness around their necks.

Kim Loo got the wagon over to a rock formation. Unhooking the horses, he hobbled them to protective cover.

"Come, missy. We get under wagon," he said, raising his hand to assist Darcy from her seat.

Her foot slipped when she gained the ground, but Kim Loo steadied her. They crawled underneath the wagon, which offered a small measure of protection against the raging elements.

From between the wagon spokes, on her stomach, Darcy watched the horrifying scene unfold before her eyes. The crazed cattle took flight, mud flying. Shouts went up from the drovers, and their stock whips cracked like pistol shots between the claps of thunder as they jockeyed for position to ring the herd and keep it from stampeding.

The heavens roared violently and the earth shook with hammering hooves. Darcy couldn't tell where the thundering ended and where her heartbeat began. Sharp needles of fear pricked her spine.

She searched frantically for Jim, but she couldn't him. Dear God, please keep him safe, she prayed.

Everything happened so fast that Jim didn't have time to ask for protection.

He sawed on the reins and spurred his horse in pursuit. He half stood in the stirrups and leaned forward in the saddle, giving his horse its head as he applied the reins across its bunching shoulders.

Jim dodged and ducked brush that threatened to unseat him by stretching low over the bay's neck. Nostrils flaring wide with exertion, the animal devoured the distance in ground-eating strides. The horse's every muscle strained, driving to overtake the cattle.

Jim narrowed his eyes against the stinging rain, looking through blurring drops at the terrain beyond. A hazy clump of brush came into view. If he could get the mob leaders to go for the thick growth, it would act as a barricade. Then there might be a chance of containing them.

The bay moved fluidly as Jim angled it toward the herd. Some sixth sense alerted him to Newley's presence on the far side. He knew his mate had the same plan in mind.

Suddenly the bay staggered, breaking its stride, and went down on its front knees.

Jim pitched forward in the saddle but quickly righted himself. Pulling hard on the reins, he lifted his horse's head, and the animal was able to regain its footing.

The gradual thickening of the brush and an indentation in the land created enough obstacles to slacken the crazed cattle's frenzied pace. It was all the time Jim and Newley needed to begin calming the herd, since the rain had slowed to a drizzle and the thunder had abated.

By now, five other drovers had reached them. The men soon had the cattle encircled.

Satisfied that the situation was under control, Jim turned his horse toward those left behind.

Darcy.

Fear for her safety knotted his stomach.

Dave Patterson never knew what hit him until his horse pitched forward. Thrown from the saddle, he cursed his bad luck as he landed on the wet ground with a thud. Almost simultaneously, he heard a sickening crack.

The blow to his head blurred his vision, the

impact echoing through his throbbing skull. He was only faintly aware of the light rain falling on his neck and arms.

Dazed, Dave tried to raise himself. The movement brought a shattering agony tearing up his right leg. He collapsed onto his back, his breath labored from pain.

Unconsciousness washed over him.

Time seemed suspended until, at last, Jim found Darcy. His shoulders sagged with relief. Then his blood chilled at what he saw.

Amid the mud, debris, and gentle rain, Darcy sat cradling Dave Patterson's head. Not four feet away lay the broken body of Patterson's horse.

Rivers and the Aborigine ringer, Pumpkin, stood nearby, hats in their hands.

Jim quickly reined his horse to a halt and dismounted. His spurs jingled in the damp air and his boots sloshed through puddles as he rushed to Darcy.

She looked up at his approach. Her hair had come undone and streamed in wet sections down her back and across her shoulders.

She saw the question in his eyes and answered, "His horse threw him. I'm afraid his leg's broken."

Jim's gaze traveled down Patterson's prone figure until it rested on the drover's right leg. Below the kneecap it bent at an unnatural angle.

"Can he be moved?"

"The leg will have to be set first. I've sent Kim Loo for my bag."

At that moment Kim Loo came running up to them, Darcy's medical bag in his hand. "I find like you say, missy." Breathing hard, he placed it beside her on the ground.

Darcy smoothed away the damp hair from Patterson's forehead. Although he was still unconscious, his face registered shock and pain.

"I'm going to need one of you to take my place and cradle his head."

Rivers came forward. "I will."

Darcy carefully eased Patterson's head off her lap, allowing Rivers to replace her.

She wiped her dirty hands on her soggy skirts before getting a clean piece of cloth and disinfecting the inside of his forearm with alcohol.

Darcy looked at Burleson. "I'm going to give him something for the pain. I don't think he could stand the setting of his leg otherwise."

Jim's gaze fixed on the fallen man, and his voice was soft with understanding. "You're the doctor."

"When he comes to, he'll probably be cursing me. His leg is going to hurt like the devil."

Darcy took a syringe and a vial from her bag. She carefully filled the syringe, held it to the gray light, and slowly rubbed it between her hands to eliminate air bubbles from the liquid. That done, she administered the injection.

In a matter of minutes the tension melted from Patterson's young body.

"I'll want something for splints," Darcy asserted.

Rivers eased Patterson's head off his lap and went in search of sturdy tree limbs.

In the meantime, Darcy produced a roll of bandage material and a pair of scissors. By the time she had arranged her instruments, Rivers had returned with two suitable pieces of wood.

She moved to Patterson's feet and knelt. Quickly, and with an economy of movement, she cut away his pant leg along the inside seam.

Varying shades of purple discolored the skin, and the shin area had begun to swell.

Darcy took a deep, steadying breath, ready to perform her healing task. Her hands sure and deft, she straightened and positioned the leg, then splinted and wrapped it.

Finished, Darcy pushed strands of dirty hair from her mud-smeared face and relaxed.

"You earned your keep today," Jim said.

Her heart fluttered at his praise. "Did I?" she asked wearily.

"Yes. I'm glad you were here. For Patterson's sake."

"He's lucky he didn't break his neck."

"He's lucky you're a good doctor." Her eyes widened, but he couldn't hold her gaze. It was too dangerous. Instead, he whirled and strode away.

Darcy rode the entire way to Kopperella in the back of Kim Loo's wagon with Patterson.

He revived briefly, but when the jarring motion of the wagon intensified his pain, Darcy gave him another shot of morphine. He slept with no further discomfort until they reached the compound.

After she got him settled in his quarters,

Darcy, weary and exhausted, sought her own room. Not bothering to remove her clothes, she dropped facedown atop her bed and slept.

But her sleep was not to be peaceful.

She dreamed of a tall man with blond hair and keen blue eyes.

Eyes that could see her very soul.

Eyes that drew the breath from her body.

And hands that touched and stroked her.

Caressed and whispered across her skin.

Jim stood inside the doorway leading into Darcy's bedroom and listened to the soft, easy cadence of her breathing as she slept.

She deserved her sleep.

She deserved more.

So much more. More than he could give.

He quietly went to the end of the bed and gazed at her. She looked so peaceful, her features in repose, her mouth slightly open. Careful not to wake her, he unlaced her shoes and slipped them off, then turned and left.

Darcy awoke and blinked. Movement near the bed caught her eye. She closed her eyes, then opened them.

She wasn't alone.

Someone was watching her.

She gasped. Two large black eyes were staring at her. Then she realized to whom those eyes belonged—Rosie.

Darcy released the air trapped in her lungs, swung her legs over the side of her bed, and sat up. "If you wanted to frighten me out of my wits, you succeeded."

A smile split Rosie's face. "I miss you."

Darcy's heart swelled. "Not more than I missed you."

Seeing that sweet child's face filled her with joy. Rosie was the only person who had been completely honest with her from the beginning and who demanded nothing from her besides companionship. She seemed the only stable thing in Darcy's otherwise upside-down world.

"You want me work for you?" the youngster asked.

"Yes, of course. We had an agreement."

Darcy rose, then frowned as she looked down at her stockinged feet. She didn't remember removing her shoes. She must have been more tired than she thought.

The hem of her filthy skirt caught her attention. Her nose wrinkled in disgust.

She walked over to the makeshift dresser and picked up her hand mirror. What she saw gave her a second shock. Dried mud caked parts of her face. Bits of grass and still more mud coated her normally soft and glossy hair. She doubted her own parents would have recognized her. Her nose wrinkled again as she smelled herself.

Darcy replaced her mirror and turned on her heel. "Come on, Rosie. We're going to the creek." She put on her shoes.

Before heading out the door, she grabbed a bar of scented soap, a towel, and a complete change of clothing. Then, hand in hand, she and Rosie set out for the creek.

Darcy absorbed the sights and sounds around her. Birds chattered in the trees while in the background came the distant bustle of activity. Another morning at Kopperella.

Keeping to the path, they soon came to the creek.

To her satisfaction, Darcy found a secluded spot in which to bathe. The large branches of a low-lying tree hung over the water's edge, a foot from the surface.

Perfect. She could undress in the privacy of its thick leaves and slip unnoticed into the water should anyone come by.

Rosie had perched herself in the tree. Looking up, Darcy asked, "Are you going to join me?"

The youngster shook her head.

Darcy removed her shoes and then each subsequent layer of clothing. She sat down on the bank, her bare bottom tickled by grass, and inched into the water. The cold water caused her to gasp. Taking a deep breath, she immersed herself in it. Surfacing with a toss of her wet mane, she smoothed the strands away from her face, her teeth chattering.

Darcy wasted no time in lathering first her hair, then her body. Sighing, she felt the grime lift from her body, and along with it, her troubles. The cleansing served as a baptism to renew her body and spirit.

After a quick rinse, she was finished. She waded back to the bank, grabbed her towel, and dried off. Once dressed, she dried her hair, then combed and secured it with a ribbon. Darcy called to Rosie and they retraced their path to the compound.

Darcy noticed a great deal of activity at the station store. A line of Aborigines snaked out the door, across the veranda, and into the yard.

She altered her course with Rosie still in tow. As they stepped into the shadowed interior, Darcy nearly collided with Newley, who stood at the front, dispensing supplies to the Aboriginal workers.

A moment of uncomfortable silence passed before Newley went about his business. Darcy tugged Rosie behind her and moved toward the back of the store.

Funny, she hadn't noticed what the store contained when she'd briefly stayed in the rear room with Burleson. The line of her mouth straightened. No wonder. She had had enough on her mind.

Now she explored in earnest. A wide variety of goods jammed the building—everything that Kopperella needed for survival, from foodstuffs, leather products, pots and pans to clothing.

While going through the piles of pants and shirts, Darcy found one of each that she thought would fit her. She hadn't abandoned the idea of wearing men's clothes for convenience. A dress, and all that went with it, were a liability in the Outback.

Dirty clothes on one arm and new attire on the other, Darcy started for the front when small packets caught her eye. Anyone would have thought her discovery to be a king's ransom the way she hugged the packaged seeds.

Joy rushed through her. She turned to the little girl beside her and beamed. "Oh, Rosie, we'll plant ourselves a garden! We'll have carrots, onions, potatoes, cabbage, and anything else I can find."

A garden would be life renewing itself. How wonderful to feel that sense of accomplishment. And a garden would keep possibly idle hands busy.

Rosie smiled, apparently sharing Darcy's enthusiasm. Darcy wondered briefly if the child understood most of what she said. If she didn't, she could learn. Rosie was very much like Darcy at the age of eight years. She saw in the child's eyes the same hunger for knowledge.

On her way out the door, Darcy spied Pumpkin. "If I can get you more supplies, would you do some work for me?"

Newley overheard the conversation. He moved toward them as they stood on the edge of the porch. " 'Ey, what's this?"

Darcy bristled with irritation. "I don't believe I was talking to you." She turned a cold shoulder.

"Well, I'm talking to you. You can't go around promising things to these blacks without permission."

She wanted to scream. Was there no end to his rudeness?

"Then he can have part of my rations. Either way, it's none of your business."

"I've always 'eard 'ow slow you Yanks are,

but I think you're setting a new record," Newley taunted.

Darcy dragged air through her lungs and released her breath slowly. "You'll find I don't intimidate easily. I think trying to bully women makes you feel like a big man."

Newley seized her upper arm and tugged her closer. "Would you like to know what makes me feel good?"

She knew what would make her feel good— her fist on his arrogant chin!

"I advise you to get your hand off me. If not, I intend to scream at the top of my lungs. Then we'll see what happens."

For a minute he looked as if he meant to call her bluff, but then he seemed to think better of it. His hands fell away.

Rubbing her arm, Darcy dismissed her adversary with a turn of her back.

She faced Pumpkin. "Well? Will you work for me?"

"You help me before. I help you now."

Respect shone from his dark eyes, and her chest filled with happiness. "Wonderful. Come by my quarters tomorrow."

After Darcy and Rosie had left, Tom Rivers approached Newley. "I 'eard 'ow you talked to Dr. McCall. You leave 'er alone. She's done nothing to you."

"You going soft on 'er, too, then?"

"She's a good woman. Not the kind you're used to. Maybe that's why you don't know 'ow to talk nice to 'er."

"That's what *you* know, old man. I wouldn't go sticking my nose where it don't belong."

"You be mindful of my words."

"Or what?"

"I've got a trick or two. Just don't you go and give 'er any more trouble."

"The only trouble around 'ere is 'er."

"At first I might 'ave agreed with you. But not now. She's a right decent person. And she took proper care of me."

Newley grunted and returned to dispensing rations.

And while he continued with his job, he thought about Darcy McCall.

She would be sorry she had crossed him. Very sorry.

Chapter 9

Brilliant moonlight bathed the compound in a silvery glow. Darcy had already checked on Dave Patterson, and was sitting on the veranda. She breathed in the night air. Above the sounds of the humming insects and croaking frogs came a faint chanting from the Aborigines' huts, a soft cadence of voices that blended naturally with the velvety night. Woodsmoke drifted from glowing campfires.

Darcy sighed and leaned her head against the back of the chair. The tranquility of the night helped soothe her nerves. She hugged this quiet time to her heart and savored it.

Alone, she didn't have to keep her inner self hidden away. Freedom, however brief, was hers to enjoy.

But then she heard footsteps and looked in the direction they were coming from.

The moon illuminated a man's figure. As he drew closer, Darcy recognized Tom Rivers. He came to the end of the porch. He smiled, his hair and beard shot with threads of silvery light.

"Thought you might care for a bit of company," he said in greeting.

"Mr. Rivers. What a surprise. Please sit down."

"Thank you." He settled in the chair next to hers and gazed at the stars for a moment before he said, "I'd like it if you called me by my given name."

"Then Tom it is. But only if you'll call me Darcy."

A flash of teeth showed beneath his whiskers. "Right-oh."

Darcy hugged herself. "Isn't the night wonderful?"

"Haven't seen one better in a fair bit."

They lapsed into a companionable silence.

In the distance, a round of loud calls broke the thumping and singing of the Aborigines. The sound jarred the night.

It startled Darcy. "What do you suppose they're doing?"

"They call it a corroboree. It's a celebration of sorts."

Her curiosity stirred. "What do they celebrate?"

Tom shrugged. "Just about anything. Sometimes hunting. Or they might act like different animals or birds. Or even like the different types of storms in these parts."

"When I have the opportunity, I intend to study their ways."

He quirked an eyebrow. "Pardon me, Darcy, but why?"

"Because I know so little about them. And I

find them fascinating. I'd like to help them if I could."

"I'll give you fair warning about those blacks," he said with quiet emphasis.

Her forehead furrowed. "Warning me against what?"

"Getting involved with them. They've got strange ways. They don't believe the same as you and me. Take medicine. They believe in magic and curses and such."

Tom rubbed the side of his face. "They follow laws 'anded down by elders who 'ave these dreams during trances. They call them visions. And I've seen with me own eyes a black fella lay down and die because 'e believed someone put a curse on 'im."

"Has no one tried to help them understand our ways?"

"I don't know. But stay clear of them."

Darcy sighed her discontentment. "So everyone keeps telling me."

"We're only doing it for your own good."

"Coming from you, Tom, I believe that. But not from others on Kopperella," she said with quiet conviction.

"Don't you give what others think any notice."

Darcy sensed she could confide in Tom. She needed to release some of the feelings burdening her. "How can I not? Ever since I arrived, the others have resented me. I'm no threat to anyone. I only want to do my job."

"I'll tell you something about bushmen. They

don't show their emotions none too easy. Especially to a woman. It's not considered manly."

Irritation tightened her mouth. "So they shut themselves off to any emotion. Except arrogance. The men around here have an abundance of that, it seems."

" 'Owever the men feel, you've got to stay and give it a fair go."

Conviction underscored her words. "Oh, don't worry. I have no intention of being bullied off Kopperella. I've faced worse." She allowed herself a reflective pause. Vulnerability crept into her voice. "It's just that I had hoped it would be different here."

She didn't voice how fervent that hope had been.

"If you don't mind me asking, why would a pretty woman such as yourself come thousands of miles from your 'ome to a place like this?"

She moistened her lips. "The only answer I can give you is I had something to prove. In America, people aren't ready to accept women doctors just yet. And if they are, it's only as second best. I'm a good doctor and wanted to prove it. But I needed a chance to practice medicine. So when I saw the advertisement from the agents in London, I applied. It seemed Australia was the only place desperate enough to take me on."

"I 'ave to tell you straight that I didn't take to you at first. Maybe I was just as bad as all them others, I don't know. But I've changed my opinion. I know you to be a good doctor. Don't let anyone tell you any different."

His confidence showered her like a gentle spring rain. "You don't realize how much that means to me. Just hearing that makes my job here a little easier." She laughed. "I'm not sure that the remaining ten and a half months is long enough to bring the others around, though."

"If you're talking about the boss, he'll see things in the right light. Just give 'im time."

"Why does he resent women? Or is it just me?" she asked.

" 'E likes them right enough. It's just that the bush is hard on women. I guess 'e remembers 'is mom." He hesitated as if reflecting on what he had said. "Australians are a stubborn lot."

"Never truer words have I heard."

"Just remember, it takes a woman just as stubborn to bring an Aussie around."

Their shared laughter mingled with the night chorus.

Still smiling, Tom rose. "I'd best be bedding down for the night. Morning comes soon enough."

"Good night, Tom. I've enjoyed our talk. Come whenever you like."

"Right-oh." He strolled toward the men's quarters, humming.

Darcy rose, stretched, and moved into the house.

Just remember, it takes a woman just as stubborn to bring an Aussie around, Tom had said.

If Jim Burleson had any doubts as to what "stubborn" meant, Darcy intended to define the word. With that thought on her mind and a smile on her lips, she went to sleep.

* * *

Darcy made an early morning call on young Patterson. The speed of his recovery pleased her, and his leg showed every indication of healing strong and straight. But his willingness to allow her to examine him pleased her more.

With a light spring in her step, she hurried back to her house. She correctly guessed Pumpkin's time of arrival and wasn't surprised to find him not far behind her.

"Good morning," she called to him as he walked up the path to the veranda.

He nodded in greeting. "I come like you ask."

"Thank you. I knew I wouldn't be able to get the garden ready without help."

Pumpkin seemed different from the other young Aboriginal men. Perhaps because he dressed like the drovers and spoke clearly, Darcy felt comfortable around him. Whatever the reason, she didn't fear him. She hoped her trust would be a foundation for friendship.

"I'll only be a minute. You can sit on the porch if you like." She disappeared inside the house.

As she walked to the bedroom, boot heels clicking across the wooden floor, she smiled impishly. Today she intended to do a shocking thing. She intended to wear a man's pants and shirt. The garden seemed a perfect excuse.

She closed the bedroom door behind her and changed. Yet when she stood on a chair and glimpsed herself in the small dresser mirror, for one craven moment she thought to abandon her idea.

She had wrongly estimated the size of the pants, for they hugged each and every curve and line of her hips and legs. And the shirt did little to hide her femininity. Not wearing the usual restraining undergarments allowed her full breasts the freedom to fill out the front. The sensation was sinfully wonderful.

Where's my sense of adventure? she asked herself. By coming to Australia and living with all these men, she had already defied the customs of the day. What could happen if she wore men's clothes?

Darcy found out.

She and Pumpkin worked all day. They divided the garden plot into two parts. During the morning, Darcy discovered just how hard clearing rocks could be. That afternoon, she hoed until her aching fingers cramped, and she had to stop. At long last, the ground was ready for the seed.

Darcy looked upon their accomplishment with pride. "Pumpkin, I don't think anyone else could have done a better job."

Pumpkin smiled broadly, his white teeth contrasting with his black skin.

Darcy picked up a packet of seed and began at the top of a row. Bending over at the waist, she poked a hole with her finger and dropped several carrot seeds into the depression.

At that moment Jim walked by. What he saw caused him to stop in his tracks. A shapely rear was pointed toward the gate. He realized it belonged to Darcy McCall.

A possessive, illogical anger gripped him.

Her bottom belonged in the house!

Never had he seen such a delicious sight, except in a whorehouse. But this wasn't a whorehouse; this was a cattle station. What was the woman thinking of? Who else had seen her? He would have to teach her a lesson; he had no choice. She couldn't go parading around in revealing clothes like that. Certainly not in front of the men!

"What the bloody hell?" he yelled.

Startled, Darcy spilled the remaining seeds as she straightened and whirled around. Jim Burleson came striding toward her. A very angry Jim Burleson. His face resembled a storm cloud.

"I beg your pardon?" Darcy looked composed, but inside she was a bundle of nerves.

The muscles in his jaw were tight with disapproval, as were his firm, masculine lips. "Get in the house and change your clothes right now, or I'll take you over my knee and give you the spanking you deserve."

The very thought stirred depths of outrage in Darcy that she had never experienced before. Damn him! Damn his censure and his insults! "Don't you dare come to my house and order me around."

"Your house? It belongs to the company, like everything else on Kopperella. And I'm the boss of Kopperella."

Her eyes narrowed. "A fact you never let me forget."

Jim stopped mere inches from Darcy, his

booted feet trampling that section of the ground.

Her gaze sliced downward and then shot to his face. The nerve! "You're ruining my garden."

Darcy was caught by surprise as he grabbed her arm and wrenched her close, so close that she could feel the hard, lean length of his thigh against her own.

"Damn your garden!"

His harsh tone restored her equilibrium. "Oh, really?" She arched a delicate brow. "Not half as much as I curse your overbearing nature."

"Just what do you think you're doing parading around here like a whore?"

Crimson flooded Darcy's features. The accusation stung and tears of humiliation threatened. By sheer will, she held them back. "I'll do what I want, *Mister* Burleson. And you can't stop me." She longed to slap his arrogant face.

Suddenly movement came from behind them, and Darcy, looking past Jim's broad shoulder, saw Pumpkin nearing Jim.

She read the intent on his face and warned, "Don't, Pumpkin. I can handle this. You can go now."

Reluctantly, the Aborigine left the two combatants alone.

Darcy felt the tension and heat of Jim's whisper as he growled, "Are you going to change on your own, or am I going to have to do it for you?"

Taking a deep breath, she started counting to ten.

She never passed *two*.

Her trembling body and thundering heart kept her from going on. She meant to answer him with defiance, but his nearness unsettled her. She despised her vulnerability. She hated his ability to make her forget herself.

"Well, are you?" Jim repeated.

Darcy swallowed the urge to comply. He must never know her susceptibility to him. "Go to hell!"

"Have it your way."

Before Darcy could react, Jim dipped and threw her over his shoulder, carrying her inside the house like a sack of potatoes. The action caused hairpins to fly from her hair, red strands cascading downward.

She pummeled his back with her fists. "You have no right to treat me this way. Put me down."

He whacked her bottom. "Be still."

"I will not." She struggled harder to free herself from her ignominious position.

He gave her another whack. "Oh, yes, you will."

Caution overrode anger, and Darcy went limp.

Jim strode into her bedroom and dumped her on the bed. She quickly raised herself up on an elbow and pushed the hair from her face. Then she gasped. Several of the buttons on her shirt had worked themselves free, and the curve of her breasts peeped from behind the material. She bolted upright and pulled the fabric together with one hand, all the while glaring at Jim.

His eyes met hers, burning blue with stark warning.

She refused to back down. "Satisfied?" she flung at him.

"Not as satisfied as I'd like to be."

A charged silence followed, during which Jim couldn't stop his mind from playing out the scene his body longed to enact. His heart began pounding in his ears at the thought of having her long, slender legs wrapped around him, of easing into her soft center. He grew heavy and full.

"I'll change my clothes," Darcy said at last. "Just get out."

But he acted as if she hadn't spoken. His eyes darkened.

"Do you hear me?" She stood, still holding her shirt together, and walked to the doorway dividing the front part of the house from her bedroom. She pointed with one hand to the front door. "I want you to leave."

Jim came over to her and grasped her shoulders. Gently but firmly, he pushed her to the left and pressed her against the wall. She was trapped between the hardness of his body and the unyielding wall behind her. He placed one hand beside her head; the other parted her shirt-front and stroked the underside of one breast.

Darcy closed her eyes against the assault on her senses. She tingled all over: from her head to her aching breasts to her somersaulting stomach to her toes.

"No, you don't," he said raggedly. "What you

want has nothing to do with my leaving, but everything to do with my staying."

She opened her eyes. She fought to draw a breath. "You're conceited."

"Just sure of what we both need and want."

"You don't know the first thing about what I truly need. And certainly not what I want." Her lie sounded hollow in her ears. Or was that her racing pulse echoing through her brain?

"I know better than you."

His hand left her breast and went to the waistband of her pants. Darcy sucked in her breath, and her stomach became concave as his fingers deftly undid the buttons and trailed inside until they rested on the soft, springy hair below.

Why did he torture her so? Why did her body find such pleasure from his touch?

He slipped his hand between her thighs. "And this is how I know."

Shock waves passed through Darcy. She felt herself grow warm and wet. Turning her head, she closed her eyes again. She hated him for making her admit her desire, but she was powerless to make him stop.

Jim buried his lips against her neck, his tongue laving her skin. "I've thought about us often. Tell me you have, too."

Coherent thought was impossible for Darcy. Desire was being telegraphed to every part of her body. She was a mass of quivering nerves.

Parting the lips of her sweetness, he stroked the tiny bud of pleasure. Darcy shuddered and then moaned. She felt as if her world were threatening to splinter apart into a million pieces—pieces she couldn't put together again.

"Tell me," he urged thickly and rubbed her sensitive place between his thumb and forefinger.

Darcy's eyes opened in drowsy sensuality. "Yes, damn you," she rasped.

Jim bent his knees and settled his hips against hers. She felt his maleness begging entry to her womanly paradise. In unison they groaned at the contact.

Rocking against her, Jim whispered heatedly, "I want you."

Darcy's legs felt like water as his hips quickened their dance of persuasion against her. She knew how it felt to be touched by this man who ached to possess her and who was on the brink of losing control.

The thought scared Darcy. She was in danger of forgetting herself, jeopardizing everything. She couldn't allow that. "Jim, stop," she cried, trying to squirm out of his arms.

"You've said that before."

"And I meant it. I mean it now."

His lips thinned. "You don't know what you're saying."

"Yes, I do. It would be disastrous for both of us if I allowed this to go any further." Conviction lit her eyes and underscored her words.

His words were softer-spoken, but carried no less certainty. "The disaster would be in not going through with it."

"I can't willingly give myself to a man out of

wedlock. It goes against everything I've ever been taught."

"You're making excuses."

"I'm telling the truth."

He leaned into her again, his chest rubbing against her still sensitive breasts. "But your body is saying something different."

Darcy groaned her frustration. "You may be able to seduce my body, but you can't seduce my heart. That is mine to give to the man I choose to love and marry. And you can bet he'll be someone who really cares about me."

"For a woman who's taken up a man's job, not to mention a man's clothes, you certainly have double standards," he ground out.

"Double standards? Look at you. You're fighting me unfairly."

Jim pulled back, still keeping her imprisoned between his arms. His frustration soared like the temperature outside. "What are you talking about?"

"You use my body against me."

"That's not how I'd like to use your body." He spoke low, provocatively.

"That's all you think about."

"What the hell else am I supposed to think about when you go sashaying around like that?" he exploded. "What do you imagine all the rest of the men will be thinking about? That's why you've got to clear out."

He was fuming now, and it gave Darcy decided satisfaction, because she had the upper hand. Her eyes narrowed. "I find it strange that you only bring that up when I stop you from taking advantage of me."

He snorted and shook his head.

"It seems to me that if you can't have me, you want me to go away." Her voice rose and gained strength. "Well, believe it or not, I've got a job to do out here that doesn't have a thing to do with you, and—"

A knock sounded at the front door.

Darcy glanced past Jim's face, noting that it was red with anger. At the open door stood Rosie.

Jim turned and saw the girl, too, then growled low in his throat and with a great deal of effort pulled away.

Darcy quickly righted her clothing and smoothed the hair from her face. "This can't happen again," she whispered.

A shade of a threat tinted his voice. "I can't promise that."

Darcy said nothing in reply. With as much dignity as she could muster, she made her way to the front door.

"What are you doing here, little one?"

Rosie stepped just inside the room. "Be dark soon. I have no place to sleep. I stay with you?" Her dark eyes shimmered with hope.

Darcy touched the top of the child's head and smiled. "Of course you can." She looked down at the youngster's dirty dress. "I have the most beautiful nightgown. It's so soft. Would you like to wear it?"

Rosie hugged her in thanks, and Darcy wrapped her arms about the girl's frail shoulders. Her heart swelled with compassion for Rosie. She cried out for love and Darcy had so much to give.

They remained in each other's arms until the staccato sound of boots striking wood brought Darcy's attention back to the present. Jim emerged through the bedroom doorway.

Darcy stood and guided Rosie toward a chair. "You sit while I talk to Mr. Burleson. Then we'll find something for you to sleep in."

She tried to keep her voice steady, as if having a man materialize from her bedroom were a common occurrence.

Jim pulled Darcy off to the side. "Now hold on. You can't do that. She'll come to expect special treatment."

"And who says she doesn't deserve some?" Darcy hissed under her breath. She already knew where this conversation was leading.

"I'm not saying she doesn't, but you can't interfere."

"Why not?"

"She's not like you. She doesn't think the same as you."

Darcy rolled her eyes in exasperation. "I've heard that a hundred times, but that's not a valid argument for letting the child go hungry, or for not giving her a place to sleep."

"The point is, the Aborigines won't like it. They don't want whites interfering with their people."

She flung her hands out. "I can't believe they'd mind if I took care of this child. After all, she's an orphan."

He gripped her shoulders and looked her square in the eye. "I don't want to see you get hurt. And you will in the end. She'll walk out on you."

Her voice tensed with aggravation. "That's not what this is all about. You're afraid of what the men will think. Your ego couldn't stand it if they thought you couldn't control me."

Jim gritted his teeth. "You're as stubborn as a mountain brumbie."

"A Missouri mule's got nothing on you."

A muscle knotted in his jaw. "When will you listen to reason?"

"When I hear some. So far, all I've heard is a lot of talk from some very bigoted people." Her words simmered with fervent emotion.

"You're here to doctor these men, not be their conscience."

"I disagree. The soul and the body aren't separate."

"Leave their souls to their Maker."

"And in the meantime allow them to deal out misery to others? No, thank you."

Jim pulled her closer. "Maybe I should give you that spanking. It might do some good."

She cocked her chin. "You can beat me until I'm black-and-blue, but I won't change my mind."

"All right. But have you thought of what will happen to that girl when you leave? If her life's been hard up to now, what of it then? Do you have an answer for that?"

There was a sinking feeling in Darcy's stomach. He was right. She hadn't given any thought to the future. What would happen to Rosie?"

Darcy shrugged off his hold and stepped back. "I don't know." Her voice lowered in concession, then rose with conviction. "I'll come up with something."

"Well, in your self-righteous campaign, don't forget her. She'll pay for it in the end." Jim tilted his head back and sighed deeply.

His expression and his voice softened as he reached out to touch Darcy's cheek. "I'm not the monster you think I am. I know you mean well, but I just want you to realize what you're doing."

"I'm doing what I feel is right." Darcy placed her hand over her chest. "My heart tells me to. I can't turn my back on her. I just can't."

They walked onto the veranda.

Jim started down the steps, then stopped and turned. "The men and I are leaving on another muster tomorrow. I want you to stay because of Patterson. We won't be gone but a couple of days." One corner of his mouth lifted. "Think you can stay clear of trouble until I get back?"

"You know me."

"Yeah, that's what bothers me."

With that Jim left.

Darcy stared after his retreating figure. Uncertainty weighed heavily on her shoulders. She sighed.

Had she gotten herself in over her head? Would she have the fortitude to deal with this situation? She wished she had answers for the questions that plagued her. But she didn't. She only had faith in her convictions.

She rubbed her throbbing forehead and went back into the house. The door closed slowly behind her.

Chapter 10

Darcy and Rosie were sitting on the front veranda eating lunch when a strange drover
rode up, scattering pebbles and dust before him.

The exhausted man checked his lathered
horse and lifted his battered felt hat, revealing
dirty, matted hair. "I was told to look for a
woman. Would you be the doctor?"

Darcy put down her half-eaten chicken leg
and walked to the edge of the porch. "I'm Dr.
McCall. What can I do for you?"

Fatigue etched the man's face. He inhaled
deeply and tried to catch his breath. His words
tumbled out. "The name's Edgar Green. I'm
from the neighboring station, Manalee. The
boss's wife, Mrs. Miller, is in bad need of a doctor. She's 'aving a baby. The boss 'eard about
you and sent me to fetch you."

The urgency in his voice tugged at Darcy. The
desire to help swelled within her, but thoughts
of Dave Patterson quickly crowded her mind.

She frowned. "I've got a patient here who
needs my attention."

"You don't understand," he said desperately.

"Boss says the baby's turned wrong. You've got to come."

The muscles in Darcy's neck and shoulders bunched. A breech birth! Kim Loo would have to care for Patterson.

"I'll get my bag." She whirled on Rosie. "Go tell Kim Loo to saddle a horse for me. Hurry."

Rosie ran down the path to the kitchen, disappearing in a small cloud of red dust.

Darcy's attention swung back to the drover. "How far is this station?"

"A day."

Darcy knew they had no time to waste.

"Then we'd best get moving."

Darcy wrenched the door open and fairly flew across her examining room to her bedroom. She grabbed a change of clothes and stuffed them into her carpetbag. Quickly she retraced her path to the front room where she checked her medical supplies. Satisfied, she snatched up both bags and was out the door in a flurry of skirts.

Suddenly Darcy remembered her hat. She raced back inside and halted by the hat rack near the door. She set down her bags and tied the hat atop her head, then picked up her things and hurried for the gate.

Kim Loo soon appeared, leading a black horse. Darcy paid no heed to the lack of a sidesaddle. Amid the creaking of leather, she hauled herself up and sat astride, petticoats, stockings, and laced boots showing. The Chinaman tied her bags across the saddle tree.

Fitting the reins between her fingers, she said,

"Kim Loo, tell Mr. Burleson where I've gone if he returns before I do. I'll be back as soon as I can. I'm depending on you to see to Patterson. Keep him in bed for several more days."

"I do. You take care, missy."

"I will."

Kim Loo moved around to the stranger. "I fix food. You take." He handed a canvas bag to the drover.

"Thanks," Green replied.

"Look after Rosie, too," Darcy called over her shoulder to Kim Loo as they headed southwest.

Darcy and her escort maintained a jarring but steady pace for Manalee. Her backside hurt and her inner thighs felt raw from rubbing against the saddle. Circular patches of perspiration darkened the sides of her bodice. She didn't dwell on her discomfort, however. She focused her thoughts on reaching Mrs. Miller in time.

The empty track bisected a sparsely covered landscape. They stopped only long enough to water the horses and themselves and eat their meal. And when they did pause, the plaguing flies quickly descended on them. When darkness fell, the stars paved their way.

Manalee appeared before sunup the next day. An ominous silence greeted the riders as they rode up to the main house. Above, the waning stars and moon were obscured by a thick layer of clouds, and only the eerie glow of a lantern from inside the house dispelled the murky gloom.

Darcy's anxiety heightened. She prayed they weren't too late.

They stopped at the gate. The drover took Darcy's reins. Dismounting, she untied her bags and went into the house.

Once inside, Darcy called, "Hello? I'm Dr. McCall from Kopperella."

A tired, leaden voice came from the next room. "In 'ere."

Darcy followed the thin ribbon of light which spilled across the floor. It led her to a dimly lit bedroom; the only source of illumination was a low-burning lantern on a table adjacent to the bed. The pale yellow glow cast the room's occupants and furniture in a spectral light.

Sitting on the side of the bed, a man bathed a woman's face with a damp cloth.

Darcy drew closer.

Sweat plastered curly blond hair to the woman's temples. Against an ashen complexion, her brown eyes appeared sunken and large, underscored by dark crescents. At intervals she moaned, a pitiful cry from deep in her throat.

With an experienced eye, Darcy took in the woman's distended stomach and pallid, spent face. She had tended many such women while she was a medical student and knew a difficult time lay ahead for her patient.

She came alongside the bed and spoke over the man's shoulder. "Mrs. Miller, I'm Dr. McCall. I'm here to help you."

The woman's head lolled to one side on the damp pillow, and her chalky lips parted, but no sound came out.

"Save your strength. There's no need to talk," Darcy reassured her.

Mr. Miller's gaze never left his wife as he said, "Thank you for coming. I'd about given up all 'ope."

"There's always hope. But you must let me tend to your wife."

Mr. Miller stood. He was a big man, with a dark complexion and broad shoulders. Several days' growth of black beard filled out the curves and hollows of his face.

Darcy had to bring him out of his worried stupor. "I'll need some water, please."

The bear of a man blinked his eyes twice before his gaze focused on Darcy. "Yes, of course."

Mr. Miller moved with a wooden gait, slow and shuffling, to an adjoining room. He soon reappeared through the doorway, carrying a pitcher of water for the basin on the washstand. He set the container down and looked at Darcy. A silent plea pinched his features.

Darcy tried to sound calm. "I'll do what I can."

Without hesitation, he responded. "I understand. But if it comes down to the missus or the baby, save my Mary."

"Let's hope it doesn't come to that."

Secretly, Darcy wasn't so sure. The woman was too weak to be of much help.

"One more thing—is this her first baby?"

"Yes."

"Thank you. I'll call you should I need you."

The quiet giant left the room, shutting the

door behind him. Soon another door closed, the sound echoing through the house.

Darcy rolled up her sleeves and washed her hands and forearms with the harsh lye soap she had brought. Scrubbed and cleaned, she positioned herself beside her patient.

"Mrs. Miller, can you hear me?"

Faint acknowledgment flickered in the dull brown eyes.

"Good, I see you do. Concentrate on the sound of my voice." Darcy felt the woman's wrist to gauge the strength of her pulse. "I need to examine you."

Darcy scooted the table and the lantern closer to the foot of the bed. She turned up the wick and the light grew stronger. Drawing back the twisted, sweat-dampened sheet and blanket, Darcy slipped her arms under Mrs. Miller's legs to reposition them.

Looking up the birth canal, Darcy saw the unborn infant's legs. For a second, her heart constricted, and she prayed for the mother's life.

Darcy came to Mrs. Miller's side and leaned near the woman's face. "I'm going to press down on your stomach. I want you to try and help me. We've got to get his baby out."

She kneaded the swollen stomach.

Mrs. Miller cried out weakly as a contraction gripped her enlarged middle. "Dear Lord, let me die."

"God doesn't want you to die. He wants you to fight. Keep pushing."

"But it hurts . . ."

"I can't do this myself. You've got to help. Now push."

Mrs. Miller gritted her teeth and feebly did her best. Her work-worn hands twisted the sheet beneath her as she grunted.

"Let go of the pain, Mrs. Miller. Breathe."

But with each ragged breath from Mrs. Miller, Darcy shared in her agony. She'd handled breech births before, but this time something else was wrong.

An hour later, the ordeal ended. Luckily, the baby had been small and Darcy had easily turned it. She followed up by coaxing the lifeless form down the birth canal. The umbilical cord had become wrapped around the baby's neck, cutting off oxygen and nourishment.

She washed the infant tenderly and wrapped the body in a clean piece of white linen.

Anger gripped Darcy. Senseless death always made her angry. Her throat worked and she fought to stem the scalding tears that threatened.

Darcy laid the baby aside. She bathed and redressed her patient and changed the bloodied sheets. Once that was done, no evidence of the life-and-death battle that had taken place remained, except for the still bundle.

Mrs. Miller's eyes fluttered open. She moistened her lips with her tongue and rasped, "May I see my baby?"

Every fiber of Darcy's being ached. Never in her life had she felt so helpless, so inadequate.

She was spared a reply. "My baby's dead."

Mrs. Miller's words were neither question nor statement. Only stark fact.

The woman stared wordlessly at the ceiling. A long sigh of suffering trembled on her lips. Tears trickled from the corners of her eyes and dampened the pillowcase.

Darcy picked up the bundle and moved beside the bed. "Would you like to hold your baby, Mrs. Miller?"

She lifted her glistening gaze to Darcy's face and nodded weakly. Darcy gently settled the infant in the crook of Mrs. Miller's arm.

Turning, Darcy busied herself with washing her hands and arms in the remaining water, and dried them on a scratchy towel. Next she cleaned and put away her instruments to give Mrs. Miller time with her baby.

She waited as long as possible before taking the bundle from Mrs. Miller.

Extracting a small bottle of laudanum from her medical bag and pouring a sufficient amount into a spoon, Darcy cradled her patient's neck and administered the medicine to her. Then she slowly lowered the woman's head.

She pressed a cool hand to Mrs. Miller's fevered brow and brushed the damp hair from her face. "Go to sleep now. I'll check on you later."

Before leaving, she straightened the room.

She found Mr. Miller sitting alone on the veranda, staring out into the early desert morning. His broad shoulders were slumped. By his drawn expression, Darcy knew his thoughts dwelled on his wife and the child he would never know.

She attempted to lighten his burden. "Mr. Miller?"

He looked at her. His large hands gripped the arms of his chair. "She's dead." The flat note of his voice hung in the still air.

Darcy sat adjacent to him and reached out to touch his hand. "Oh, no. On the contrary, she's going to be fine. It'll take time, but her health will return."

A poignant pause followed.

"And the baby?"

Darcy shook her head.

The man braced himself. "Boy or girl?"

A lump tightened Darcy's throat. "A boy."

Dismal silence separated them. A steady breeze rose and scattered the clouds shrouding the pale sun.

Tears rolled from the crinkled corners of Mr. Miller's eyes. His chest puffed out and his body trembled. Then his form grew rigid, as if he remembered himself.

He looked at Darcy. "I know you did your best and I'm grateful for it."

"If only I could have done more."

Haunting words.

If only . . .

Darcy remained on Manalee for two days, during which she came to know the Millers well.

Despite his large build, Joseph Miller was a caring, sensitive man. He delegated his chores to the drovers and attended his wife. He loved her very much.

Such devotion warmed Darcy's heart. She purposely kept her examinations brief when Mr. Miller was home so the couple could spend time together, alone.

When the opportunity presented itself, Darcy visited with Mrs. Miller. She, too, despite the hardships of the Outback, had not lost her sensitivity. Her genuine regard for her visitor was not lost on Darcy. Although weak, Mary, as she requested Darcy to call her, was ever attentive to Darcy's comfort and instructed her husband accordingly. The two of them welcomed Darcy with open arms.

Having another woman to talk to proved a godsend for Darcy, and they quickly formed a friendship. Two hours in the morning and another two in the evening were spent in idle conversation.

When the time came for Darcy to leave, it was difficult for everyone.

Wrapped in a blanket, Mary sat on the veranda with Darcy beside her.

"Just as I ordered. Sunshine to bring the color back to your cheeks," Darcy said. "Half an hour every day will do you a world of good. But no more. I don't want you taxing what strength you have."

Mary took Darcy's hand in her slight, toil-marked one and squeezed lightly. "I'll never forget what you did for me."

Darcy opened her mouth. "I—"

Mary's brown eyes searched Darcy's face.

"You did nothing short of a miracle, and I'll always be grateful. I would 'ave died without you. God sent you when I needed you most."

"God did us both a favor. I found a friend."

Mary smiled. "As soon as I'm able, Joseph and me will 'ave a party for you. Promise you'll come back."

"How could I stay away?"

"Then it's settled."

The sound of approaching hoofbeats broke into their good-byes. Joseph had brought Darcy's horse to the gate.

Darcy looked at her bags sitting on the edge of the porch. Reluctance to leave shadowed her green eyes.

She forced a light note into her voice. "It seems it's time to go."

Mary smiled wistfully. "I suppose it is."

Darcy stood and leaned over to hug her. "I'll miss you," she whispered against her friend's ear.

"Not 'alf as much as I will you," Mary returned.

They broke off and Darcy straightened, running the back of her hand across each eye. "Remember, don't overdo for at least another week. I've left specific instructions with Joseph. He knows what to do."

Mary nodded.

"Good-bye." With her back ramrod straight, Darcy turned on her heel and walked to the gate.

Joseph handed her the reins and took her

bags. He cleared his throat. "My man will see you back."

Darcy touched his forearm fondly. "Thank you."

She mounted and held out her hands.

Joseph lifted her bags and she secured them to the saddle tree.

With a wave, Darcy reined her horse to follow the drover and urged the mount into an easy canter, not wanting to linger.

She dared not look back for fear she would embarrass herself with tears. She was a doctor first and a woman second. She mustn't forget that fact.

Yet for a short while it had been wonderful to have another woman to talk to. She had been made to feel a part of this tiny piece of the Outback. But now duty forced her to return to the familiar hostility and turmoil of Kopperella. Her heart betrayed her by quickening at the thought of seeing Jim Burleson.

Weary and dirty, Jim Burleson rode into the compound of Kopperella. Drovers and a mob of brumbies followed. Unconsciously, he quickened his pace and reined his horse in a southerly direction.

Not until he reached Darcy's gate did Jim realize his actions. Yet oddly enough, he didn't care what she made of them. The best thing would be to leave her alone. But logic had nothing to do with his feelings for Darcy. Since he'd left on muster, he'd been unable to think of anything except her. Not the doctor, but the soft, beautiful woman.

Jim dismounted and strode up the path. His boots stamped a staccato rhythm against the porch's wooden planks.

He removed his hat and knocked.

Anticipation clawed at him.

Impatient, he knocked again.

Rosie answered the door. When she saw him she skidded to a halt and her beaming face fell.

Jim frowned. "Where's Dr. McCall?"

"She not here."

Jim's stomach felt as if someone were twisting a knife in it. Damn her! Why couldn't she do what she was told? He clenched his teeth until the veins along his neck stood out.

He hit the doorframe with his palm. "Where the bloody hell is she? I gave her orders to stay with Patterson."

An unaccustomed feeling of fear passed over him. He straightened. She'd be here unless . . .

Jim shouldered past Rosie and strode into Darcy's room. His gaze scanned the interior until it settled on her trunks. He released his pent-up breath. She hadn't gone back to the States.

But where the devil was she? He walked back to Rosie. The girl's eyes widened and she inched away from him.

Jim regretted his earlier tone and he softened his words. "I'm sorry. I'm tired. Can you tell me where the doctor went?"

Poised for flight and her eyes trained on him, Rosie answered, "Man from Manalee come seven days ago. He say boss's missus sick, need doctor. So doctor leave. She not come back."

Jim ran a hand through his short blond hair and jammed his hat atop his head. "Manalee, is it?"

He pivoted and walked out to his horse. The heels of his boots crunched against the pebbles strewn along the path, the sound matching his irritation.

Even if she'd stayed a couple of days, she should have been back by now. Unless something had happened to her.

His raw nerves throbbed with the need to find Darcy. Was she lost? Was she lying out there somewhere, hurt?

Was she alive? his heart echoed.

Jim led his mount to the corral, tethered it to a rail, unsaddled it, and headed for the kitchen.

Ignoring Newley, who sat at the table eating, Jim strode over to Kim Loo.

"I'm going out again." Jim paused long enough to have a drink of water. He wiped his mouth and tossed the dipper back into the bucket. "I want a bag of tucker."

"You going after missy, boss?"

"Yeah."

The Chinaman's eyes sparked. "Good. I worry."

Newley pushed his plate aside, tin scraping against wood. He leaned nonchalantly back in his chair, the front legs coming off the floor. "Eh? Now why would you be worried about 'er? She gotten 'erself in trouble?"

Jim turned and faced Craig. "Joseph Miller

from Manalee sent for her. Darcy hasn't been seen or heard from since."

"Calling 'er by 'er given name, are we?" Newley sneered.

His jaw tight with annoyance, Jim answered, "What I call her is none of your business."

Newley appeared unaffected by Jim's heated reply. "Calm yourself, mate. I reckon a spitfire like 'er can take care of 'erself."

"Well, you reckoned wrong. You know how it can be out there. She doesn't stand a chance if she's alone."

"What makes you think she's alone? A woman like 'er attracts men. I reckon one's sniffing along behind 'er. Maybe Miller 'isself, what with the missus sick and all. I'm sure 'e 'asn't been lifting 'er skirts lately."

Outrage roared through Jim. He threw himself at Newley. The impact sent both men crashing into the far wall.

Jim maintained the advantage, his strength fueled by anger. He dragged Newley up by his shirtfront and pinned him against the wooden barrier, his forearm pressed against Newley's throat.

"You bastard! If you ever say anything like that again, I'll give you the thrashing you deserve."

Hatred shone in Newley's eyes as he surveyed Jim's taut features. "I don't think you're man enough," he rasped, his throat restricted by Jim's arm.

Blood pounded in Jim's temples and aching savagery tightened every muscle in his body.

"That's your mistake." Anger—bitter and black—overrode sanity.

For Jim Burleson, the ensuing moments were lost in a fog of hostility. Finally, when the haze lifted, Newley was lying on the floor in a collapsed, groaning heap, his hands cupping his groin, blood streaming from his nose and split lip.

Bile roiled in Jim's stomach and burned in his throat, but he felt no regret. He grimaced as he flexed his bruised hand.

He faced the cook. "I won't be back until I find Dr. McCall."

Jim retrieved his fallen hat, crammed it on his head, and picked up the bag of food. He started for the door.

Kim Loo called after him, "What I do about him?"

In answer, Jim kicked a chair out of his path and strode from the kitchen.

Darcy felt as if she had been riding for an eternity. The ache deep inside her bones, of weariness and thirst, convinced her of it.

She pulled her horse to a halt and looked up at the sun in an attempt to get her bearings. The Manalee drover had seen her to the border of Kopperella, where she'd convinced him to let her go on alone. The track before her seemed clear, and without ever having been told, she knew that the Millers needed every spare hand to keep the place running. But before she'd realized it, she'd found herself off the track, and lost. She had no compass and the unfamiliar terrain offered no landmarks by which to journey. And she couldn't judge direction by the stars. That only left the sun. Yet it gave her no mercy as it beat down savagely on her exposed head. Her shoulders burned from the onslaught.

Her heart took on the pounding tempo of her head. Her cracked lips formed a silent entreaty.

Craig Newley tried to raise himself. His body wouldn't cooperate and he collapsed against the rope-frame bed. Pain sliced through his groin. Sweat broke out on his forehead and upper lip.

God, he hurt. He didn't think a square inch on his body had been spared.

He looked around the drovers' quarters. No one else was there.

" 'Ey! Can anybody 'ear me?" The effort cost him and he swallowed a groan.

Momentarily, there came the sound of boots against wooden planks, followed by the creaking of rusty hinges as the door opened.

"What's all the yelling about?" Rivers asked.

"Get your bleedin' ass over 'ere," growled Newley.

Rivers stepped near the bed. With a dispassionate look, he asked, "What 'appened to you? Looks like you went waltzing with a wild boar."

"Shut your fucking mouth."

Rivers chuckled dryly. "Now is that any way to talk to your mate?"

Newley cast an arm across his forehead. "Just get me a bottle."

Rivers chuckled again—this time deeper. "Just

what you need." He turned and left, his footfalls growing fainter with each step.

Newley recalled Rivers' words. *Looks like you went waltzing with a wild boar.*

His breath came tight and hard. Burleson. The bastard.

Fury replaced a portion of Craig's pain as he remembered the beating Burleson had given him.

He swore revenge.

Darcy twisted in the saddle and looked back in the direction she had come from. There were no tracks, no signs that she had passed that way. It was if the earth had simply swallowed up all signs of her.

She turned around and stood in the stirrups, trying to ease her cramping muscles. She was losing body fluids faster than she would have liked, but she dared not squander her meager supply of water. She had to consider the horse.

Darcy eased her bottom against the leather and passed a weary hand across her face. She winced at the contact with her sunburned skin.

She had two choices. She could remain where she was in the hope that someone would find her. That could take days. Or she could go on, trusting she was heading in the right direction.

Both alternatives could conclude with the same result—death from lack of water and exposure to the elements.

Underlying all her other emotions was a fierce tenacity to cling to life. She refused to relinquish her hold without a fight.

Darcy urged her horse forward. The animal reluctantly moved, laying its ears back and tossing its head in protest.

Time seemed suspended. For Darcy, one hour blurred into the next. Maintaining her presence of mind was difficult.

Eventually, pressed beyond her limits and unable to continue, she stopped to rest on the side of a sandhill as the sun reached its zenith. She watered her mount, using her hands to hold the water, then drank sparingly herself from the water container.

She sat and had a simple meal of cold damper. The tasteless bread resembled dry wood. Swallowing proved difficult because of her raw, parched throat.

Darcy drew her knees to her chest and hugged her calves. Slowly lowering her head, she pressed her forehead against her kneecaps. She felt like crying; she wanted to cry. But her dust-clogged tear ducts and dwindling body fluids robbed her of even that small self-indulgence.

Darcy remained that way until she glanced up to see the sun setting in an orange glow on the horizon.

She forced herself to stand and walked on shaky legs to where she had unsaddled her horse. Having no hobbles, she had tied him to a shrub. She retrieved her tent and rigged it to a low-lying bush.

Sitting inside the small entrance of her tent, she stared at the sky. It appeared unblemished and crystalline, apricot to peacock blue at the horizon, pale blue and gray at the zenith. The first stars materialized.

Using the saddle blanket for extra cover, she lay down.

Her body curled into a ball against the cold, Darcy slept fitfully that night, and dreamed.

She found herself standing naked, her hair a mantle about her, in a secluded grove. It was neither day nor night, but a strange twilight. Calm blanketed the scene, and not a single tree whispered in the breeze. The moon rose over a mountain.

In the distance, Darcy observed twin flames. Each burned equally bright. The small tongues of fire drifted closer together, their glow intensifying, until they merged. The single brilliant flame nearly blinded her.

Darcy heard a man. His voice sounded like a murmuring river. He then appeared before her, naked as she. On his forehead burned another tiny flame of fire, pearly white in color, resembling a star.

Suddenly Darcy felt energy rising up her spine. A living current of desire.

The man walked toward her, his eyes encompassing her like an embrace. She looked at him and saw not only his handsome face but also a reflection of herself. Her whole being surged with a primal feeling that confirmed inner ties to this stranger. Freely she moved into the circle of his outstretched arms. He bent his head, pressing his mouth to hers, and kissed her passionately. Her parted lips trembled as his tongue softly outlined their fullness.

With that kiss, their souls joined.

Her arms crept up and twined around his back and neck to press him closer. She returned his fervent embrace and kiss. Hungrily, impatiently, her lips fused with his. Her tongue darted inside his mouth. Her body quivered like the taunt strings of a guitar strummed by a master.

He wrapped his fingers in her red hair. Strands the color of a fiery sunrise streamed past her slender shoulders as his lips trailed across her soft cheek. She whimpered low in her throat while his mouth sought her eyelids and temples to brand her as his alone.

His warm breath fanned her like a hot, humid breeze, and the sensation tickled. She laughed softly as she writhed against him. Her nipples hardened into buds against his lightly furred chest.

The man laughed, too, huskily, before claiming her mouth again, urgently now, demandingly. His tongue plunged between her pliant lips and filled her with molten desire. His hands, still tangled in her mane of thick hair, gripped her tighter. His callused palms caressed her body, slid down her back to cup her buttocks, and pulled her to him. She felt his rising passion pressed against her thighs.

Darcy flung her head back. He nipped the sensitive skin of her bare throat with his teeth. His masterful lips moved lower and roamed the valley between her breasts.

Impatiently his hands kneaded her moist flesh, heated with desire. His hands possessed her breasts. Thumbs and forefingers flicked the stiff peaks, taunting, teasing, until they strained against him, aching for more. His head dipped and his lips captured and savored one rosy crest. She arched against him and whimpered with unleashed emotions. Her flesh burned where his tongue lingered. An uncontrollable spasm of delicious agony radiated from the center of her nipple, causing her body to catch aflame like a fire out of control. Her blood boiled and her flesh tingled as though it had been scorched. An almost painful ache blazed at her very core. It grew hotter and hotter until she felt as though it would consume her. She cried out, but the man's mouth never left her bosom, and the fire continued to rage past all constraint.

Startled, Darcy awoke. Gasping, she bolted upright. Goose bumps cropped out along her skin. She touched her parted, parched lips with trembling fingers. The dreamy passion and pulse of his kiss still lingered.

The dream had been so real, so vivid. The stranger's image burned in her memory.

It was the heat spiraling from his eyes ...

Eyes of blue.

Jim's eyes.

Chapter 11

Darcy must have drifted back to sleep, because an unnatural calm woke her. She lay there for a moment. Drawing a long, waking breath, she coughed. Dust permeated the air.

She peered out from her swag. The scene had the intense irrational quality of a dream. The sky appeared dark, yet the temperature was climbing, and the sun was a pale yellow imitation of itself, wearing a dusty veil.

Darcy tentatively placed her fingertips against her crusty eyelids and lashes. Red earth was everywhere. In her clothes. In her hair. In her nostrils and mouth. It even gritted against her teeth. This was no dream.

Her mind sharpened. Inexplicable dread pierced her. Something was wrong.

Her gaze swept the area where she had tethered her mount. Her eyes widened. The horse was gone.

Darcy heard a roaring in the distance. Panic doused her like cold water, and her breath left her in a rush. She tried to stand, but her legs wouldn't support her. She sank to her knees and rocked against her heels.

Only a small ration of water remained, her food was gone, and now she had no horse.

Willing herself not to despair, Darcy stood. The wind picked up and stinging sand pelted her. Her reddened eyes narrowed against the onslaught of the bellowing cloud rolling across the landscape.

The urgent need for self-preservation mobilized her senses. She scrambled to make a shelter out of her swag. Wedging herself between two boulders, Darcy anchored the canvas sheet with large rocks to create a sanctuary. There was nothing to do but wait out the storm. She had her medical bag and her tin of water. It would have to be enough.

Almost instantly the flies swarmed about her, making her skin crawl. Darcy sought the scissors from her bag. She cut away part of the bottom section of her skirt, a section sufficient to cover her face. Quickly shaking off the dust, she wrapped the cloth around the back of her head and over her eyes, then pulled the fabric high enough to cover her mouth and nose.

The air beneath the swag was like the fiery breath of a furnace, the temperature climbing rapidly.

Suddenly a roaring and driving wind lambasted her crude shelter. Needles of sand pierced the edges of the swag and dug into Darcy's skin.

Breathing through the material of her skirt was difficult and she tried to drag air into her lungs. The horrifying feeling that she might suffocate all but overwhelmed her.

Clenching her teeth and squeezing her eyes shut, she valiantly tried to occupy her mind with reflections of home, family—anything but the raging storm swirling around her. Nothing worked. The smothering feeling gripped her tighter.

She squeezed her eyes harder and welcomed the pain of imbedded sand against her eyelids. Pain would help her ignore thoughts of being buried alive.

A warm, salty liquid stung her cracked lips. She tasted blood. In her anxiety, she had bitten her bottom lip.

The wind blew all that day and into the night. By rationing her water, Darcy fought to stay alive. But the thread of hope to which she clung was thin.

Out of the storm's path, farther up the track, Jim desperately searched for signs of Darcy's whereabouts. Fear that he wouldn't find her alive raged within him as he knelt and touched the still warm carcass of a horse bearing the Kopperella brand.

He knew Darcy was on foot now. But where? With no horse, her chances of survival were reduced by half.

Jim closed his eyes tightly, squeezing dire images from his mind. Fatigue hammered at him. But then he got up, steeled himself, and went on.

* * *

When at long last the wind ceased its howling and the driven sand lessened, Darcy crept from her swag into the sunlight. Her cramped muscles screamed in protest and she had to straighten by degrees.

She unwrapped her headcloth and looked up at the pale, hazy sky. Her gaze lowered and stretched out across the land. There was nothing on the horizon but an empty plain, some half-dead trees with their exposed, wind-eroded roots twisted in torturous loops, and endless sand hills.

Darcy knew she had to press on while she still had strength and water.

Resigning herself to the journey ahead, she rummaged through the swag for her water tin. She stopped short. Covered by dirt, the container lay on its side, the top askew. Unknowingly, she must have knocked it over during the storm.

Shock and disbelief broke across her face. She picked up the tin with trembling hands. Empty. No, it couldn't be! Darcy shook the tin, then with a strangled cry hurled it as far as she could.

She drew several sobering breaths to clear her mind. Think, she told herself. *Think.*

Only one course of action presented itself. She had to forge ahead in hopes of being discovered. Perhaps if she could make the sand hill some one hundred yards away, she might be able to see something.

Squaring her shoulders, she forced one foot in front of the other. Slowly she waded through the cresting waves of sand, then made better time over the flat, hard terrain of a claypan, until she reached the foot of the small hill.

Resolve infused the blood in her veins, giving her weary body the strength she needed for the climb ahead. Midway up, the sole of her boot slipped against a rock and she stumbled to her knees. Gasping for breath, she rolled onto her backside and sat for a moment.

She studied the hill with its gently sloping sides. The heat of the morning sun was sapping her strength. Maybe if her mind had been clearer, she would have listened to common sense and waited until nightfall. But time was a precious commodity. Every day—no, every hour, every minute—was critical now.

Darcy willed strength into her tired, quivering limbs, and rose.

At last she reached the top and gazed at the terrain beyond. There were no signs of life. On her way down the other side, she rested again, supporting her face in her hands.

Ten minutes later she gained the level ground, and began crossing the claypan. Her nemesis, the sun, had begun to set, but she felt no relief from the heat.

Tormented by thirst and exhaustion, Darcy crossed the open expanse. Suddenly she floundered through the soft sand, lost her footing, and fell face-forward.

She lay sprawled until she summoned the last of her energy to rise.

On sheer determination, Darcy made it to a

clump of scrub brush. Under a meager amount of shade, she collapsed.

Jim's sharp eyes spotted a dark shape on the red plain, but the descending twilight made it impossible for him to tell if it was human.

He whipped his horse into a gallop. He couldn't distinguish between the pounding of the horse's hooves and the thundering of his heart.

Hurriedly, he dismounted and knelt beside the prone figure. His stomach plummeted as he looked down at an unconscious Darcy.

Please.

Not realizing he was holding his breath, he eased her onto her back and pressed an ear to her chest. He heard the soft passage of air through her lungs and felt the shallow rise and fall of her chest. He lifted his head and his own breath came out in a soft rush.

His shaky fingers brushed her dirty, stiff hair from her face.

A stunned hiss escaped him. "Jesus!" The word hung in the air.

The exposed areas of her skin were fiery red, contrasting with the white lines about her mouth and eyes. Sand coated her fissured lips, and her tongue appeared swollen.

"Don't you die on me," he growled, unable to separate pain from anger. "Do you hear me, Darcy McCall? Don't die, dammit."

Uttering a curse, he hurried to his horse, grabbed his water tin, and returned to Darcy. He tore the kerchief from around his neck and soaked it with water. Dropping to his knees, he cradled Darcy's head in his lap. Gently, he passed the wet cloth across her face and pressed it to her mouth.

"Come on, Darcy, take this," he half pleaded, half commanded.

Darcy shuddered and opened her eyes. Comprehension slowly dawned in the green depths as she looked up at Jim. Gradually, she was able to suck the moisture from the wet cloth.

Relief came as a raw, tremulous sigh for Jim, and his throat ached with emotion. "Good girl. You're going to make it."

Blackness, thick and heavy, covered Darcy. The sounds that penetrated her darkness were garbled.

Was she dead?

No, she felt pain. Ceaseless, throbbing pain.

Darcy clung to that agony like a lifeline. Pain meant she was alive.

She sensed movement around her, and she heard voices. But whose? She couldn't tell.

Eventually the enveloping darkness dissipated like early morning fog, leaving a misty veil draping her perception.

She concentrated on one thing—reaching Jim.

Bright sunshine skipped across Darcy's face, teasing her into awareness. She blinked against the light. The movement of facial muscles and stretched sunburned skin caused a twinge of pain. She grimaced.

Beneath her hands, Darcy felt sheets instead of sand. The softness of a mattress supported her back, instead of red earth. Tears of relief spiked her lashes, and her breath trembled past her lips.

She turned her head to the side. Kim Loo sat nearby in a chair, asleep, his chin resting on his chest. On a pallet, curled into a ball, lay Rosie. She, too, slept.

Somehow Kim Loo sensed Darcy's gaze on him, and awoke. He looked over at her.

A grin split his face. "Oh, missy." He rose and shuffled toward her. "You feel better?"

Darcy moistened her lips and croaked, "Yes."

"I tell boss you wake. He tell me get him quick." Kim Loo left.

His voice must have awakened Rosie, for she sat up and stretched. When the child saw Darcy, a joyful expression played across her young face. She was beside the bed before Darcy could blink.

A small hand touched the wispy hair at Darcy's temple. "I glad you not die."

The reminder of her horrifying ordeal evoked fresh tears. Darcy didn't care. She was alive!

"Me . . . too," she rasped.

Rosie regarded Darcy's sunburned skin. "You should take care of skin like black fella. He no let burn."

"In this case, I should have." Darcy raised herself slightly and repositioned her pillow at her back. "Have you been here all the time?"

"Plenty time."

"All by yourself?"

"No. Cook and boss. They stay, too."

A lump of joy formed in Darcy's scratchy

throat, but she felt no discomfort. They cared for her, her mind sang. They *really* cared.

Obviously unaware of Darcy's preoccupation, Rosie continued merrily. "Boss found you."

At the mention of Jim, Darcy's attention focused on the child. "He one stay most. First days he not leave ever. He wash and feed you like baby. He say no one see you but him." She giggled. "But I sneak in sometimes."

"He did that?" Darcy gasped.

Normally, she would have been appalled that he'd tended her in such an intimate way, but somehow in the here and now she didn't care. The rapid beating of her heart invigorated her weary, aching body. Despite everything, Jim Burleson was far from indifferent to her! The fact that he'd risked his life for her proved that.

When Jim appeared at her bedside minutes later, Darcy's heart sank. Fatigue painted deep grooves near his mouth, and several days' growth of beard shaded his face. His wrinkled clothes testified to his lack of sleep. Compassion tugged at her heart.

Yet beneath the layers of fatigue she recognized the man she knew. She remembered those same strong features, that same solid frame. He was as rugged as the land. He was, she thought, the vital, beating soul of the Outback.

Their gazes met and held.

"Thank you," she said softly.

To Darcy, those two words seemed inadequate for what he'd done, but Jim seemed pleased and smiled.

"You're a great deal of trouble, you know that?"

Darcy returned Jim's smile. "So you keep telling me."

"And you talk too much. Don't overdo it. I want you to rest now." He rubbed his chin. "We'll talk later, when you're stronger. And when I've had a shave."

Darcy wanted to argue, but was too weak. Instead, she nodded.

He knelt and leaned near her. "I'll be back," he promised.

His manly scent, carried on the heat of his skin, wrapped around her senses. It was the scent of dust and horses and the sweat of hard work done under the hot sun. His nearness was reassuring.

"Jim?"

His fingers caressed her cheek briefly. "What?"

Darcy couldn't speak, couldn't think. Her heartbeat accelerated as delicate, hidden emotions whirled inside her and threatened to erupt. He had touched her as a lover would. As someone who truly cared.

She focused her attention on his face until she was capable of speech. "I don't remember much, but Rosie told me everything you did for me."

A crooked smile played at his lips. "Not quite everything," he drawled softly. The timbre of his voice stroked her in secret places.

"You didn't—"

Jim interrupted her. "I said we'd talk later. If you're good, I'll give you details then."

He rose and started for the door.

Darcy couldn't bear for him to leave. "Jim?"

He pivoted in the doorway and frowned in feigned impatience. "Now what?"

"Thank you again."

The warmth of his smile wafted across the room and touched her.

As Jim walked to his quarters, his thoughts dwelled on Darcy. He sighed, and one side of his mouth lifted. She was safe and mending. Nothing else seemed important.

He stopped in mid-stride.

He should insist she leave for her own good, he knew that. The Outback had claimed much stronger people than she. Her near brush with death brought that point home forcefully. But then the thought of her going caused a sharp pain in his chest.

Sweet Jesus, what was she doing to him? She was clouding his judgment. Someone had to do the thinking for her, because she was to full of pride and defiance to do it herself.

Tonight, when they talked, he would insist she leave.

"Damn," Jim breathed aloud.

A voice broke into his thoughts.

Tom Rivers approached. "Don't mean to bother you, boss, but I wanted to know about Dr. McCall."

Realizing Rivers had heard his curse, Jim said, "Sorry, that wasn't meant for you. I was just thinking to myself." He cleared his throat. "I

just came from her house. She's awake now."
His gruff tone surprised him. Judging from the
look on the man's face, it surprised Rivers, too.
"Sorry."

"Got things on your mind, do you?"

Did Jim detect a knowing gleam in those cunning eyes, or was his imagination playing tricks
on him?

"I've just been preoccupied. Haven't gotten
much sleep lately, either."

"We've all been worried about the doctor."
Rivers coughed and spit to one side. "Well, most
of us anyway."

Jim fought to maintain a relaxed stance, but
a frown etched a line between his brows.
"Newley?"

"I'm not one for giving you advice, but if I
were you, I'd keep one eye open when I sleep.
'E's changing by the day, and I don't like what
I see."

"We all change."

"Not mean like 'im." Rivers took a step closer.
"I'm going to talk straight."

"I've never known you to do otherwise."

"When Newley was on the mend, laid up in
'is bunk, 'e got drunk. Muttered 'ow 'e was going to get even," Rivers said.

"Don't worry, I can take care of myself."

"It's not you that I'm worried about. It's Dr.
McCall. I wouldn't leave 'er alone."

Jim's hands clenched into fists. "If he so much
as touches her, he's a dead man."

"Why don't you sack 'im?"

"I've thought about it. But I can't until we're done with the mustering. I have to do the fair thing."

"Just don't let that fairness do you in."

"I'll wait it out."

"One more word."

Something in Rivers' expression made Jim brace himself. "What's that?"

"Newley's brother is back in the district. 'Eard 'e's running with a mob of bushrangers. That's trouble for sure."

Jim's insides coiled like a tightly wound watch.

That evening, Jim returned to visit Darcy as promised. He came bearing a supper tray and a bouquet of wildflowers, feeling more like a green boy than a full-grown man.

"Looking at all this food, you'd think Kim Loo was afraid you'd starve." He set the tray down on a small table and moved it beside the bed.

Darcy reclined, pillows at her back, dressed in a fresh gown and robe. Her hair was combed back and held with a ribbon.

She smiled. "And the flowers? Do I have Kim Loo to thank for them as well?"

The lantern light was soft; the glow from the fire was soft. And her eyes were soft.

Jim half groaned to himself. Convincing Darcy to leave would be hard. The hardest thing he'd ever done.

"I thought you might like them."

"They're lovely. Thank you." She laughed and

gazed at the coverlet, making a show of smoothing out the wrinkles.

"What's funny?"

She looked up at him, and the scent of her hair came at him in a sweet, inescapable rush. "It seems 'Thank you' is all I ever say to you lately."

"I don't mind hearing it."

Her shoulders moved in a fetching shrug. "Then I won't apologize for saying it."

At the tender expression on her face, Jim's throat tightened and his mouth grew dry. If he didn't break the spell she was weaving, they'd both be lost.

"That's enough talk for now. Let's eat before the food gets cold," he muttered.

He lifted the cloth covering the plates, removed his, and set Darcy's, tray and all, on her lap. He pulled a chair to the table and sat.

They ate in companionable silence.

Outwardly, he seemed absorbed with his food. But inwardly, Jim was all too aware of Darcy. Each bite she took, each time she raised her glass to her lips, he knew it.

For the briefest second, he imagined what it would be like if Darcy stayed, if he asked her to share his life with him. Ever since Cynthia, he'd resigned himself to solitude. But in a way, Darcy—with her damned foolish pride and defiance—was more dangerous out here than a soft kind of woman. She was always getting into scrapes and arguing. So he told himself to stop daydreaming and say what was on his mind.

Darcy's voice broke the mellow quiet. "Tell Kim Loo the roast beef was wonderful." She wiped her mouth with the napkin and folded it atop her plate.

Jim rose, picked up the tray, and placed it back on the small table. "He'll be glad to know that. He's been worried. They've all been worried about you."

Suddenly a fierce need rose in Darcy. Unexplainably, it mattered to her how Jim felt.

"And you?" She held her breath.

He straightened, his body silhouetted by the firelight behind him. She couldn't see his face clearly.

She felt his words as his silken tone glided over her skin and senses. "What do you think?"

"That I was very lucky you found me."

A silence fell between them, wrapping the atmosphere in lush folds of velvet warmth.

Darcy perceived Jim's uncertainty.

His actions confirmed her feeling. He turned and moved to the fireplace. He picked up the poker and jabbed the logs. The fire hissed as ruddy sparks showered upward, glowing dark red and yellow.

As Darcy watched him, something deep inside her let go. Having faced death, she realized how much she had denied herself. She wanted to feel Jim's arms around her again, to feel his lips on hers. She wanted him to love her. She wanted Jim, no matter what.

The sound of his approaching footsteps roused her from her thoughts.

He sat beside her on the bed. "Darcy, we need to talk."

"About what?"

"Us."

"What is it you want to say?" She smiled up at him almost coquettishly.

"A great deal." He yearned to taste the soft skin at her throat with his lips. The feeling was so strong that he had to look away.

When she slid her hand over his and let it glide up his strong, corded forearm, he almost gasped. She touched his cheek, gently forcing him to look back.

He groaned at the nearness of her, the visible softness of her lips.

Did she understand what her body was saying? Did she want this as much as he did?

Suddenly Jim backed off. "Darcy ... do you know what you're doing?"

She could only look at him. Her green eyes had darkened. He could see the firelight reflected in them. He saw her own passion burning within them.

He moved closer until only inches separated them. Her body heat wafted to him like so much smoke, lingering, titillating, curling around his heightened senses.

In a low, deliberate tone he asked, "You want me to stay?"

She nodded and moistened her lips.

"I won't be able to stop this time."

Again she nodded. The truth was, she'd never cared about what the world would say. That had only been an excuse, just as Jim had claimed. She'd been afraid. But now she didn't want to be afraid anymore.

His lips brushed her temple, the sensitive, tingling skin beneath her ear, the hollow of her throat. His soft, rumbling groan fanned the flames of her desire.

Darcy broke the contact and inched away to make room for Jim. No words were needed as he joined her atop the bed.

God, how she looked at him with such yearning in her eyes. It was more than he could bear.

With deft fingers, he untied her robe, slipped her out of it, and tossed the garment aside.

Kneeling, facing her, Jim encircled her waist with one arm and drew her gently against the lean, hard lines of his chest, his hips, his thighs.

He imagined that she grimaced. "Does my touching you hurt?" he asked, concern simmering in his words.

She looked at him with large, languid eyes. "Not as much as if you didn't."

His head dipped. "Then I don't want you in pain," he murmured against the lushness of her bottom lip.

While he kissed her, he unbuttoned her nightgown. And while he unbuttoned the nightgown, his mind took flight with visions of Darcy naked and willing in his arms, and a half cry rose from his chest.

His hands sought the hem of her nightdress. Slowly, sensuously, he inched it upward, his roughened fingers skimming the warm, silken contours of her thighs and hips.

At her waist, he stopped and gathered the

loose garment in one hand. He cupped her buttocks and his free hand skimmed across her hip, passed between their bodies, and dipped into the soft, curly hair of her womanhood.

His fingers parted the quivering, moist lips and stroked the center of her pleasure.

Darcy gasped against his mouth as rivulets of shock and excitement ran through her. His arm tightened around her to support her sagging body as her legs turned to water. A tremor began in her stomach and spread outward like ripples across a pond. Her breath came tight and fast.

"You like that, don't you?" he whispered as her head dropped against his shoulder.

"Yes." The single word came as a soft rush of air, damp and heated against his ear. "Oh, yes."

Jim removed his hand. "Look at me, Darcy."

With a great deal of effort, she raised her head and stared wordlessly at him beneath drooping lids. Drowsy sensuality suffused her face.

His hand traveled to her throat. His fingertips lingered on that spot at the base of the slender column where her pulse beat strong. "I want you."

"I want you, too."

"Do you truly know what that means?"

"It means I want you to keep on touching me and kissing me."

Her eyes were wide and innocent. It struck him then that, doctor or no, she didn't know the first thing about what really went on between women and men. She was offering herself to him—all of herself—without even knowing what it meant.

"I can't stop with just that. There's so much more."

She was silent for a moment. Then, softly but clearly, she said, "Show me."

His heart filled, and every fiber of his being yearned to do just that. But he knew that if he took her now, she would give herself to him body and soul. He didn't know what he could give her back—except an impossibly hard existence in the Outback. They spent most of their time arguing as it was. How would it be when she finally realized what kind of life—and man—she'd committed herself to? And though he sensed that he cared for her more than for any woman he'd ever met, that was all the more reason to treat her gently and well, to see to it that she left.

It took all of his willpower to pull her arms away from him and get up. The sight of her wide, stricken eyes and the sound of the sob that escaped her branded themselves in Jim's memory.

"Darcy, I . . ." But suddenly he didn't know know what to say, how to explain himself. "I . . . Darcy, you've got to go away from here."

That was the last thing she'd expected to hear. She'd opened herself to him and, despite all her better instincts, let herself be vulnerable. All he'd had to do was accept her—all of her. But he couldn't. Humiliation flooded her. The only thing he'd ever really wanted was her body. But clearly, even his lust was short-lived. Darcy retaliated because he had hurt her, struck her at the core of her being.

"I'm sorry you feel that way, but I'm not leaving until I'm ready. And that won't be until I fulfill my contract. I've given my word, and I intend to keep it. You'll have to send that letter you threatened me with before. That's the only way I'll leave."

She drew a quivering breath. "But let me assure you, I won't be able to leave here fast enough once my year is over. You're suffering from disillusionment if you think I have any other reason for staying."

Had she had more presence of mind, Darcy would have seen the wounded look in Jim's eyes. Perhaps it was the strain of her ordeal, the strain of being at constant odds with this man, or the fact that she desired him. But whatever the reason, Darcy's wounded pride demanded satisfaction.

"Our intimacy was a mistake. I see that now," she said with quiet dignity, although her chin trembled from the effort she made to maintain her composure.

"Darcy, listen—"

"Oh, spare me!" Her control snapped and she flung the bouquet of flowers at him. They struck his chest and fell to the floor. "Now, if you have nothing further to say, I wish you'd go."

He stood, his own private despair visible in the broad set of his shoulders. He'd only been trying to do what was right. But she was too headstrong to see that.

His sense of injury evaporated, replaced with unadulterated anger.

He spun on his heel and left.

The slamming of the front door marked his passage.

Chapter 12

Jim sat on the front steps of the store, rum bottle in one hand, tin cup in the other.

He closed his eyes and drew a ragged breath. Pain broke over him.

"Boss?"

He looked up to see Tom Rivers standing at the bottom of the steps.

Rivers' gaze dropped from his face to the rum bottle he held. "Saw you walk past my quarters. Thought you might like a bit of company."

With his teeth, Jim uncorked the bottle and splashed a liberal amount into the cup. He spit the cork out. "Well, you thought wrong."

Obviously, Rivers wasn't going to take no for an answer. He joined Jim. "You know what they say about drinking by yourself. Gives people the wrong idea."

Jim raised the cup to his mouth, tilted his head back, and took a deliberate swallow. The rum burned a fiery path down his throat and warmed his stomach.

"Suit yourself. But I don't have another cup."

Rivers grinned. "Don't need one when you've got the bottle."

Jim passed the bottle. "Help yourself."

Focusing his attention on his own drink, Jim downed the remaining liquor in one gulp. Finished, he wiped his mouth on his shoulder.

"Is Dr. McCall all right?" Rivers asked.

Jim's glare sliced over Rivers. "I wouldn't know."

"I think you do, and that's why you're sitting 'ere, intent on getting yourself drunk."

Growling, Jim snatched the bottle from the other man's grasp and filled his cup.

"That's what I reckoned." Rivers retrieved the bottle from Jim and took a long drink. Then, sighing his appreciation, he continued. "Even when the liquor's as fine as this is, it won't solve your problems."

"But it helps you forget."

"For a while, but the pain comes back. You'll find no answers in a bottle. Living life, now there's where you find answers."

"Sometimes life is too painful."

"That's when you take what comes like a man. You stare your problem in the face."

"Sometimes it's not so easy. Not when you hurt people."

" 'Ave you got matters straight? Did you 'urt someone, or did that person 'urt you? You sound like a man with an ailment."

Jim gave a humorless laugh. "I doubt anyone has the cure for what ails me."

"Except the woman herself."

Jim's head snapped around.

Now it was Rivers' turn to laugh. "Don't look so surprised. I've 'ad my suspicions for quite some time."

"You're—"

"Wrong? Not this time." He took another sip. "I knew your father. And 'e didn't raise a fool. Don't lie to yourself."

"He raised a bigger fool than you think."

"Oh, we certainly can act like fools, that's for certain. But 'ere." He jabbed a finger at Jim's chest. " 'Ere is where you know the truth."

A brutal headache grasped the back of Jim's neck, throbbed in his temples. "It's not that easy."

"Because you don't want it to be."

"Because she's like no other woman I've known." Jim's tone conveyed his frustration— and something more.

"Isn't that why you're drawn to 'er?"

Jim groaned. "Nothing of the sort. She's bloody frustrating. Just when I think I've got her figured out, she goes and does something else." He passed a hand over his weary eyes. "And she's stubborn as hell. Won't listen to reason."

"Like someone else I know."

"Threatening her with a letter to the agents in London didn't even do any good."

"You wouldn't 'ave done anything so stupid." Rivers paused. "It would 'ave been the biggest mistake of your life."

"Now hold on. . . ."

"Don't go getting your nose all twisted. You wouldn't get angry unless I was right."

"You're taking a lot upon yourself, talking to me like this."

"Maybe. But somebody's got to talk to you straight." Rivers sighed. "I 'ave other reasons. I like the doctor, and I don't want to see 'er get 'urt. By you, or anyone else. She's been through a lot and doesn't deserve any more grief. So quit putting yourself first and do what's right by 'er."

Jim's face twisted. "Don't you think I've tried? I tried to convince her to leave, that Kopperella was no place for her. For the love of God, she nearly died out there."

His last words were spoken with quiet conviction. "I don't want her death on my conscience."

"Stop comparing 'er to your mom." Rivers raised his hand against Jim's growl. " 'Ear me out. Your mom, God rest her soul, made her choice. She chose to stay with the man she loved. She knew the risks. You've got to let the doctor make up 'er own mind, too."

"She doesn't realize the danger."

"I think she does. She's 'ad to fight to get where she's at. After all, she's got pride, too. And determination. 'Ow many times must she prove 'erself?"

Jim tried to answer, but swallowed back the words.

What was he afraid to confront?

One answer came to mind—loving someone to distraction, and being loved back.

Rivers must have sensed his difficulty, and his inner confession. "If you love 'er like I think you do, then put your faith in 'er. And your 'eart. She won't let you down."

Jim shrugged, feeling far from indifferent. "The rum's gone to your head."

Rivers laughed into the night. "Not yet, but I intend for it to."

Neither man noticed the shadowy figure that had been hovering at the side of the building, and now blended into the darkness.

The next day, for Rosie's sake, Darcy put on a brave face.

While the morning remained cool, Darcy rested in a chair on the veranda. The sunshine and fresh air helped to revive her lagging spirits.

Rosie sat at her feet, leafing through Darcy's copy of *Fairy Tales of the Brothers Grimm*.

Her fondness for the little girl grew daily. With Rosie, she could relax. They shared a delight in simple pleasures. Rosie was the only person who demanded nothing, but gave her unconditional adoration.

Darcy remembered her own youthful, carefree days at home, where her parents had nurtured her with love. But here at Kopperella, cut off from that security, she felt a part of her was withering. She wasn't the type of person who could exist without affection.

At Rosie's exclamation of wonder as she viewed the drawings, Darcy roused from her thoughts and asked, "Haven't you ever seen a book before?"

"No. Most wonderful." Rosie frowned and pointed at the printed page opposite the illustration. "What this?"

Darcy leaned forward. "Those are called words. People know what the book says by what's written down. It's called reading."

Rosie's frown deepened. "How you tell? Nothing like black fellas' paintings."

"No, they're not. Each letter is a symbol. A picture of sorts. Black fellas' paintings have symbols. But it takes lots of white fellas' symbols to make words."

Rosie's eyes lit in wonderment. "You do this thing called reading?"

Darcy smiled, delighted by Rosie's earnest interest. Her eagerness and thirst for knowledge were touching. Whoever said the Aborigines were stupid didn't know this wonderful child.

"Yes," Darcy said simply.

"You wise."

"I'm not wise. I know these things only because someone taught me." An inspiration struck Darcy. She didn't know why she hadn't thought of it before, but it was the natural thing to do. "I could teach you."

It would help keep her mind off her pain and confusion, and Jim. Distraction was the best medicine for her now. Her body, mind, and spirit were in need of healing.

Rosie thrust the book into Darcy's lap and hovered over her shoulder. "You teach now."

Darcy laughed. "Eager, aren't you?"

What an amazing child she was. Intelligence shone from her dark eyes.

Teacher and pupil happily spent the morning in the pursuit of knowledge. They shared the experience, Darcy learning as much as Rosie.

Jim, on the other hand, wore a dour face, suffering a hangover, as he and the other drovers broke in the new brumbies.

The holding paddock buzzed with activity. Drovers perched on the top railing and talked, waiting for the buck-jumping to begin.

Dave Patterson, balancing on his splintered leg, opened the gate for Craig Newley.

Wearing a crooked grin, Newley sauntered toward his waiting brumbie, acknowledging the rowdy encouragements of the other drovers. "Don't place any large bets against me, mates. This is going to be a short ride," he boasted.

"Judging by the 'orse's looks, this one just might be the one that tosses you," one man called out.

"Then put your money where your mouth is. Patterson can 'old the money," Newley returned glibly.

His expression sobered and his gaze skirted the area. His eyes, hard and cold, settled on Jim. "You placing any bets against me?"

"Depends."

"You should go with the winner."

"I'll remember that," Jim said evenly. Only the tic in his cheek indicated his hostility.

"Best ride to the best man." Newley continued toward his mount. Behind him, his challenge hung in the air.

Tom Rivers stood at a post centered in the paddock, with a lead rope running from it to the brumbie's bridle.

Wasting no further time, Newley gained his seat in the saddle and adjusted the reins between gloved hands. With a toss of his head, he signaled Rivers to release the horse.

Newley took up the slack on the reins and jabbed the horse in its flanks.

Instantly the animal became a whirlwind of motion. Nostrils flared, ears laid back, the brumbie lowered its head between its front legs and bucked, plunged, twisted. Bits of earth went flying, along with Newley's hat.

Pounding hooves, jangling spurs, and labored breathing blended in a chorus of struggle. Flecks of foam and sweat covered both man and beast.

Shouts of "Stay with 'im, Newley" and "Don't let the bugger best you" resounded from the drovers.

The horse changed directions abruptly. Newley couldn't correct his posture fast enough. The brumbie bucked rider and saddle over its head when the girth broke.

Newley landed with a jarring thud. For a moment he lay sprawled on the ground, the wind obviously knocked out of his lungs, before he

raised himself on hands and knees. He stood
slowly and shook his head.

He bent to examine the underside of the saddle. There was a rigid set to his shoulders when
he straightened. He walked slowly to where
Tom Rivers leaned against the fence on the inside of the paddock.

Rivers had no time to react as Newley
grabbed his shirtfront, pulled him forward, then
slammed him back against the railing. "You bastard. There's no crupper on that saddle."

Breathing hard, his own anger surfacing, Rivers replied, "It's not my job to check the bloody
thing. You should 'ave done it yourself."

"I say you did it purposely."

"You're making excuses. The fact is that the
brumby bucked you straight off, and you're not
man enough to admit the horse got the better of
you."

"Maybe it's time someone got the better of
you."

Newley drew one hand back in a fist. His arm
arched high.

Rivers' knife, staring him in the face, changed
his mind. He obviously had misjudged the older
man's speed, for proof of his mistake glared at
him in the sunlight.

"You'd do well to let go of me." Rivers' strident tone underscored his words. "Now."

"You're going to be sorry you did that."
Newley drew back his lips, revealing slightly
yellowed teeth. "I don't take to being shown up
in front of my mates."

Rivers pressed the knife point to Newley's throat. "Not 'alf as sorry as you'll be if you don't get your bleeding 'ands off me."

Grunting in disgust, Newley threw his hands off and stalked away, disappearing through the gate.

Jim came over to Rivers. "You all right?"

Rivers wiped the sweat off his forehead with his sleeve. "I reckon."

"I stayed clear of it, knowing you'd want no interference."

Rivers snorted. "I may be getting older, but I can still take care of myself."

"Never doubted it. But it seems that word of caution you gave me now holds for you. Don't turn your back on him."

Rivers dropped his voice. "I won't breathe easy until 'e's gone."

Jim shared that sentiment with a grave nod of his head.

Newley went inside the bunkhouse. Bloody hell! He was tired of people interfering with him. It seemed everyone on the station had turned against him, and it was Dr. Darcy McCall's fault.

He walked to his bunk and kicked the leg with his booted foot. Damn her soul. She had been nothing but a thorn in his side since the day she arrived. She had countered his orders; she had challenged his authority. And the worst of it was, the men had accepted her.

It would be difficult, but not impossible, to get rid of her still.

His dark thoughts turned to Burleson.

Well, mate, he thought, it seems we've come to the end of our friendship.

Newley laughed into the quiet air. "Well, it's not going to be me who sees the last of Kopperella." His deep voice resounded with self-confidence. "It bloody well isn't going to be me."

Rosie's first reading lesson had gone so well that Darcy decided there were other things she could teach her.

Not wanting a confrontation, she waited until after the men had breakfasted before taking the child to the kitchen. Besides teaching Rosie how to use a fork and a knife, it would give her a chance to visit with Kim Loo.

She greeted him in a warm tone. "Is there anything left for us, Kim Loo?"

The Chinaman looked up from his chores. His face broke out in delight. "All time for you, missy."

He shuffled to the stove, spooned portions of eggs and beef onto two plates, and set the plates side by side on the table.

With a wave of his hand, he said, "You eat now before get cold."

Darcy and Rosie sat.

Darcy unfolded her napkin in her lap. Rosie, on the other hand, immediately stuck her fingers in her food in her customary manner.

Darcy placed a hand atop Rosie's to stay the motion. "Today, I'm going to teach you how to use a fork and a knife." She smiled. "But first, you unfold your napkin and place it across your lap as I have done."

The girl's eyes dropped from Darcy's face to her lap. A line creased her brow as she concentrated on her task. Once completed, she looked to Darcy for approval.

"Good girl."

Next, Darcy touched the knife. "This you hold in your right hand." She then touched the fork. "This one in your left. White fella eat with these."

Rosie had trouble mastering the utensils. They obviously felt awkward in her hands and she dropped them several times.

Finally she managed to hold on to them. She looked to Darcy for further instructions.

"Now comes the hard part. You use the knife to help you put food on the fork, and the fork brings the food to your mouth."

Darcy demonstrated by pushing bits of egg onto the fork, curved side down. She slowly raised the food to her mouth.

Chewing first, Darcy said, "Now you try."

Rosie, tongue peeking from the corner of her mouth in concentration, managed to direct egg onto her fork with her knife. But the second stage was her undoing. As she lifted it to her mouth, the egg fell back onto her plate.

Wordlessly, she tried again. This time, with a grunt, she pushed egg onto her fork and hurriedly brought it to her mouth. Again the food fell.

On the third try, she raised her fork so quickly that Darcy, fearing Rosie would hurt her mouth with the utensil, stopped her in mid-motion. As a result, bits of egg flew across the room, toward the door.

And hit Jim Burleson in the face.

Kim Loo dropped a pan. Rosie gasped. Darcy's eyes widened.

The three culprits held their breath and waited.

Slowly, Jim wiped the bits of food from his face and shirt with a pass of his hand. Without a word, he strolled into the room and to the stove.

Darcy felt as if she awaited the guillotine. A slender hand fluttered to her graceful throat, bared by her unbuttoned collar, and she swallowed.

Jim poured himself some tea and began to sip it, staring at Darcy over the rim of the cup.

Say something, she thought. Yell, scream, curse, anything.

Finally, nerves stretched taut, Darcy burst out, "Kim Loo and Rosie aren't to blame. It was my fault. Don't be angry with them. If you're going to take it out on anyone, it should be me."

She stopped and her cheeks colored.

Jim's blue eyes seared her. He looked as if he was about to say something, but then he stopped. Instead, he put his cup down and strode out, leaving Darcy behind, feeling like an idiot.

* * *

Half an hour later, a frustrated Darcy stood inside the barn.

Her eyesight adjusted to the dimness as she scanned the interior for Jim. She saw him by one of the stalls and walked over to him.

He turned around and gazed at her with an intensity in his blue eyes that made her feel overheated.

She cleared her throat. "I thought we should talk."

Jim flashed her an infuriating smile. "About what?"

"We can't keep going like we are."

He wiped his hands on a rag. "And how's that?"

Darcy felt the color rising up her neck. "You know. Why must you make me say it?"

His eyes darkened. "Because I want you to tell me what we are to one another."

"Nothing. We're absolutely nothing," she said quickly.

Jim snorted. "We're anything but that."

"Why must you make this so hard?"

"It's no harder on you than it is on me."

Suddenly the memory of the way he'd left her last night, half naked and aching in her bed, flowed over her. Her cheeks grew hot. "Everything comes easily for you."

"There's a great deal which doesn't come easily to me. But I don't expect you'd understand it."

She released a ragged sigh, "We fight too much. It's got to stop."

"I agree."

Darcy stomped her small foot. "I should have known you'd make this difficult."

"You're the one making this difficult. If you'd just do what I ask—"

"What? Leave? No, thank you. Why is it every conversation we have always comes around to this?"

"Because you don't realize what you're doing."

Darcy was furious. But not so furious that she couldn't find words to express herself. "Men always think they know what's best for women. I'm sick to death of having men tell me what to do." She straightened her spine. "And most particularly, I'm sick of you telling me what to do."

Jim grabbed her tightly by the arms. "And what about me? Don't I have some feelings that count? Because what I'm sick of is you trying to prove yourself equal to men." His words were laced with exasperation.

"Oh, you are, are you? Well, let me tell you something."

"Something I haven't already heard, I hope."

Darcy's eyes flashed her irritation. "You're the most infuriating man I've ever met."

"You've already told me that."

"Maybe you need to hear it again."

"What I want to hear is that you've decided to listen to reason and return to the States, where you belong."

"I've earned the right to stay on Kopperella." Her eyes misted despite her attempts to stem her emotions. "I nearly paid for the privilege with my life."

Jim's tone softened and his hold on her relaxed. At the look on his face, Darcy's thoughts skidded to a halt.

"That's just it, Yank. You nearly died. I don't want that to happen to you." He leaned near and his lips brushed hers. "I don't want anything bad to happen to you."

Darcy stiffened, gaining a small degree of control over her emotions. "Then I suppose we'll have to keep our relationship strictly business."

He leveled an appraising look upon her. "You know that's not possible."

"It has to be."

"It's more than I can promise. I'm only human." In a deceptively casual move, he captured her wrists, pulling her to him so that her hip pressed against his thigh. "Can you promise that we won't be involved?"

She moistened her lips. "We both know it would be disastrous. Nothing good has come of it so far."

Her eyes darkened and Jim knew she lied. Joy surged through him. "What a cool liar you are."

Her warm flesh came alive beneath his heated touch, but she broke away from him. "You always twist my words and actions around to fit what you're thinking. You manipulate me and make me feel like a fool. But I tell you, I won't let you make me leave. I came here for a reason, and no matter what's gone on between us, that still means something to me. So, Mr. Burleson, you're just going to have to act like an adult."

"Jesus, woman . . ."

Darcy drew a shuddering breath, spun on her heels, and stormed from the barn.

Chapter 13

The room hummed with a mixture of sounds. In one corner a piano's off-key tinkling competed with clanking mugs, shuffling cards, and raucous laughter. Pungent odors punctuated the musty air of the grog-house, a combination of tobacco smoke, spit, stale liquor, unwashed bodies, and cooking food.

"Well, look who's 'ere," remarked the petite blonde serving drinks behind the bar.

Her red lips puckered enticingly as she watched the man's broad shoulders clear the doorway. He was tall and sturdily built, with black hair and green eyes—enough to make a woman pant. That was Edward Newley. Her tongue moistened her painted lips in appreciation.

The outlaw sauntered up to the bar, folded his arms, and leaned forward. He raised one hand, tipped his black hat back, and grinned, " 'Ello, love."

"Been a while."

"That it 'as." He gave her an assessing look. "You 'aven't changed much in two years."

She lifted one shoulder suggestively, the gaudy satin rosette on it bobbing. "Depends. In some ways, I'm much better."

He winked. "You can show me later 'ow much you've learned."

"You're a bold one, coming back 'ere," she said on a serious note.

"Don't worry, Nettie. I can take care of myself. They 'aven't caught me yet."

The whore came around the bar. Newley turned to meet her. She threw her arms around his neck and rubbed her body wantonly against him.

"I've missed you," she said huskily.

Newley anchored one hand on her hip and wedged the other between their pressed bodies. His fingers dipped inside the plunging neckline of her satin dress and closed around one breast.

"Because I'm the best you've ever 'ad." He squeezed the fleshy globe. "And I reckon the biggest."

Nettie groaned when he left off his petting, only to moan in eagerness when he thrust his hand between her inner thighs and grabbed her through the fabric of her dress.

"You been keeping it warm for me?" Newley nuzzled her neck.

"It's never been cold when it comes to you." She laughed throatily.

Newley broke off the contact. "You keep it that way."

"But—"

"First things first."

He ignored Nettie's pout and walked over to a vacant table next to the wall. He pulled out a chair and sat down.

Edward tossed his hat down and crossed his forearms atop the table. "I'll be wanting something to eat." He smiled devilishly, lowered one hand, and cupped himself. "Before I 'ave my desert. And bring rum and two mugs."

Nettie soon returned. "You going to be long?"

She set a tin plate of beef and potatoes in front of Newley. The requested rum and mugs followed.

"Depends. I've got business to see to."

She leaned over the table, giving him a clear view of her breasts. "You know where to find me," she breathed.

He produced a roll of bills and peeled off two notes. Elbow on the table, he waved the money between two fingers. "Since I'm paying for the entire night, you'd best get some rest, Nettie. You're going to need it."

Taking the money, she sauntered away.

Edward dug into his food.

Fifteen minutes had passed when Craig Newley walked through the door. His gaze swept the room before he caught sight of his brother.

Craig wove his way through the crowded tables to the far corner. Edward, his shoulders resting against the wall behind him, leaned back in his chair. His arms were folded against his chest and his eyes were closed, making him appear to be dozing. But Craig wasn't fooled by

Edward's indifferent air. He knew that his brother sensed his every move.

"Been 'ere long?"

Edward opened his eyes. "Long enough to 'ave some tucker. And a drink."

"What, no woman?" Craig asked laconically as he dropped into a chair.

"She comes later."

Craig splashed rum into a mug. After taking a drink, he said, "What I've got to say won't take long."

He took a letter out of his pocket and slid it across the table to Edward. "I 'ad someone write this. I want you to see that it gets posted to London."

Striking a match on the sole of his boot, Edward lit a cigar. He took a drag and let the smoke out slowly, a thin ribbon curling above his head. "London? What for?"

Craig's features tightened. "I've got a score to settle."

"Why not with your fists?"

"I've got my reasons. Just do what I ask."

"Consider it done." Edward raised a brow. "But what about the other? You said you'd 'ave something for me and the boys."

" 'Ow many do you 'ave riding with you?"

"Six."

"That should be enough." Craig drained the last of his rum. "You're going to do some paddy dodging."

"Steal cattle? Where?"

"Kopperella."

Edward's voice registered surprise. "Isn't Burleson still boss?"

"Yes. What of it?"

"Why go against 'im?"

Craig's eyes were hard as emeralds. "Let's just say I intend to teach 'im a lesson."

"If your plan doesn't blow up in your face."

"I'm going to make bloody sure it doesn't. Nothing's going to stand in my way."

Following a week of rest, Darcy and Rosie set about to tame the riotous garden of stubborn weeds and grasses.

To do so, she enlisted Pumpkin's help, knowing it would take all three of them to accomplish the goal in a day.

He arrived Saturday morning, early.

Darcy greeted him, sipping a cup of tea and wearing her men's clothing. She'd long since decided to ignore Jim Burleson on that score.

His broad features lacking expression, the Aborigine studied her appearance.

"Don't worry. Mr. Burleson won't dare say so much as a word to me," she reassured him. "Why don't you get started while I get my hat. I've put out the hoe."

"Whatever you say, miss."

She turned and went to the table where Rose sat. "When you've finished practicing your letters, you may come out and help in the garden."

Rosie glanced up, and Darcy touched the child's cheek and smiled. "I'll save some weeds for you."

Darcy grabbed her hat and joined Pumpkin in the garden.

He had already made progress halfway down one row. The sound of crunching earth and shifting dirt filled the morning air.

As they hoed side by side, she wondered if Jim had given him any grief about coming to work for her today. "Did the boss say anything to you about coming here?"

Pumpkin didn't look up. "No, miss."

Darcy bent and pulled a clump of weeds from atop a dirt mound. "That's good. I didn't want to cause any trouble for you." She tossed the weeds to the side and wiped the sweat off her brow with a sleeve.

She moved down the row until she was even with the Aborigine. "How long have you worked on Kopperella, Pumpkin?"

"All life."

"Were you born here?"

"No, miss. I brought here when baby."

"Your parents, are they alive?"

Pumpkin didn't answer.

Thinking he couldn't grasp her question, Darcy rephrased it. "Do your parents live on Kopperella?"

The ringer looked uneasy. "No, miss."

Understanding dawned on Darcy. "They're dead, then."

"Black fella not talk about dead. Very bad," he said gravely.

Darcy quickly changed the direction of their conversation. Between swatting flies, she asked,

"Do you want to learn from the white fella, Pumpkin?"

"What mean, miss?"

"Maybe I'm not saying this right," she said, more to herself than to Pumpkin. "Would you let someone—say me, for example—teach you white fella's things?"

"Black fella know plenty. Know everything he need to live in Outback."

Darcy returned to her hoeing. While working, she kept reframing the same question in her mind. She had given a great deal of thought to helping the Aborigines, but didn't know how to go about it.

She stopped and leaned against the hoe. "Pumpkin, I want to know something."

He kept to his chore, attacking the weeds and clumps of earth.

"Please look at me. I want to make sure you understand what I'm saying."

He stopped. His gaze reluctantly met hers.

Darcy took a deep breath, desperately hoping to enlist the Aborigine's support. "I've been thinking lately. About helping your people. I know they won't come to me, but I was wondering if they'd allow me to go to them."

"Black fella no like white fella's help."

"But you work for white fella. Most of your people take white fella's tobacco and food. You yourself wear white fella's clothes."

"Not same. Black fella have own special medicine."

"What your people practice is not really medicine. It's—"

His broad nostrils flared. "You not go." He began vigorously hoeing again.

Darcy crossed the distance between them and laid her hand on Pumpkin's arm. "Why? I could help the babies and the older children so they wouldn't get sick and die."

"Old ones stop you."

"Oh, for heaven's sake, I'm no threat to your medicine man." Frustrated, Darcy raised her voice. "Don't you understand? I care."

The ringer clutched the hoe's wooden handle. "You not go."

"Why won't you help me?"

Pumpkin was slow to answer. "Old one put curse on me."

"Superstitious nonsense," Darcy mumbled under her breath. Louder, she said, "I was hoping you'd take me to your village. Perhaps if they saw you with me, they wouldn't be afraid."

"No!" Pumpkin threw down the hoe and walked away.

Unnerved at his vehemence, Darcy didn't stop him. Besides anger, there had been fear in his eyes. Was he afraid of her? Or of what his people would do to him if he helped her? She kicked a pile of wilting weeds and sent them flying through the air.

Fine, she thought. This is just fine. Now I've managed to alienate someone else.

"Damn!" she said aloud.

She clenched her hands and looked at the ground. Stooping, she seized a dirt clump and hurled it as far as she could. The clod thudded against a fence post and crumbled.

"Taken to the habit of throwing things?"

Startled at Jim's voice, Darcy whirled. She lost her footing and, with a yelp, fell on her hands and knees among the cabbage.

Frustration, anger, and pain at seeing him pounded inside her head. It was the proverbial straw that broke the camel's back.

She glared at him. "Mind your own business."

Jim picked his way between the green rows and reached out to her. "Here, let me help you, milady."

She rose to her knees and brushed away his proffered hand. "This isn't amusing."

"From where I'm standing it is."

She got to her feet and brushed off her clothing. "Then go stand somewhere else, because you're not wanted here."

Seemingly unaffected by her taunt, he asked, "Is it just me, or do you always greet your company this way?"

"Company isn't what I'd call you."

Jim lifted a brow. "Oh?"

Darcy knew she was behaving like a shrew, but she couldn't stop herself. "Bastard is more what I had in mind."

She retreated a step when his face darkened. Her bravado melted like snow.

"You won't let up, will you?" Jim ground out.

"How am I supposed to act?"

Why should she back down from Jim Burleson?

She felt the keen edge of pain because of him. So why shouldn't he suffer, too? She hadn't considered that a hurting heart never gives sound advice.

"Maybe like a lady for a change. Or is that too much to ask?"

The lines framing his mouth deepened. "Ever since you got here, you've acted just the opposite. Well, you're not a man. Stop trying to prove that you're as tough as one. Let yourself be a woman. There's no shame in that."

A tense, thundering silence fell.

The truth of his allegation struck Darcy with an unsettling impact. But how could she allow herself to be a woman, and a competent doctor, without appearing vulnerable?

His accusation agitated her into reprisal.

"I've never been ashamed of who I am."

His eyes raked her. "If you insist on acting like a man and dressing like one, then you'll be treated like one. From this point on, no one on Kopperella will make any concessions to you because you're female."

"I've never asked for any!"

Jim thrust a thumb over his shoulder. "Have you forgotten your house, for instance?"

Burning anger blackened the edges of her thoughts. "That's not fair. I couldn't share quarters with the men, or with you."

"All right. The next time you get into an argument with one of the drovers, I'll let him settle it the way men usually do."

"Now why doesn't that surprise me?" Darcy

taunted. "Violence is nearly always the first thing men resort to."

Jim remained maddeningly unruffled. "Remember, no special treatment. You're to be treated the same as any other drover on this station. No exceptions."

"No exceptions."

He tipped his head to the side. "And what would be proper punishment if you break our agreement?"

"Is this to be some sort of a bet?"

"Why not?" he drawled. "Afraid you'll lose?"

"Certainly not!" Darcy snapped, although thorny doubt pricked her.

"Good. Then you won't object if I name the terms of our wager."

She nodded curtly.

"If you lose, you'll forgive me for hurting you."

Her mouth opened in a little *O* of amazement. What was he up to now? she wondered.

"You can't dictate what my thoughts shall be. I can think whatever I like," she managed to say at last.

He hurled one final barb, served with a slow, lazy grin. "May the best *man* win."

As he walked away, Darcy silently called him every vile name that came to mind, and told him what he could do with himself. Suddenly she saw what he was trying to do. He was planning to make life so miserable for her that she ended up leaving Kopperella of her own accord. Well, she'd show him how wrong he could be.

Darcy decided to leave off her gardening and go to the kitchen. In all the commotion, she hadn't realized how hungry she was. Her stomach grumbled in protest and she pressed a hand to it. After she ate, she'd bring Rosie something. Her foul mood didn't warrant company.

Heedless of her men's clothing and the stares from the drovers leaving the kitchen, Darcy trudged inside.

She dropped into a chair, suddenly feeling the weight of the day's earlier events on her shoulders. Sparring with Jim always drained her.

She needed food to restore herself. "Kim Loo, may I have something to eat?"

The Chinaman looked up from his cleaning. The deep lines around his mouth bespoke his uneasiness.

"Boss, he say no feed you if you late."

"I don't understand."

"You eat with men or no get food."

"I've never eaten with the men. What are you talking about?"

"Boss, he say you like drovers. Eat when they eat."

Darcy's temper was a short fuse on a powder keg. "He did, did he? Well, I'll give him credit, he didn't waste any time." She slammed a small fist on the table. A forgotten cup rattled ominously.

Kim Loo tucked in his chin and lowered his voice. "Sorry, missy."

Immediately contrite, Darcy went over to Kim Loo. "*I'm* sorry. I shouldn't take my anger at

Burleson out on you." She touched his shoulder. "Forgive me?"

His face brightened. "No worry, missy."

"At least I still have a few friends left on this station." She sighed and started for the door.

"Missy, wait." Kim Loo shuffled toward her and took her hand. He placed a piece of damper in her palm. "You not tell, all right?"

Darcy smiled. "I not tell. All right."

She tucked the morsel away in her pants pocket. "I just remembered. Today's Saturday. I'd best be going so I can get my supplies at the store. 'Bye, Kim Loo."

" 'Bye, missy."

Her spirits buoyed by Kim Loo's kindness, she walked more lightly as she went to the store.

She waited in line, not daring to go out of turn. Thirty minutes later, she found herself in front.

Tom Rivers was doling out the supplies from behind the counter. "G'day, miss."

"I'd like—"

Bewildered, Darcy silently watched him set four ounces of tea, two pounds of sugar, and some beef on the counter.

But when he added four ounces of tobacco, her temper flared anew. Frustration gathered in her breast. "Just what am I supposed to do with tobacco?" she asked through clenched teeth.

Rivers stroked his beard. "The boss said you were to—"

She held up a hand. "Don't tell me. I'm supposed to get the same rations as the men, right?"

"That's about the size of it."

The regret in his eyes helped to soothe her. "I'll take everything but the tobacco. You can have it. I'd much rather have had my writing supplies."

"Thanks, miss."

She walked away stoically, but inside she was a bundle of vibrating nerves. Her mind tumbled apace with her agitation.

For some unexplainable reason, she hadn't really thought Jim would go through with this stupid bet. Why, she didn't know. He'd always kept his word to this point.

Well, she'd show him. She'd win his little game.

Briefly, she basked in the warmth of that small confidence.

Reaching her house, Darcy returned to her gardening with a vengeance. She showed no mercy to the remaining weeds. Even an occasional carrot suffered a premature yank. She smiled briefly when, later, Rosie joined her, though the child kept to herself at the other end of the garden.

They toiled until late afternoon. Sore, protesting muscles finally halted Darcy in her work. Taking weary steps, she ushered Rosie inside. Leaving the child to rest, Darcy gathered clean clothes and a bar of soap, and headed for the creek. She wanted nothing more than to forget today and soak her aching body.

The murmur of the slow-running creek was

like a siren's song, beckoning Darcy to come closer and immerse herself in its delightful, restorative waters.

Earlier frustration and anger forgotten, Darcy stripped beneath the low-lying limbs of her protective tree and inched into the cool blueness. Cramping muscles relaxed, and she nearly dropped her scented soap. She sighed. The water felt heavenly. She took a deep breath and ducked beneath the surface. Emerging with a toss of her soaked tresses, she smoothed the strands away from her face. She lathered her limbs, then her hair, feeling the day's dirt and perspiration dissolve. Finished, she tossed the bar of soap on the grassy bank.

Invigorated by her cleanliness, Darcy indulged the urge to frolic in the creek like an otter, gracefully cutting through the water, diving and surfacing.

Then something registered on her carefree mind. She turned in the direction of the bank. She thought she'd heard a splash. Yet there was no sign of anyone. Must have been water in her ears, she thought, dismissing the sound.

Suddenly a pair of strong—and decidedly male—hands grabbed her waist and pulled her under. Her frightened protest came out in a rush of air bubbles.

Frantic, Darcy clawed at the imprisoning fingers and kicked at her assailant. Somehow she gained her freedom and fought her way to the surface. Sputtering and gasping, she pushed the hair away from her face and blinked the water out of her eyes.

She made a mad swim for the bank, but the intruder caught her beneath the low-lying limbs of the gum tree.

Hidden within the secretive shade, Darcy found herself staring into Jim Burleson's amused face.

Embarrassment and anger hotly stained her cheeks. "What do you think you're doing?"

"I reckon it's obvious. I'm taking a swim."

"But you can't."

"Why? Because you're here?"

"Of course because I'm here. Have you lost all sense of decency?"

Jim's eyes darkened momentarily. "There's nothing wrong with swimming with my mate. Or are you going to tell me that I can't swim with you on account of you're a woman?"

The wager. Blast him! "You're deliberately trying to make me lose."

He smiled. "I don't recall anyone saying I couldn't."

"That's because you made up the rules to this stupid contest."

His arm encircled her waist, and he drew her to him. His thumb traced the outline of her wet lips. Her nerves hummed at his closeness, so naked and threateningly male. Previous hostility dissipated like so much smoke.

"It won't be stupid when I win."

She trembled. "This is cheating."

He laid a hand to her breast and made a circular motion. "Not as much as this."

She felt her nipple harden against his palm.

Her breathing became shallow and sporadic. "Stop ... don't ..."

"Darcy."

His voice, rich and resonant, played havoc with her senses.

Beneath the water's surface, one hand journeyed to the base of her spine while the other continued its sensuous caress of her breast. His hand skimmed downward to her buttock. Much to her chagrin, she instinctively arched against him and thrilled at his hard male need.

Darcy rallied the remnants of resistance. She pressed her hands against his chest to push him away. Her nerve endings registered the feel of his strong heartbeat and the ripple of his muscles.

"Jim—"

"You want this as much as I do. Besides, I'm sick and tired of trying to do what's right. You don't seem to appreciate it."

He lowered his head. Darcy battled her rioting senses as he suckled one breast.

"Damn you!" Frustration and sweet agony throbbed in her voice.

And then he covered her lips in a slow, wet kiss of enticement.

Strong hands lifted her. "Open your legs, Darcy," he whispered against the lushness of her mouth.

"You make it sound so simple."

"It is. All you have to do is enjoy."

"Is that all you can think about? After what you've done?" she gasped.

He frowned. "What do you mean?"

"Oh, just leave me alone!" She freed herself and ducked beneath the water.

With each stroke, she wanted nothing more than to put miles between her and Jim. And her emotions.

She never reached the river bank.

Jim grabbed her and pressed her tightly to him. She felt every wet, sensuous line of him, including that which begged attention.

"Sweet, Yank. It's not that easy. You can't swim away from what's between us."

"I can swim away from you."

"That's only a temporary solution. You know I'll always come after you. I can't help it, I guess."

"The only thing between us is what's between your legs," she said, disgruntled. "It seems that's all you think about. You want me to give in to you easily, and I won't do it. You haven't a care about my feelings."

"Jesus, woman, for once why don't you just shut your mouth and listen to me. You try my patience."

"Not half as much as you do mine."

Her feet touched the rocky creek bottom. Tight-lipped with anger, she dressed hurriedly. She denounced her brief abandonment of principle in allowing him to yet again carry her past reason and vowed not to betray herself again. She prayed it was a promise she could keep.

With a lift of her chin, she stormed off.

Stepping onto the bank, Jim watched the sway of her hips, encased in men's pants, as she walked away.

She stopped briefly and glanced at him over her shoulder. She watched Jim struggle to keep his balance as he tugged his trousers over wet legs.

Catching the look in her eyes, Jim felt his stomach knot furiously. Her expression appeared so grim, so miserable. Was she hurting on the inside like him?

She snapped her head around and continued on her way, her back ramrod straight.

Damn! She most probably hated him—he'd certainly given her reason. He wished she could understand his actions. For that matter, he wished he could understand them. He suddenly recalled when she'd been so willing, when she'd offered herself to him. He should have seen where this was leading and taken her then.

But all that was in the past.

Jim balled a hand into a fist. Try as he might, he could no longer deny his love for Darcy McCall.

After dinner that night, Darcy paced inside the front room of her house. The conflict and worry of the past few days fermented in her mind. She desperately needed something to calm her down.

After spending several minutes walking about the room, Darcy eyed a decanter of port which she had brought with her. Maybe a glass of it would help her relax, and sleep.

Crossing the room, she filled a glass with the rich liquor and sipped it. The drink tasted good. She poured herself another and, with bottle in

hand, sat down on the veranda. The stars twinkled in the black sky, and in the distance she
could hear the sound of drums from the Aborigines' camp.

Suddenly she felt light and easy. She knew it
was the port, but what did it matter? No one
would bother her this late. So she refilled her
glass and stared into the ruby-red liquid. She
didn't give a twit about Jim Burleson. To em-
phasize her thought, she snapped her fingers,
but they wouldn't connect. Odd. Oh, well. She
shrugged and lifted the glass to her lips again,
then hiccuped.

The music from the encampment swirled
through her head.

Rising, Darcy swayed precariously, and she
closed her eyes against the dizziness. When the
feeling subsided, she brushed the tumbled hair
away from her face and leaned against the railing.

Across the way at the Aborigines' village a
fire had been built, circled by tribesmen. The
sounds of their drums and sticks thundered in
Darcy's head.

Craning her neck, she saw a man appear from
the darkness and enter the circle of firelight—a
young Aborigine stomping his feet to the beat.
Soon others joined him.

Her head throbbed and, bringing a palm to
her brow, Darcy wondered why she couldn't be
carefree and enjoy herself like that.

The longer she stood there, the more en-
thralled by the raucous vitality of the music and
the dancers she grew. They fired her blood. Sud-

denly the night seemed impossibly hot. She unbuttoned her blouse, exposing her creamy neck and a fair portion of her breasts.

Compulsively, Darcy swirled and danced in the shadows of her porch. Her red hair cascaded over her shoulders and chest as she tilted her head back, lifted slim, graceful arms high, and swayed sensually to the drums.

Darcy's movements spelled out an age-old message. A soul possessed, she felt strange, untamed abandonment. With her eyes half closed, she gazed about until she focused on a man, tall and blond, standing on the bottom step. Unconsciously she began to dance for him—and him alone!

Her slender hips swayed in time with the music, her arms appeared to seek his embrace, and her breasts, barely concealed, beckoned to him. Suddenly the searing glance of Jim's eyes jolted her back to reality. She stumbled and dropped to the floor. When she opened her eyes, she was looking up at Jim.

She knew she should cover herself, but she couldn't. Her pride told her to ignore him. Her heart would not.

"I'm afraid ... I'm ..." She hiccuped.

Jim bent and pulled her to her feet. He caught her shoulders to steady her. "I came by to apologize for the way I acted this afternoon. But I can see you're not in the mood to talk." Compassion and amusement played across his face, and his voice carried a gentle reprimand. "You shouldn't drink too much when you're not used to it."

Giggling, Darcy reached up and tapped his nose with her index finger. "Don't worry. I feel ... fine."

Jim half groaned, half laughed. "Wait until morning."

She traced the fullness of his lower lip with a fingertip. "Why are ... you ... being ... nice?"

"Because I care about you." Somehow he could say it to her now, when she looked so utterly defenseless, though he hadn't intended to.

Darcy frowned. "Then why are you always angry with me?"

Jim rubbed his cheek against the top of her head. "You're always getting yourself into a mess."

"Am I in a mess now?"

"Yes."

"Oh."

"Darcy?"

She snuggled her face against his chest. "Umm?"

Jim trembled. "What shall I do with you?" His hold on her tightened.

"I—I don't know."

"Do you still hate me?" he said slowly.

Darcy's brow furrowed. "Hate? No."

"Then why can't we stop fighting?"

"I wish we could."

"We can."

Darcy sighed. "I've never been drunk before. Liquor makes you feel odd ... have strange thoughts."

"Such as?"

"Well, for one, if you weren't so overbearing, I think I could like you."

His heart beat a nervous cadence. Yet Jim urged himself to observe caution, for he knew the wine was liberating her thoughts and her tongue.

He forced his voice to maintain a level tone. "Anything else?"

"Actually, yes. No man's ever made me feel the way you do. I think it's your wicked mouth and naughty hands." She hesitated, then placed a finger to her lips. "But, shh. Don't tell anyone."

Jim scooped her up into his arms. He considered kissing those tempting, parted lips, but the idea evaporated when her head lolled against his chest.

He carried her inside, to the bed and gently deposited her on it, then tucked her beneath the covers.

He looked down at Darcy's sleeping profile. He drew one raspy breath, then another. He felt something akin to regret. Perhaps he shouldn't have gotten involved with her. Yet, even now, his body reacted to her despite his efforts to control it. If he put his hands on that silken skin, it would be much later before he found his way to his own bed.

She was the most beautiful woman he had ever known.

And her beauty and purity of spirit bound him to her as securely as any rope. His reason dwindled with the tumult of his passions.

Before it all ended, he would have to have his

fill of her. And leave her most decidedly satisfied.

Perhaps they were meant to be together after all.

Chapter 14

Sitting at a table in the middle of the men's quarters, Jim waited for the game of seven-card stud to begin.

With a deft wrist movement, Tom Rivers dealt cards to the other four players in a clockwise motion. First Jim, next Dave Patterson, followed by another drover, then Craig Newley, who sat across from Jim, and finally himself.

One of the ringers brought a round of rum and vanished through the door, swallowed up in the smoky haze blanketing the room.

Patterson, his youthful face revealing his eagerness, leaned forward and flipped a coin into the table's center. "I'll 'ave a go at your money with my pair of tens."

He stretched his splinted leg to the side and settled back in his chair.

Without glancing at his hole cards, Jim regarded the exposed aces in front of him before matching Patterson's bet. "I reckon my pair is worth a fair bit."

Grimes anted up.

His expression carefully blank, Newley fin-

242

gered his revealed seven and nine. He tossed in his bet. "I'll take you on." His gaze cut to Jim on the last word.

Jim read the dare within Newley's stare. Instinct told him that Newley's words weren't idle and that Kopperella's second-in-charge was bidding his time. But for what? And when?

Be patient, Jim counseled himself. He'd have to wait Newley out. His own gaze remained unwavering.

The tension thickened to match the cigar smoke snaking over the men's heads. It broke momentarily when Rivers commented, "I'm out." He pitched his cards down.

"Let's see how far it goes." Strident challenge echoed through Jim's statement. He would play Newley's cat-and-mouse game.

Eventually everyone folded except Jim and Newley.

"You reckon Lady Luck will be good to you?" Patterson asked Newley, yawning behind his hand.

"She's in my 'ip pocket tonight," Newley drawled.

He shifted his position, laying his fanned cards atop the table, and draped one arm over the back of his chair. With his other hand he reached for the rum bottle. Glass clinking against glass, he poured himself a drink. He tilted his head and gulped down his drink, then passed his sleeve across his mouth and smacked his lips.

He set his glass down with a rap. "Speaking of Lady Luck, I saw the doctor this afternoon. Didn't look like much of a lady, if you ask me."

Straightening, he dragged the final card he'd just been dealt to the table's edge to steal a look. He checked his cards close to his chest and gazed about the silent party of men.

Outwardly, Jim appeared relaxed. Inside, his gut tensed, then twisted like a coiled serpent. He refused to take Newley's bait.

Revived by the stimulating morsel of gossip, Patterson asked, "What do you mean?" Inquisitiveness burned two bright spots on his cheeks.

"Wearing men's pants, she was. And tight ones." Newley clucked his tongue and shook his dark head. "Why, they were so tight you could see those neat curves plain as day."

Jim had an instant vision of Darcy. He also had the urge to wrap his hands around Newley's throat and squeeze.

Glancing up from his cards, Newley smiled his obvious satisfaction, a corner of his mouth curled in a taunting salute toward Jim.

Nonchalantly, he tossed another coin on the growing pile and a comment at Jim. "It's your call."

His calm demeanor hid the burning anger raging in Jim's mind. Like seared parchment, his voice crackled. "Still feel lucky?"

"Like a cat with nine lives."

"Curiosity killed the cat."

Newley laughed. "Did it, now?"

Placing his cards facedown on the table, he retrieved a cigar from his pocket. He sliced the end of it with his knife, then placed the stogie in his mouth to moisten the exposed end. He produced a match from behind his ear and lit it on the sole of his boot.

Dragging slowly on the rolled tobacco, Newley drawled, "It'd take more than curiosity to kill me." He clamped the cigar between his teeth, the tip glowing red.

The mocking, self-assured thrust of Newley's jaw caused Jim's hand to curl around his cards. "I wouldn't want to find out, if I were you." He tossed a bill onto the pile.

"Stakes are 'igh. Getting 'igher all the time," Newley said.

"Don't play if you can't afford the risk."

"You know me. I'm always one to take a risk."

"I call you, then." Jim's eyes were like chips of blue ice. "Let's see if you're bluffing."

"You never know when I'm bluffing."

"Don't be so sure." A current of steel flowed beneath Jim's words. "Winner take all."

Newley laid down his cards. "Two pair. Sevens and nines."

Jim flipped over his hand. "Aces over sixes."

He recognized the anger that flared briefly in Newley's eyes and knew a moment of grim gratification.

"Seems you've won." Newley removed his cigar, dropped it, and ground the tobacco under the heel of his boot. "For now."

Darcy looked at the letter through eyes glistening with joy. Sweet Mary! She hadn't forgotten her promise of a party.

A smile trembled on Darcy's lips. It would be wonderful to visit with her again. She had missed her dearly.

She scanned the letter a second time. Her joy dimmed behind a frown. Mary had invited all the drovers on Kopperella. That meant Jim was expected to attend. And that meant trouble. Mary mentioned that all the neighboring settlers would be in attendance. Darcy couldn't go to the Millers' affair in her men's clothing. But if she wore a dress, would she lose her bet? Her desire to be treated equally with any other male doctor was quickly becoming a double-edged sword.

Oh, but to see Mary and Joseph again. Her initial joy rebounded and a smile tugged at her lips once more.

They were expected tomorrow. No time for subtleties. A direct attack seemed her only course. She would have to convince Jim Burleson that attending necessitated her wearing a dress and shouldn't be considered a violation of their agreement. Surely he would relent.

Scouring the compound, she found him at the second paddock, overseeing the vaccination of the recently mustered cattle. She decided it was best that she not enter the paddock. Instead, she watched from the fence.

Newley and Rivers, at each end of a yearling, pulled their ropes tighter, stretching the animal's limbs. The Hereford bawled and wiggled when Jim administered the syringe of medicine. Finished, Jim straightened. He must have sensed her presence, because he turned in her direction. His face registered brief surprise. He walked toward her, removing his leather gloves and holding them in one hand. He leaned against the fence and contemplated her between rails.

He tipped his hat back on his forehead. "You looking for me?"

Darcy breathed deeply, then expelled the air in her lungs in one slow motion. "I need to talk to you about a certain matter."

He grinned lazily. "That certain matter wouldn't be Joseph Miller's party, would it?"

Darcy's face cataloged her astonishment. "Why, yes. But how did you know?"

"You forget, nothing happens on Kopperella that I don't know about."

"It must have slipped my mind," Darcy said dryly.

The skin around his eyes crinkled as his smile broadened, straight white teeth showing. "Must have."

Irritated by his sarcastic tone, and by the way the very sight of his handsome, almost boyish features made her pulse accelerate, she snapped, "I suppose you know why I'm here, then?"

His gaze slowly took in each button of her shirt before returning to her face. "I reckon you want to wear a dress."

Darcy's knees nearly sagged from relief, but she forced herself to remain still. "I'm glad you agree, then."

"I didn't say I agree—only that I knew what you wanted."

"What do you mean?"

"You can wear whatever you like. But if you put on a dress, then I'll have won our bet. Remember, no exceptions."

Darcy gasped her indignation. "Surely you can't expect me to meet the neighbors dressed like this."

"Why not? It doesn't seem to bother you to wear these clothes around here. I don't see why the Millers' party would make a difference."

"Because I've never met the majority of the people invited. What will they think?"

"Yeah, what will they reckon? But it shouldn't matter to you, Dr. McCall."

"You know very well that's what I said. But I couldn't have foreseen something like this."

"I'd say that was a serious error on your part."

"Then you won't consider dropping this ridiculous bet just this once?"

"No. You're the one who insists on being treated as a man and an equal. I'm only doing what you say you want."

Darcy tried to swallow the cold lump of pride in her throat. "And I suppose you want me to beg, is that it?" She nearly choked on the words.

"That might be nice," he drawled.

His casual attitude rankled Darcy. She'd be damned if she'd give in to him. "You'll have to wait until hell freezes over before I'll bend a knee to you."

"I've got time. Do you, Yank? Can you outwait me?"

"I can and I will."

"We'll see." He smiled, the corners of his eyes

crinkling. "I reckon I'm getting used to your new way of dressing. Of course, it'll be interesting seeing how you explain your pants to the Millers."

His broad shoulders shaking with laughter, he returned to the drovers.

Darcy stamped her foot in vexation. Tom Rivers had warned her about that damned Aussie pride.

Darcy and Jim, along with Tom Rivers, Dave Patterson, and Craig Newley, arrived at Manalee at dusk of the following day.

How different her arrival was this time, Darcy thought as they neared the heart of the compound.

Tonight, lights—myriad tiny, dancing flames suspended against a black sky—greeted the travelers. Darcy soon realized the wavering fingers of light were gaily colored lanterns strung on ropes across the yard. She could hardly believe her eyes at the festive glow. The scene warmed her heart.

As they drew closer, more ribbons of light appeared, streaming from every door and window of the Millers' large house. People were everywhere, either standing in groups, milling about, or dancing.

A small stage had been built to the left of the main house. A spontaneous gaiety floated on the cool breeze as young and old entered with zest into lively folk dances, while musicians made brave accompaniment on concertina, fiddle, tin whistle, and flute, and willing songsters rendered traditional ballads.

The Kopperella group halted their horses at the front hitching post and dismounted. Newley, Rivers, and Patterson immediately blended into the crowd.

Darcy's feet had no sooner touched the ground than Mary Miller hurried toward her, arms open wide in greeting. "Oh, Darcy. I've counted the 'ours for the last two days until you came. I thought you'd never get 'ere."

The two women embraced.

When she was able to speak, Darcy disengaged herself from Mary's fierce hug. Gently, she placed her hostess at arm's length. "I've missed you."

"Not 'alf as much as I 'ave you," Mary said with a laugh. She kissed Darcy's cheeks and gave her another quick hug.

"How pretty you look," Darcy commented as she took in Mary's green lawn dress and her blond hair arranged atop her head.

"And you look ..." Mary paused, taking in Darcy's pants and shirt. She grinned. "Different."

Darcy spread her hands wide. "It's part of a bet." She glanced over her shoulder at Jim. "I'll tell you about it later."

Mary nodded. "Say no more. I can well imagine."

Joseph Miller came to his wife's side, placing his arm around her slender shoulders. "Now, don't be forgetting our other guest."

Mary looked at Jim. "I'm sorry. Where are my

manners?" Her hands fluttered to her throat. "You mustn't think badly of me, Jim Burleson. It's just I'm so happy to see Darcy again."

"No worries, Mary. You two women go ahead. I'm sure Joseph can show me where he's keeping the rum." Jim winked at Darcy over his shoulder as the two men strolled away.

Darcy's stomach fluttered in response. It was maddening the way she kept reacting to him.

Suddenly she felt dowdy in her pants and shirt. The men had washed and changed their clothes at the last watering hole, but Darcy had waited until arriving at Manalee to don her party clothes.

She untied her bag from her saddle and asked, "Is there some place where I might change?"

"You just follow me." Mary giggled, a knowing glint in her eyes. "I imagine you would like to freshen up a bit."

Three-quarters of an hour later, the two women emerged from the main house.

Pausing on the veranda, Mary gazed at the peach satin and white lace creation that Darcy wore. "You look beautiful in that dress, with all the lace and ruffles, and your 'air all done up, right soft about your face. You're going to turn a few 'eads tonight."

Secretly, Darcy wanted to turn only one.

She laughed. "I don't know what made me pack this dress. I never dreamed I'd have a place to wear it."

"Good thing you did."

"Mary, you're a marvel—the way you've arranged this party and all."

"I didn't always live in the Outback, you know." She linked her arm in Darcy's. "Now, let's go enjoy ourselves. After all, this is in your 'onor."

Darcy was soon caught up in a rush of introductions, of warm embraces from the women of the neighboring stations and firm handshakes from the men. A sea of smiling faces welcomed her to the Outback.

At some point, it occurred to Darcy that the married men were much more accepting than the single ones. Married men looked upon women as helpmates and not as hindrances. The thought was a heartening one.

Eventually, Mary led Darcy to a long table laden with food. "You've got to be famished. I want you to eat something."

Someone called to Mary, who pivoted and waved.

She turned to Darcy. "I'll be right back. You 'elp yourself." She hurried off, amid the rustling of stiff skirts and petticoats.

Darcy had never seen such a feast. Big tureens of soup, whole poultry and a side of beef roasted to perfection, and several large cakes rich with butter and eggs graced the table. Also, there were scones, home-baked loaves, small pots of preserves, cheeses, and spiced meats.

She was reaching for a scone when a man's warm, callused hand covered hers and stilled her motion. "You've lost the bet, Yank."

At the sound of Jim's deep, rich voice, her

limbs felt like jelly, and Darcy had to set her plate down before she dropped it. She forced her eyes to meet his.

Her lips lifted slowly in a grin. "Oh, no, I haven't."

"Either that or my eyes are failing me. Isn't that a dress you're wearing?"

"Why, yes, it is," Darcy replied sweetly.

"Then I've won." He tapped his chin thoughtfully with a finger. "Let me see, how shall I have you pay the wager?"

"Don't think on it too long, because I haven't lost the bet." She slowly lifted the hem of her dress. "You see, I'm wearing my pants."

Jim looked down at the trousers Darcy wore beneath her dress. He broke out laughing. "I should have guessed."

"Never count me out," Darcy quipped.

"Never for a minute, Yank."

Satisfaction lit her features. "Now, if you'll excuse me. I'm hungry." She reached again for a scone.

He eyed the table. "Try the cake instead."

"Are you an authority on food as well?"

"I know what's good," he murmured.

His mood had changed from teasing to serious. She pulled her hand from beneath his. "Do you?"

"Thought you knew that by now."

Darcy's toes curled at the silky quality of his voice. She tried to dodge his remark. "Everything looks so good, I think I could eat all of it."

Jim chuckled. "Right now I'd rather fancy a sweet, delicious peach. A ripe, juicy one that I could sink my teeth into." His gaze moved slowly over Darcy's dress.

Darcy didn't know whether to be outraged or excited at his remark. The defenses around her heart were in peril of crumbling.

He was strikingly handsome in the soft glow of the lantern light.

Too handsome for her to keep her wayward emotions in check.

Too handsome for her to remember all the reasons that she should be angry at him.

And disarmingly engaging at the moment.

Jim cast his eye about the table. "But since I don't see such a treat, I'll sample the cake."

She watched his sun-bronzed, lean fingers close about the knife's handle. Irresistibly and hopelessly drawn, her eyes tracked his hand's movement as he cut a slice. Oh, how she remembered what it felt like to have those same hands hold her.

Suddenly he was lifting the piece of cake toward her. Her gaze darted to his. How could a single piece of cake throw her into such turmoil, causing her heart to thump against her rib cage?

He gently pressed the morsel to her mouth, tantalizing her lips. "Have a bite."

She did so, the confection sweet on her tongue. She swallowed, then licked away the sugary remnants.

He brought the remaining cake to his own lips. He opened his mouth. "I like it when the insides are moist and warm."

Darcy's senses vibrated at a higher frequency,

making her painfully aware of Jim's every move.

"Hmmm." His tongue ran over his lips; then he licked his fingers. "Once you've had something this good, you crave it all your life."

Jim's hand reached out and wiped away a forgotten crumb from Darcy's bottom lip. He consumed it. "Can't afford to waste even the smallest bit."

She tasted the sweetness where his finger had lingered. His nearness was like a drug, robbing her of the ability to think.

Loud clapping from appreciative dancers shattered the fragile moment.

"I think I'll go find Mary," Darcy said too quickly, too breathlessly.

Jim's laugh followed her as she wove her way through the crowd. Both of them knew she was beating a coward's retreat.

Stopping at the far side of the dance area, Darcy looked around. Everyone was having a wonderful time, dancing and talking. These people seldom had the chance or the reason to gather and celebrate. When given the opportunity they relished the occasion.

" 'Ow do you like the party so far?" Mary asked, appearing at Darcy's side.

Darcy hesitated as she thought of Jim and the way he made her feel. On one hand, she felt self-conscious and miserable. On the other, she felt carefree and delighted. To be around Jim was a heady thing. "It's lovely," she answered shortly.

A knowing look entered Mary's eyes. "Could

it be a certain drover is weighing 'eavy on your mind?"

Dear Mary, Darcy thought. Nothing escaped her. "Perhaps. But don't let me spoil your fun."

"I won't. But don't you miss out either."

Why should she? Darcy wondered. Why should she deny herself a release from the daily hardships she'd encountered since arriving in Australia? Didn't she deserve some pleasure?

Darcy smiled. "After coming all this way, I'll say not."

Mary winked. "Good. Because 'ere comes Jason Thornton. 'E's 'ad 'is eye on you ever since you got 'ere."

"Oh."

"Don't worry, 'e's 'armless enough. It just gets lonely way out where 'e lives."

Mary turned to leave.

"Don't go," Darcy called, feeling uneasy.

Mary patted her hand. "One would think you were married or something, you not wanting to dance with other men."

Darcy snatched her hand away. "Of all the silly things!"

"Of course," Mary replied slowly, smiling. She made her exit.

Jason Thornton walked straight to Darcy. Tall and thin, he looked to be in his forties, with graying hair and a sweeping mustache.

"G'day," he said. "Or should I say evening?"

"Good evening."

"The name's Jason Thornton. But then I reckon Mary told you who I was, seeing 'ow you two were talking when I walked up."

Darcy felt as awkward as she had at the dances they used to have back home in Boston. But this poor man looked every bit as uncomfortable as she felt.

"She did mention you," Darcy said, trying to put him at ease.

"I live past Manalee to the west." He fingered his mustache. "I was wondering if you'd care for a dance."

In the background, the band played a lively tune.

What could Darcy say? And then she thought of Jim most probably watching her, wondering himself why she didn't dance. That thought alone caused Darcy to accept.

"I'd be honored."

Mr. Thornton grinned and swept her into his arms and onto the dance floor.

Darcy learned what an experience it was trying to keep up with a spry bushman who hadn't had a woman's company in some time. She didn't think her feet touched the ground the entire time they were dancing.

Yet despite her earlier discomfort, Darcy found she enjoyed his company, and soon she lost herself in the fun.

At the end of the tune, a slightly breathless Darcy thanked her partner. "You . . . certainly do enjoy dancing."

"Never get much chance. Especially with so fetching a woman, I might add."

Mr. Thornton's smile was contagious and Darcy returned it. "Why, thank you."

"Would you be wanting something to drink, Dr. McCall?"

"That would be nice."

"I'm afraid she doesn't have time," came a familiar voice behind her "This dance is mine."

Darcy stiffened. Had Jim been there the entire time? She turned. "I don't remember—"

"Promising me this dance. Why, Doctor, is your memory failing you?"

"Sorry, didn't realize she was with you," Mr. Thornton said.

Jim smiled broadly. "Neither did she," he whispered softly for Darcy's ears only.

She blushed. The man certainly had his nerve! She had a good mind to dispute him. But when he looked at her with those compelling, searching eyes of his, she forgot everything except his nearness.

"Come, Dr. McCall." He took her into his arms and directed her onto the dance floor.

The tune was slow and Jim held Darcy close to him. Slowly, intimately, he guided her among the other dancers.

This time Darcy knew her feet touched the ground, but somehow she couldn't feel them. What she felt were her breasts pressed against his solid chest, his muscular thighs brushing her, her hand atop his broad shoulder.

But that wasn't all she felt. She felt his strong arms encircling her waist and holding her so close that she imagined she couldn't breathe. His cologne and the faint smell of rum drifted to her on the night breeze. Her senses tingled with awareness.

Sweet Jesus, the power he had over her! She was trapped between heaven and hell.

"What's the matter, Darcy, am I stepping on your toes?"

"What?"

He laughed. "By the pained expression on your face, you'd think I was trodding on your feet."

Pained expression, Darcy thought. Sweet, agonizing pain.

"No, it's not that," she managed to say.

"Then what?"

"It's nothing."

"You're a poor liar." His warm breath fell softly on her face.

"Am not."

"Don't bother trying to deny it. I always know when you're lying by your eyes. They give you away every time."

Darcy tried to be angry at his assertiveness, but found she couldn't. "I didn't realize I was so transparent."

"There are a lot of things you don't realize."

"Such as?"

"How much you enjoy being in my arms."

"I—"

"Do not? There you go again. When will you give up?"

"I'll never give up when it comes to you." Didn't she mean she'd never give in to him? She was having trouble discerning her own thoughts. "What about you? When will you quit?" she countered.

"After you've said yes."

Her blood thrummed wildly. They both knew what he meant, yet she denied his words. "That won't happen."

"I remember a time when you wanted it to."

Her cheeks grew hot and pink, for she remembered it, too.

"It *will* happen." His lips brushed hers. "Sooner than you think."

Her heart pounded against her rib cage. Or was Jim squeezing her? She wasn't sure.

She wasn't sure of anything except that she had to put some distance between herself and Jim.

She stopped and pulled out of his embrace. "I think I've had enough dancing for a while. If you'll excuse me."

The rest of the evening and into the wee hours, Darcy tried to take in the gaiety of the occasion. During the process, she consumed a fair amount of punch, liberally laced with rum.

Joseph and Mary said their good-byes to the last of their guests, many choosing to be on their way only a couple of hours before dawn.

Joseph left his wife and Darcy standing at the gate and went to extinguish the hanging lanterns.

A weary but happy Mary turned to Darcy. "Did you enjoy yourself?"

"Oh, very much. I can't thank you and Joseph enough for the thoughtfulness of having this for me."

"Nonsense. It was our pleasure. Couldn't 'ave done nothing else for such a dear friend." Mary yawned. "I'm all done in. Come on, I've made up a room in the house for you."

"Mary, if you don't mind, I'd like to take a walk before I go to sleep. I'm afraid I drank too much punch. I need to clear my head."

"I should 'ave warned you about that punch."

"And take away my fun?" Darcy teased.

"You go ahead with your walk. No one on Manalee will bother you. I'll leave a lantern burning in your room."

"You're a dear."

"Ah, go on, now." Mary smiled. "Take my shawl, though. Don't want you catching a chill."

Darcy accepted the garment and threw it across her shoulders, pulling the wool close to her. "Now you sound like the doctor."

"Somebody's got to look after you. Might as well be me."

"Good night, Mary."

Darcy watched Mary disappear into the house before beginning her stroll. After all the laughter, dancing, and music, she welcomed the quiet of the compound. Aimlessly, Darcy walked, hoping to exorcise her restlessness.

She hadn't realized where she'd been headed until she came across the barn. Impulsively, she went inside.

The air was thick with the sweet smells of hay and leather and the soft, warm sound of the horses' nickers. Silvery beams streamed through the gaps in the wooden slats, allowing a small measure of light by which to navigate. Darcy giggled, recalling tales that her father used to spin of fairies frolicking on such moonbeams.

She tilted her head to one side, smiled, and extended her arms out to the sides. Imagining her shawl to be her spritely wings, she began to dance whimsically across the hay-strewn floor.

Closing her eyes, she moved to the music playing silently in her head. She dipped and swayed as much as her form-fitting gown would allow.

Delightful moments passed until Darcy whirled into a pair of strong arms. Her eyes flew open.

His legs braced apart, Jim held her close to him. He smiled down at her and tapped the end of her upturned nose with a finger.

"Couldn't you sleep either?" The question stroked her like a velvet caress in the stony silence of the barn.

The suddenness of his appearance and the heady rush of passion inundating her senses at his nearness caused Darcy to be startled for an ephemeral pulsebeat.

"No," she said breathily.

Jim touched her cheek. The warmth of his hand felt pleasant. And very unnerving. He cupped her chin. Her gaze locked with his and she felt her world compress to the limits of those sensual blue orbs.

His lips curved seductively. "I couldn't sleep for thinking of you." He lowered his head. "And doing this."

He kissed her ... slowly ... tenderly. ...

Heat throbbed deep inside her womanly core, a heated desire she'd fought valiantly to denounce ... quell ... pretend didn't exist. But now, despite all prudence and reason, he was a temptation she had no will to resist. Sighing her surrender, she wrapped her arms around his neck and leaned into him. She returned his kiss fervently, her breath punctuated by feathery moans.

Feeling the corded length of his body, his explicit arousal hard against her stomach, she felt secure in his embrace. Too secure . . .

Darcy broke away from him. "I should go," she whispered, as if the words alone could stop the delicious trembling of her body.

"I know."

There were a thousand reasons for her to leave, but only one for her to stay.

One that had everything to do with desire and fulfillment. And the love of one man.

"But I can't," she confessed in a soft drift of words.

"Only a fool remains blind to the truth. I've been one long enough." Jim's gaze searched her face. "I know what I want. I love you, Darcy. But I need to know what *you* want."

His words of love rang true inside her. They were what she'd been yearning for him to say, though she hadn't really known it. Somehow, they changed everything.

She said very quietly, with heartfelt sincerity and simplicity, "I want you. I love you, too."

Jim swept Darcy into his arms and showered kisses across her face.

It felt so right to be in his arms . . . so right to feel her heartbeat mingling with his. "I should have said it long ago."

He carried his precious bundle to a stall. There he set her upon her feet, within the circle of his arms.

Looking into her eyes, Jim said, "Is this what you want?"

She nodded, the invitation in her eyes unveiled and unmistakable. Never had she wanted anything as much as she did this.

His lips brushed her temple, the sensitive, tingling skin beneath her ear, the hollow of her throat. His soft, rumbling groan fanned the flames of her desire. She quivered with need and desire. And anticipation.

Standing behind her, with deft fingers, he undid her dress. The bodice slipped down her arms to reveal the tempting sight of her breasts above the neckline of her chemise. His hands drifted across their sides and rested against their fullness. He squeezed them lightly. His thumbs teased her nipples until they puckered and ached against the material.

She sighed at the exquisite torture of it.

He slipped her out of her dress and tossed the garment aside. He turned her around slowly.

A slow smile spread across his face. "Where's your pants?"

"Oh, those. I took them off before I went for my walk."

Jim's expression grew more earnest. "I have no intention of allowing you to leave this time. You know that, don't you?"

"My values are the same as they were yesterday," she said weakly.

"But this is tonight. And it's going to be our

night." He encircled her waist with one arm and drew her gently against the lean, hard lines of his body. "Do you like my touching you?"

"Jim—"

"Just answer yes or no."

"I—"

"Don't deny us any longer, Darcy."

"With my last . . . breath." Her voice faltered.

"Your last breath of passionate surrender."

"Not surrender."

"Definitely surrender. Surrender to what we've both wanted for a long time."

"I'm still a doctor."

"You're a woman first. And I intend to make you realize just how much of one."

"Why do I feel as if I don't have the power to tell you no any longer?" Darcy groaned.

"Because you know this is right. It's meant to be." Jim paused. "Now, tell me, can you deny that you like my touch?"

She looked at him with unfocused eyes. "Umm."

His head dipped. "Then I'll continue," he murmured against the lushness of her bottom lip.

While he kissed her, he unbuttoned her chemise. Then his hands sought the straps and slowly, sensuously, he eased it down her shoulders, his roughened fingers skimming the warm, silken contours of her collarbone and arms.

He drove her past distraction. He drove her beyond the earthly boundaries of time and place. She soared toward heaven on the wings of her heightened senses.

"Your skin is so soft, so white," he murmured.

The chemise soon joined the discarded dress. Darcy felt the night air against her flushed skin. She shivered. Her body screamed with expectation.

Darcy licked her lips. "Please . . ."

With an impatient growl, Jim divested Darcy of her underclothes and tossed them to the floor then undressed himself.

Desire peaked like a storm in the stillness of the barn, and the air vibrated.

As he stood before her in his perfection, Darcy keenly knew the difference between viewing a man in a clinical sense and viewing a man as her partner in lovemaking. His eyes had darkened, and she knew what it meant to be sought by a man who burned for her.

Jim never seemed so tall, so proud. Her gazed dropped to his broad chest and followed the contours of his body along his thickly corded arms and long, muscular legs. Finally, she gazed at the proof of his manhood. Swallowing, she experienced a moment of apprehension as her imagination conjured a picture of her absorbing his maleness.

She looked up at Jim. Their eyes met. In the moonlight, her face had taken on a wild, pagan beauty while her skin gleamed like satin. Jim felt powerless to control the primitive desire she aroused within him. His gaze moved to the white column of her throat, and he ached to plant his lips there, to feel the heat of her flesh and the tremor of her body as he touched her.

"There are things I'd like to teach you," Jim said, reaching out to slide his fingers through the burnished curls on her shoulder. "So very many things that bring pleasure."

Her pulse leaped as his thumb moved to her mouth, parted her lips, and slid across the ridges of her teeth. His tongue then probed with delicate inquisition. With a wild shyness that suited her feelings, her arms circled his strong neck and, shockingly and boldly, she met his tongue with hers. He drew hers slowly into his mouth. Her low moan escaped in a breathy, feathery exhalation.

Jim locked his hands against the small of her back while his lean hips moved in a slow rhythm against her soft curves. His uneven breathing fell upon her cheek. The taste and feel of him whetted her appetite until she hungered for more.

Strong, tanned hands stroked a warm spine. . . .

Slender white finger caressed a corded bicep. . . .

A firm mouth possessed. . . .

Parted lips quivered. . . .

Shadows and muted light played across their bodies.

Darcy's senses floated as his tongue slid along her throat to her earlobe, and she felt the hardness which promised ecstasy against her stomach.

Jim whispered heated words into her ear—an

invitation to paradise—and Darcy trembled. Her eager hands glided over the warm, tanned skin of his back.

Jim drew back his head. "Look at me, Darcy."

She complied.

He reached out and softly touched her cheek with his fingertips, then her mouth and throat. Delicately, he brushed downward until his palm caressed her taut nipples. He watched the enjoyment on her face as his hand moved back and forth.

Her beauty fed his hungry gaze and made him ache with a need that demanded the total giving of herself.

Jim kissed her again, while at the same time lifting her atop a box. The edge pressed into her buttocks and her legs draped over the sides.

Easing between her long, dangling limbs, Jim leaned over and cupped her breasts. Lush sensuality infused her as he stroked the soft rise of one.

"Does this please you?"

She opened her mouth to speak, but his thumb and forefinger touched her already cresting nipple. The words lodge in her throat. Slowly, gently, he rubbed and teased each peak.

"I've thought about you like this," he murmured, "so soft."

His mouth moved over her swollen nipples, his tongue playfully flicking, then circling. Suddenly his lips closed tightly over one, drawing hard, and Darcy gasped with startled pleasure. She trembled as she felt his silky hair brush her skin. Warmth rushed in an intoxicating turbulence downward from her sensitive breasts to her stomach, then lower.

Balancing on the dizzy brink of the unknown, Darcy whispered, "Please."

"Not yet." Jim kissed her soundly.

His hands moved down her thighs, then up between them to cover the soft mound of hair. Instinctively, Darcy tensed in shock. He watched her, his questing fingers parting her and intimately exploring her, sending melting, tingling sensations racing along her raw nerve endings.

Nuzzling her neck, Jim continued the arousing movement of his hand against her most susceptible place, his skillful fingers lingering on sensitive spots.

Kneeling, he touched his lips to the silken curls nestled between her thighs. Darcy felt as if she were dying when her body arched against this intrusion.

He stood and leaned over her. "Some of the pleasure I spoke of."

She tried to answer him, but the words wouldn't separate from the jumbled confusion in her mind as he stroked her curls.

"Good, isn't it?" Jim asked.

She nodded, her face only inches from his, her eyes so hot he felt heat spiraling out.

"It's only just beginning," he said, standing back and pulling Darcy to her feet.

His hands urgently fondled, massaged, caressed her breasts, her buttocks.

Darcy's skin burned from the onslaught of her emotions. She throbbed from wanting to draw

Jim deep within her and hold him tightly therein.

Jim shared those sentiments as his feverish mind thought of nothing save having Darcy's slender legs wrapped around him in agonizing delight. He grew heavy and full. He grew impatient.

"I'll try not to hurt you," he breathed.

Balancing on a precipice of no return, in a soft rush of words Darcy said, "I know you wouldn't."

It hurt her more for him not to take her. Her body demanded deliverance.

Jim backed her to the rear of the stall. Darcy was pressed against the wall, pressed against the unyielding wood and Jim's equally unyielding hardness. His lean hips moved rhythmically against her and voiced his yearning in body language.

Jim cupped her bottom and lifted Darcy to her toes as his maleness begged entrance.

She gave a sweet, surrendering sigh.

He planted one hand beside her right shoulder, his fingers catching strands of hair. His other hand grazed her rib cage and breasts before resting beside her ear. He leaned close. His male scent carried to her on his heated skin.

Butterflies of anticipation and dread took flight in Darcy's blood.

Their eyes met and held.

He leaned into her until her breasts were flat against the muscular plane of his chest. She saw the slight flare of his nostrils and heard his labored breathing.

He eased into her opening, then hesitated. His body demanded release, yet he didn't want to hurt her. He entered her slowly.

She gasped, breathless and startled, as pain ripped her. She tensed and closed her eyes against the sensation.

Jim paused, hot and heavy, inside her. "I'm sorry. I didn't . . ."

Darcy's pain subsided enough for her to whisper, "Shh."

Jim withdrew, only to ease again into her dewy warmth. Darcy clung to him, melted against him, and undulated her slim hips to take him deeper. Obliging her, he became one with her.

She wrapped her long legs about his waist and leaned her head back against the wall, giving him access to her breasts. She wanted his mouth on her. She wanted his tongue laving her hot, moist skin. She wanted all of him.

While Manalee slept, they climaxed together as the first rays of morning burst across the horizon.

Chapter 15

Later that morning, Darcy greeted Mary and Joseph with a cheerfulness that was nigh to bursting within her. Happiness imbued the air she breathed.

For the first time since her arrival in Australia, the puzzle pieces of her existence fit together, creating a picture of stark clarity. She loved Jim, and he returned her love. Life did not have to be a bewildering, complex chain of events. No, life came down to the bare necessity of loving and being loved.

She now knew she could be both doctor and woman. Without shame, guilt, or compromise, she was still the same person she had always been.

Darcy approached the waiting Millers, regret at leaving her friend momentarily eclipsing her joy.

Mary looked up. A bittersweet smile tugged at her mouth.

Darcy knew by her friend's overly bright eyes that Mary shared the same sense of loss.

Darcy's throat tightened painfully, and she

hugged Mary tightly. "It seems not too long ago we said our good-byes."

The two women separated and looked at each other.

Tears slid down Mary's cheeks. "I 'ave to tell you straight. I don't want you to go. But I know you must."

Darcy swallowed. "Perhaps I can come again soon, and stay for several days. That way, we'll have something to look forward to."

Mary wiped away her tears and her face brightened. "Right you are."

Darcy raised herself on tiptoe and planted a small kiss on Joseph's bewhiskered cheek. "Thank you for the wonderful party."

Joseph blushed. "Our pleasure."

Jim moved beside Darcy. He slipped his left arm around her waist and shook hands with Joseph in parting. "My thanks, mate."

"Glad you came," Joseph returned.

Jim looked down at Darcy. "We'd best be going."

Jim helped Darcy mount, then swung up into his own saddle.

As the group rode away, Darcy glanced back and waved a final good-bye to Mary.

Jim, Darcy, and the three drovers neared Kopperella's center by nightfall the next day. Sudden gusts of wind among the stringy-bark trees raised whirlwinds of leaves and dust, and the crash of fallen boughs echoed across the landscape.

Darcy's mount grew skittish, dancing sideways, fighting the bit in its mouth. She grappled to control the animal.

Jim came up beside her. "Something's not right. Your horse smells it. Take a deep breath."

Darcy inhaled. Faint woodsmoke filtered through her nostrils. "Smells like smoke. But where's it coming from?"

"I've got a bad feeling about this," Jim confided.

Her stomach tightened. "What do you mean?"

"If we make good time reaching Kopperella, things will be fine."

His scowl belied his encouraging words. Her dread blossomed, but she remained silent, not wanting to be a burden.

A grass fire twelve miles from the compound confirmed Jim's suspicion.

Fire glared through the trees. Dark figures seen in strong relief against the vivid light, beating down the flames with boughs, produced a strange, wild scene.

Darcy watched in wide-eyes horror. She gripped her reins. "Are we going to make it?"

"Don't worry. But we're going to have to ride hard to reach Kopperella before the fire does. We've got to get in front of it. Don't take your eyes off me."

Jim twisted around. "Right, men, there's nothing else for it. You know what's to be done."

Simultaneously, a yell sounded and the men spurred their horses forward.

Bending low over her horse's neck, Darcy dug her heels into the gelding's flanks and it surged ahead like a pistol shot.

All around, the flames leaped across the ground, licking up the grass and blazing overhead from treetop to treetop.

Her heart in her throat, Darcy buried her face in the horse's whipping mane. Squinting, she looked through the flying strands of dark hair. She matched Jim's grueling pace.

The riders skirted the fire. They gained a lead, and the group maintained a quarter-mile advantage.

Great numbers of animals stampeded—kangaroos leaping along in droves, emus, often with their tail feathers scorched, cattle and horses, all running for safety.

Darcy wondered if she would ever be able to forget this night. The roar of the fire and the noises of the poor beasts in terror and pain filled the air.

The riders maintained their relentless pace for seven miles across flats divided by strips of thick scrub.

Once, Darcy nearly lost her seat in the dense growth, but she had a good leader in Jim. He had taught her to lie flat along her horse's neck and keep her feet pressed against its sides so as to ride faster. And whatever happened, she was to give the horse its head. Give a horse its head and it will avoid dangerous obstacles. Try to rein a crazed animal, and the horse will fight to go in the opposite direction.

As soon as they reached the compound, Jim dismounted and ran toward Darcy.

He reached up, his strong hands circling her

tiny waist. She rested her hands atop his broad shoulders as he pulled her off his horse. She slid down the length of him until her feet were planted between his braced legs.

Jim lifted her chin with a finger. "I want you to go to your house. Gather whatever supplies and instruments you can and bring them to the kitchen. The kitchen's better located and easier to defend against this sort of thing." He gave her a quick kiss and a gentle push. "Now get going."

Darcy retreated two steps. Fear of losing him knotted in her chest.

Despite the fact that their world was threatening to break apart around them, she threw herself against him and wrapped her arms about his neck. Molding her lips to his in a kiss that conveyed all her worry, hope, and love, she clung to him.

Her soft breasts were pressed against his muscular chest. Their heartbeats mingled and became one.

At last she broke away. Dewy tears glistened on her spiky lashes like gentle rain. "Take care of yourself."

He gave her that characteristic crooked smile of his, and her heart somersaulted. She loved him so much, and she didn't think she could bear the pain if anything should happen to him.

"Don't worry. I'll come back to you."

Darcy raced for her lodgings. Only once did she hazard a backward glance. Jim was shouting orders to the drovers who had stayed behind, walking the camp's perimeter, strategically setting back fires to battle the oncoming fiery rampage.

In her haste, Darcy stumbled on the top step of the veranda. Rising, she regained her footing. Rips in her pants revealed scraped and bleeding knees. She gritted her teeth against the pain. Next to Jim, nothing mattered to Darcy except finding Rosie.

She flung the front door back on its hinges and swept her eyes across the inside. "Rosie? Where are you? Answer me!"

She frantically searched the house, calling the child's name, but found no sign of her.

Desperation clawed at her. Was Rosie trapped in the fire? Was she hurt, calling for help, with no one to hear her cries?

Darcy marshaled her emotions. She was a doctor, trained to respond calmly to crisis situations, and she would behave accordingly.

Grabbing her bag, she filled it with as many items as she could and fairly flew out the door, headed for the kitchen. With empty sacks, men beat the fire out on the far side of the compound.

She ran on. Alarmed, she watched with widened eyes when one of the smaller buildings on the compound's edge caught fire. In a matter of minutes, the structure was consumed by flames. Black smoke billowed overhead. Gum poles and walls sizzled and popped in the heat. Nearby lay the burned carcass of a trapped heifer. The stench of singed hide and hair permeated the air. Darcy released her grip on her medical bag and pressed a cupped hand to her nose and mouth.

Soon she reached her destination. Breathing hard, feeling a stitch of pain in her side, she dropped her bag and fell into a chair, then pushed fugitive strands of damp hair from her face.

Kim Loo was busily stacking food supplies at one end of the kitchen. His pigtail swung wildly down his back, matching his movements.

Between gasps, she asked, "Kim Loo . . . have you . . . seen Rosie? I can't find her. . . ." The words trailed off. He stopped and turned, a look of regret on his face.

"Sorry, missy. She go on walkabout two day ago. Not been seen since."

Darcy's body sagged. "Jim warned me against that," she very softly replied, sadness in her voice. "Perhaps I should have listened to him."

Kim Loo came to stand on the opposite side of the table.

"Do not be hard on self, missy."

Darcy clenched her hands in her lap. "Did I cause Rosie to run away? Did I expect too much from her?"

His eyes darkened, reflecting what Darcy perceived as long-held anguish. "I know how feel to be laugh at, or not wanted. Used only as servant. Until boss. He treat better. Same as you treat little black girl. She need love you give. Never be sorry."

Her brow furrowed in confused pain. "Why did she leave?" Darcy bit her lip. "I just hope and pray she's all right."

"Your God take care. You see."

Her gaze drifted to the fire burning beyond the door. Suddenly she knew she had to do something. She placed her hands on the table and rose. "I can't just sit here. I've got to help."

Kim Loo opened his mouth to protest, but Darcy had already raced out the door.

The roaring fire gave off clouds of smoke, suffocatingly thick. She coughed, then gasped for breath, but the hot air burned her lungs. In the background, she heard the horrible screams of burning animals. She pressed onward despite her rasping breath.

She skidded to a halt and watched in horrified fascination as tufts of dry grass caught fire. The blaze spread rapidly across the ground, threatening other structures. Drovers quickly took up their positions and beat at the flames.

Darcy felt as if she had been swallowed whole into the fiery bowels of hell. What should she do? Every muscle in her body tensed for flight. She stifled the urge.

Then a plan of action came to mind. The creek!

She ran to the group of Aboriginal women and children who'd collected near the paddock and told them to grab anything that would hold water.

Stopping at her house, Darcy snatched up a bucket and hurried to the creek. There she joined the women and children, who formed a line stretching from the creek to the compound and beyond to the Aborigine village.

Darcy waded knee-deep into the water alongside three other women and began filling containers and passing them to the person next to her.

Repeatedly performing her task, Darcy felt that her back was near the breaking point, and her shoulder muscles screamed in protest. Her labored breath hung in the chilly night air, although perspiration trickled into her eyes.

Her hands hurt from cut fingers and bleeding blisters. Despite the pain, Darcy refused to quit and doggedly continued to fill the containers with water.

Momentarily, she glanced over her shoulder, wondering if the fire still raged uncontrollably. She froze. Her slender body swayed as if buffeted by an unseen wind. A fiery wall surrounded the compound, consuming all within its flaming path. A roar of flames and crackling, popping wood nearly deafened her.

Embers on her skin brought Darcy out of her temporary paralysis. The stench of burned flesh and hair hung in the thick air. Black clouds drifted upward where the wind caught them, then blew the smoke down across the water brigade.

The flames inched closer.

Everyone fled. Darcy followed the Aborigines, who scrambled to their village, scooping up whatever possessions they could as they ran past empty huts. Those who were sick or old were helped by the young and healthy. Mothers, with their babies in their arms, herded older children to safety in a nearby gully.

Darcy scanned the village for signs of anyone

left behind. Her eyes widened with instinctive fear seconds later. She saw Pumpkin stoop to grab a fallen possession. As he did so, a tree fell atop him. He struggled beneath the smoking wood but couldn't free himself. All the while, the fire raced through kangaroo grass.

"Pumpkin!" Darcy cried, her scream drowned out by the fast-approaching, roaring inferno.

Ignoring the scorching heat burning in her lungs, she ran to Pumpkin. Fear infused her body with needed strength. Small teeth bared, she lifted the tree, but not before the licking blaze set his clothes aflame.

Out of the swirling confusion and smoke, Jim's soot-covered figure miraculously appeared. Together they pulled Pumpkin away from the fire.

Darcy snatched a hide from the hands of a nearby woman and fell across him, smothering the flames with her body and the pelt. Her quick action wasn't enough. Pumpkin was blinded from the fire, his face blistered and raw.

Her hands dropped to her sides and her shoulders slumped with despair.

She didn't have time to reflect further as small blazes flared all around her. Sparks landed on adjacent huts, causing the walls to smolder and burst into flames.

Clutching the hide, Darcy beat at the fires until her arms ached and she could no longer lift them. Still they raged, destroying entire huts in a matter of minutes.

The suffocating heat burned Darcy's nose and

throat and cracked her lips. She gasped for breath.

Everything around her turned to blinding orange heat. A heavy blackness engulfed her.

Distantly, she heard Jim scream her name in a roaring crescendo of anguish and alarm. "Darcy!"

She saw him lunge ahead, but the fire blocked his path. He pulled back, then shielded his eyes with an arm and started forward again.

"Jim, don't! I'm coming," she cried.

Darcy swayed and fell. The heat blasted her head, back, and legs as she lay sprawled on her stomach. The gnawing imperative to rise nagged at her, but the effort seemed insurmountable.

A sudden piercing sound exploded behind her, charging her weary body with energy, and she raised herself to her knees. Twisting her head, she looked around. A small, naked Aborigine child stood behind her. His chest expanded from deep, shuddering breaths, he wailed at the top of his lungs.

Darcy scrambled to her feet and staggered toward him. She snatched him up in her arms, clutching him to her, and, guided by instinct alone, headed for where Jim stood beyond the fiery wall.

On the other side, Jim and several drovers worked frantically to cut down burning trees and beat back the flames with wet sacks and blankets.

Through the gaseous flux of heat waves and lashing tongues of fire, Jim spotted Darcy.

He cupped his hands and screamed, "Darcy, here. Walk this way. Follow my voice!"

While Jim directed her, the drovers managed to create a tiny opening which Darcy slipped through.

When she awoke, Darcy was conscious only of the pain. Her head pounded, and her lungs burned with every breath. She tried to swallow but couldn't. Her throat felt as if it had been scraped with a razor.

Comprehension slowly dawned in her pain-dulled eyes as she became cognizant of her surroundings.

She was in her bed. How had she gotten there? The last thing that she remembered was being in Jim's arms.

Squinting, she glanced at the bedroom window and saw sunshine. The knowledge didn't warm or comfort her. Rather, she felt cold inside from a sense of dread. Dread of the unknown. What would she find outside these walls?

Was Jim safe?

Were the others?

She had no way of knowing.

Suddenly a figure blotted out the sunshine.

Sweet relief flooded Darcy's features when Jim knelt beside the bed. She reached out and touched the side of his soot-blackened yet handsome face.

He took her blistered hand and pressed it gently against his warm chest. "How are you feeling?"

"I'll . . . be all right . . . now that you're here,"

she said haltingly, trying to coax some saliva into her cotton-dry mouth.

"There was a time there when I reckoned I'd lost you."

For a fleeting moment, Darcy thought she saw unshed tears in his eyes. Her heart swelled with emotion.

Jim looked away, cleared his throat, then faced her again.

"Pumpkin?" she croaked.

Jim shook his head. "He didn't make it."

Her cheeks grew wet. "Oh, no."

"Don't blame yourself. There was nothing to be done for him."

"Any others . . . hurt?" She coughed hoarsely, a sharp pain stabbing her chest from the exertion.

"The usual cuts, scrapes, and the like."

"And the compound?"

The corners of his mouth lifted in a brief smile. "We managed to save most of it. Only those huts in the Aborigine village were burned, and one shed on our end."

"I'm glad."

"I reckon you need your rest now." He kissed her fingertips lightly before tucking her arm beneath the blanket. "I'll be back later to check on you."

Rising, Jim left.

Darcy closed her eyes and fell into a fitful slumber.

Later that night, Jim returned to find Darcy thrashing and moaning in her sleep. He stripped, washed the soot from his body, and then lay beside her. Crooning softly in her ear, he snuggled her head against his chest and brushed the hair from her face.

He didn't care if the other drovers knew about his relationship with Darcy. The only thing he cared about was her.

His stomach knotted as he thought of what Darcy had endured in the past twenty-four hours. He admired her courage and inner strength.

Never again would he doubt her ability to survive in the Outback. This woman—his woman—was a survivor, first and last.

And now that he had found her, he wanted her at his side.

Always.

He held her tight. "Shh. It's only a nightmare. I've got you. You're safe."

Her eyes snapped open. Her heart pounded in her chest. "Oh, Jim!" she gasped. "It was so real. Hold me. Please hold me."

He drew her slender frame next to his body and cradled her shoulders in the crook of one arm. She turned onto her side and rested her head atop his chest for a moment, then raised it. Her gaze melted into his, and she said with a soft, metered cadence, "Jim. Never let me go."

"You're mine forever, Darcy. Nothing's going to take you from me," he whispered.

She laid her head back down and moved closer, snuggling her body against his with a sigh. A smile touched his mouth.

As he held her in his arms, Jim felt the intense

desire to protect her against all odds. He was beginning to grow used to having her body next to his in this way, and he didn't want it to end.

"Jim, have you ever been afraid?"

"Yeah."

"I mean so afraid you couldn't think or act?"

Her head moved as he breathed deeply and his chest rose. "It happens to everyone, whether they admit it or not." He had felt that way about Darcy—scared he would lose her.

"That's how I felt when I thought I was going to die." She moistened her lips. "But why should I be afraid to die? I know there's a God in Heaven."

"It's not that you're afraid of dying. I reckon you love life. And you know you haven't finished what you were put on this earth for."

"But do we ever know what our purpose is?"

"Yes."

"How?" There was a hint of urgency in her voice.

"You feel it in your gut. And when you've felt how right something is, you'll never doubt it."

"I'm not sure I've ever felt that way."

Jim smoothed her hair. "Yes, you have. When you became a doctor. I've never seen anyone, man or woman, with such determination to prove themselves. I reckon you've known in your heart for a long time what the Lord put you here for."

"I did since I was a child, but do you know how hard it is fighting everyone? Listening to what they tell you about what's right for you and what you should be doing?"

"That's just the way a lot of people are," Jim said reflectively.

"I suppose so. But they waste so much time worrying about others instead of seeing to their own needs and lives."

"That's true. I reckon the only person we should see to is ourself."

Jim rubbed his cheek against her head.

"I could never be with someone who didn't love and respect me for the person I am. We're all individuals. God made each and every one of us special." she said.

Jim had never heard Darcy speak with such conviction. But then, Darcy always kept him on his toes. Suddenly it seemed very important to tell her what was in his heart—the new thing that had taken root as he watched her during the fire. "I'll never doubt your stamina and will again." He raised her chin so he could see her shining eyes. "I'll never doubt you. I love you."

Chapter 16

Tired and drowsy, Darcy sat in a chair before the fireplace. She yawned. "You're a hard taskmaster." Firelight played across her heart-shaped face.

Jim knelt beside her and poked the burning logs. "I reckon you'll need to learn all I can teach you if you aim to stay on Kopperella."

She reached over and ruffled his hair. "You'll never get rid of me."

He looked up at her; his eyes reflected leaping light and tenderness. "I don't want to."

She laughed, the sound ringing lightly in the room. "At one time, you would have jumped at the chance to have me off your hands."

"Hmm. But now I like you on my hands."

"You're incorrigible."

"And you're a hypocrite for not admitting how much you like it when I touch you," he teased.

"I'm not admitted to anything," she returned playfully. "I wouldn't want your head to become too big for your hat."

"That's not what grows big."

"You never give up, do you?"

"No. You should know that."

"Don't press the point."

"Hmm, now that's an idea. Want to feel?"

"Oh, really, Jim."

She smiled and rested her head against her hand. She had ridden all day at his side while he had seen to his duties around Kopperella. Though bone-tired now, she had loved every minute of it.

Almost as much as she loved . . .

Her eyes closed.

Jim replaced the poker. When he gazed at Darcy again, she was fast asleep. He studied her.

How beautiful she looked, her face in soft repose.

Too beautiful to be of this earth.

He brushed his knuckles lightly across her cheek to reassure himself of her reality.

Jim lifted her into his arms. He considered kissing those tempting, parted lips, but the idea evaporated when her head lolled against his chest. Maybe he had worked her too hard today.

He carried her to the bed and gently deposited her there. Carefully removing her clothes so as not to awaken her, Jim tucked Darcy beneath the covers.

Undressing, he looked down at Darcy's sleeping profile and drew one raspy breath, then another. She was the most important thing in his life. The thought scared him. He'd lose his mind if anything ever happened to her.

Even now his body reacted to her despite his

efforts to the contrary. If he touched her, there would be no rest for either of them.

Jim got in bed and lay down beside her. A smile touched his mouth. In her sleep, she snuggled against him. He pulled the covers up over them and put his arm around her.

Lying there, staring at the ceiling, Jim was sorry for every angry, hurtful word that had passed between Darcy and him. To hurt her was to hurt himself. He only wanted to love her.

Darcy sighed again, and Jim looked down at her. Holding her close every night was becoming a habit he never wanted to break. Her hair smelled sweet and clean, and she felt soft against him, her flesh warm and yielding.

She was the most wonderful woman he had ever known.

He could never allow her to leave him.

He would convince her to marry him.

Feeling confident, he fell asleep.

A hearty whack on her behind rudely awoke Darcy. She rolled over and bottled upright in bed. Jim stood to the side, hands on his hips and a maddening smile on his handsome face.

"Do you reckon to stay in bed all day?" He rubbed his chin in contemplation. "Of course, I don't suppose it would hurt none. I could always join you."

She came to her feet, wrapping the top cover about her nakedness.

Jim laughed. "Have no worry, darling. I don't intend to make love to you. At least, not now."

Darcy's heart pounded against her rib cage at the warm gentleness in his eyes.

"Don't you want some tucker? You have to eat to keep up your strength. Being a doctor, you should know that."

"You're hopeless."

She seized a pillow and flung it at his head.

Jim ducked.

She grabbed another and sent it sailing through the air.

Another miss.

He gave her a crooked grin. "You're still a bad aim, although you present a right fetching picture."

Spontaneously, she stuck out her tongue at him.

In the blink of an eye, Jim lunged across the bed and grabbed Darcy about the waist. They tumbled to the floor, amid covers and a tangle of legs and arms.

They wrestled like two frolicking pups.

Jim's rich laughter filled the air, along with Darcy's heart.

"I'll teach you, woman, to show the station boss some respect," he playfully warned.

His face was so near, his whisper touched her.

And then he grew still, his expression raw with desire.

Her stomach contracted. Jim was an exceptional man. He resembled a statue cast in the finest bronze, sculpted arousingly.

He alone had the ability to awaken her passion.

He alone had earned her love.

Suddenly his eyes roamed over her quite differently. They touched her with a shimmering heat. They seemed to caress her, as if he cherished her above all women.

Her lips were dry. She fought to moisten them.

His fingers threaded through her hair as he slowly lowered his lips to hers.

His touch sent a searing streak of pleasure through her. His tongue teased the edge of her mouth, causing her lips to part to the provocative demand.

Darcy groaned her disappointment when Jim ended the kiss abruptly.

"Have I told you this morning how much you mean to me?"

Darcy shook her head, red hair settling about her shoulders like a cloud, and replied, "No, and it's long overdue."

"Never keep a lady waiting," Jim teased. "I love you, Darcy McCall. But that's enough of that. I've got plans for us. First, though, we'll have some tucker."

He got to his feet and brought a tray in from the other room.

"It seems you've thought of everything," Darcy said.

His gaze took in her state of provocative disarray. "Too often."

She grinned mischievously at his less-than-subtle meaning.

They spoke little as they ate. Jim finished first

and leaned back against the side of the bed. Reaching out, he gathered a portion of Darcy's hair in one hand and wrapped the silken strands around his wrist before he raised it to his nose and inhaled the clean, fresh scent.

Between bites, Darcy glanced into Jim's smiling face. His disarming charm struck a chord of harmony within her. She would be hard pressed to deny him any request at the moment.

"Don't tell me you're not curious about what I've planned for us today," he commented as he trailed some of her hair across his cheek.

"Maybe just a bit."

"I thought you might care to go for a swim."

"I'd like that."

"But not at the creek. There's another place I want to take you."

"Where?" Her laugh and wide-eyes expression conveyed her curiosity. "Somewhere I haven't been yet?"

"I used to go there a fair bit as a boy. This water hole is fed by an underground spring and is always full."

"Why have you decided to take me there now? Why not before?"

His expression grew serious. "I wasn't ready to share my life with you before."

Like a carefree child, Darcy impulsively leaned over and threw her arms around his neck. "Oh, Jim."

He rose and extended his hand to her. "Come, Yank. Time's wasting." She placed her fingers in his palm and he pulled her to her feet, then caressed the side of her neck. "Wear your cotton day dress. The simple blue one." His words heated to a degree. "But leave your underclothes here."

"I can't dress like that in the open!" Darcy's reply was a denial, but her rapid pulse was an acceptance. "Besides, what about the bet?"

"Forget all about that. There are some things I'm willing to give up when I have other things to gain." Jim ran a finger between her breasts.

"You're mighty sure of yourself," she said, laughing.

"Very sure. The place where I'm taking you is very private. No one will see you." He looked down her body appreciatively. "Except me. And I intend to see a great deal of you."

"You take a lot for granted."

"Yeah. I'll go get my horse."

He kissed her tenderly, then left.

A curious peace descended over Darcy. She knew many people would condemn her for giving herself to a man outside the bounds of matrimony. But nothing could make her regret her decision to love Jim. They had reached a milestone in their relationship, and there was no turning back.

Darcy quickly donned the requested dress. It was a simple frock of blue cotton, with short, puffed sleeves, flaring lines, and a dipping neckline.

Ten minutes later, she found herself outside, beside Jim's horse.

He sat astride his bay gelding, grinning down

at her. His sun-bronzed fingers reached out and closed about her forearms. Darcy felt the steel-hard muscles in his arms flex as he pulled her sideways in front of him.

He tugged the reins to his left, and his arm brushed against her body. Her shoulders rubbed the solid wall of his chest as the horse danced beneath the additional weight before cantering toward the far end of the compound, onto the plain.

Jim's taut thighs burned her legs. His masculinity roused her senses, triggering a solely carnal reply. His warm breath fanned her hair and brushed her skin.

He slowed the horse's gait to a walk.

As they rode, his right hand circled Darcy's waist and moved upward to stroke one breast. Her muscles tightened and her breathing became erratic. He was a sorcerer who held her body captive with his sensual magic. He merely had to touch her to make her want him.

Contentment flushed Darcy's features. She loved the feel of the wind against her skin and in her hair. Unbound, her long tresses streamed out behind her in billowing waves. The ride was a tantalizing exercise.

They soon reached the watering hole.

Jim dismounted. His hand caressed her exposed calf and traveled up her leg to rest on her thigh. She drew a sharp breath. But when his hand wandered higher, burrowing beneath the folds of her dress and stopping only scant inches from her center, Darcy's entire body went rigid. In the span of a heartbeat she felt a tiny pulsing within her womanhood. His fingers worked their way between her and the saddle until they stroked her soft curls. Her face flamed when she felt herself grow moist against his fingertips.

Her throat closed. She fought for speech. For long seconds in which her heart seemed to beat a thousand times, she remained still.

Just when her nerve endings screamed for satisfaction, Jim's hand glided down her leg before lifting her.

"Let me help you," he drawled, the smile of a well-fed cat curling his lips.

She placed her hands atop his broad shoulders as his hands gripped her waist. He assisted her down.

Her descent was slow. His hands slipped from her waist to under her arms. Momentarily, he held her suspended, her mouth level with his, her breasts aligned with his chest. Their eyes locked.

Only a breath of air separated them. Acutely she felt his tight-knit frame against the length of her. How well she knew the hard-muscled coils and planes of his form, just as she knew the searing pulse that protruded from him and beckoned wantonly to her body as it brushed her belly.

Jim's whispered words drifted warmly across her lips. "Would you care for a swim?"

Her gaze shifted to his mouth, and she watched the movement of his tongue against his teeth as he spoke. The tip of her own tongue moistened her lips. Suddenly she yearned to be joined with him, to become one with him.

"Yes," came her single, hushed word.

Jim crushed her to him. She clung to his neck as he kissed her, skillfully, seductively. The long, loving kiss left her breathless.

Her fingertips caressed his rippling back muscles. The strength of his arms as they tightened possessively around her was comfortingly familiar. He loosened his hold slightly and her feet touched the ground, but her senses remained aloft.

Jim dragged his mouth from hers and pressed his lips to her forehead.

His breath fell like a soft mist on her skin, "Now for that swim."

They undressed. Jim held out his hand to Darcy, and she took it, letting her emotions drift with the soft breeze.

The rocks were smooth beneath her feet. Sunlight warmed her shoulders. The moist breeze off the water brushed her lips.

They waded into the pool until they stood hip-deep. Darcy leaned back against Jim's chest as the cool, refreshing water lapped about her thighs. She sighed her contentment.

Sunlight kissed her cheeks, nose, and eyes. Her thick hair cascaded over her breasts and his encircling arms, and the sensation was erotic.

He pulled her around to face him and lifted her chin. She leaned into him and their bodies touched, his hard and muscled, hers soft and yielding.

Jim lowered his head and kissed her urgently. Then his movements slowed, becoming tender and gentle, until finally he pulled away from her. He studied her, rejoicing in her beauty as he fingered the curve of her cheek.

Tilting her head back, Darcy was giddy from the desire spiraling within her She felt suspended in tenderness.

Jim murmured, "Your lips are so soft." And then, tenderly, "Kiss me again."

He brushed her lower lip with his finger. She tasted the saltiness of his touch and felt the tiny callused skin of his fingertip. Water rippled around her thighs in a sensual rhythm.

Finally she raised her chin, gazing into his eyes for a moment before she closed hers, and pressed her mouth to his in a full, open kiss. When she broke away from him, she was trembling and he had to support her with his hands.

The warm, golden afternoon fed their senses. They splashed in the cool water, played tag on the rocks, talked of simple things. And then Jim carried her to the soft bank where they made love. Their bodies were wet and glistening, and when Jim came into her it felt as if a million stars were exploding. She sang out her love. Afterward, she curled her body into him and they dozed.

Darcy looked upward as vultures circled overhead, casting ominous shadows on the ground. She shrank from the stench of death that filled the air.

Jim guided his horse around the broken and

mutilated bodies of several Herefords which littered the bloodstained ground. "Bloody hell!"

Darcy held the back of her hand to her mouth to keep herself from choking on the bile rising in her throat as she viewed the carnage.

"You all right?" Jim inquired.

"You'd think my being a doctor would make me immune to this."

His narrow gaze swept the carcasses strewn on the ground. "There's a difference. This bothers you because it's senseless slaughter."

Jim dismounted, leaving Darcy astride his horse. He knelt on one knee, reading tracks.

As a young man, he had learned a great deal about tracking animals—and the same skill could be used on men. If a rock had been moved from its customary spot, he could tell. If he saw a snapped twig, a crushed blade of grass, or a bit of weed cut off by a horse's hoof, he could make a good guess about how long it had been that way. A print made during the night would usually be marked with tiny insect tracks.

Barring specific marks, Jim could still ascertain in which direction his quarry was traveling by the tracks of the animals frightened out of its path. No movement was too slight for him to ignore, no sound too quiet for him to miss.

Jim remounted. The horse danced as he tightened his reins and pulled the animal's head down.

"Who would do this? Is it Aborigines again?"

"No. Bushrangers." He looked into her face. "Outlaws."

"Why?"

"This was done for the meat. Next time, they'll return to do a little paddy dodging. They make money stealing cattle."

"What do we do?"

"We're going to see if we can find out what they're up to." Upon seeing Darcy's startled look, Jim added, "Don't worry. We'll just look."

They rode in silence.

Half an hour later, they came upon a grouping of rocks.

"Shh." Jim raised a finger to his mouth. "They're close by."

"What do we do now?" Darcy whispered hoarsely.

"Nothing."

"The why don't we just go back to Kopperella and return with more men?" she asked hopefully, not wanting an encounter with the bushrangers.

Jim's gaze shifted to her. "Will you keep quiet? You're distracting me. Keep an eye on that spot below."

Wiping the perspiration from her forehead, Darcy closed her eyes against the late afternoon glare. When she opened them, she wished she hadn't.

She thought her heart would stop beating at any moment. Straight ahead was a small group of armed men. Carved hunks of meat hung from their saddles. The bushrangers! Her hands locked until her knuckles whitened.

What did they want? And worse—what would they do?

Jim straightened in his saddle. "Damn."

Darcy knew this was all her fault. If only she'd kept her mouth closed and allowed Jim to do his job. If only . . .

His voice sounded hollow in her ears. "Whatever happens, just do what I say. There's nothing to do now but face them."

Incredulity filled Darcy's softly spoken words. "You aren't going over there, are you?"

"I've no other choice if we stand a chance of getting out of this."

Jim lowered Darcy to the ground. He kicked the flanks of his horse and rode for the bushrangers.

Darcy watched. And held her breath.

Showing no fear or hesitation, Jim approached the man who appeared to be the leader.

Jim's horse shifted beneath him while he unflinchingly returned the appraisal in the brown eyes of the man across from him.

The outlaw spoke first, revealing stained, irregular teeth. "Look who we 'ave 'ere, boys. Jim Burleson 'imself."

"Where's your leader? I'd have thought Edward Newley would be riding with you." Jim rested a forearm across his saddle. "Or has he taken to letting others do his dirty work?"

"You calling 'im a coward?"

"Only if it fits."

The speaker grinned, but his smile never reached his eyes. "You're plenty brave, considering there's only two of you. And the other being a woman at that."

While the man spoke, Jim took note of the position of the rest of the men. It wouldn't be easy to get them all, but it could be done. Darcy's safety had to come first.

While the two men continued talking, one bushranger detached himself from the group and slowly circled Darcy. Silently, he taunted her with menacing looks. She watched the man warily. She forced herself to remain quiet and show no fear.

The outlaw stopped beside her. Inwardly, she cringed as the stench of his dirty, unwashed clothes assailed her. She stared at his rigid facial features. Weathered by the sun, his skin was dark and leathery-looking. His eyes were shadowy and cold, and the gun he wore tucked inside his belt only made him appear more dangerous.

Then he unsheathed his rifle and moved the barrel closer and closer until it nearly touched her cheek. He lifted a strand of red hair that had worked its way free of the ribbon. Cold perspiration covered her body, while the blood drained from her face. Her fear intensified with each second he stared at her.

Suddenly her tormentor withdrew as Jim made his way back to her. Breath escaped her lungs in a soft rush.

Abreast of her, he said in a low voice, "There's going to be trouble. When it starts, I want you to head for those boulders to your left. Understand?"

"Yes."

He slipped her a knife. "If anyone comes near you, use this."

She took the weapon and stared at it with widened eyes. "I don't know if I can."

"Just use the knife," he said in a clipped tone.

The group leader left his men and rode alongside Jim. "I've been giving it some thought. I want your gun."

Menacing intent evident on their faces, the rest of the bushrangers closed in a circle around them.

"Yeah. I bet."

In the blink of an eye, Jim drew his weapon and shot the leader. The bullet slammed into the outlaw's thigh and he toppled backward off his horse.

Darcy bit down on her bottom lip to keep from screaming.

Time seemed to stand still, and action blurred. Jim sank to the ground and rolled beneath the legs of his horse, firing at will. Another man dropped from his mount.

Darcy snatched her impeding hemline and bolted for the boulders, but a horse's shoulder knocked her to the ground. On her back, stunned, she peered up at the ugly face of a bushranger.

When he leveled his gun at her, Darcy instinctively tumbled toward his horse's hooves. The sudden movement surprised the outlaw and his shot went wild. Passing beneath the belly of the rearing animal, she came up on the other side and slashed the man's hamstring muscle.

Howling, he kicked himself off his horse and hit the ground on one knee, but Darcy was already running for the rock formation.

She never reached the boulders.

A spinning rope fell over her shoulders and, though she tried to throw it off, circled her waist with a jerk. She lost her footing and was dragged backward, kicking and gasping.

More gunshots were fired.

Still clutching the knife, Darcy sawed through the rope. Free and panting, she leaped to her feet and swung the blade in a glittering arc.

Dust whirled around her.

She ducked away from the bushranger, who sprang at her. Rolling, she saw a bullet kick up the dirt close beside her head and heard it whine angrily upward. Sunlight blinded her vision of her attacker, towering above her. Suddenly he clutched his back spasmodically as he landed in the dirt, facedown, blood trickling from a hole between his shoulder blades.

Jim rushed toward her, his rifle in one hand.

Dirty and gasping, her dress torn at the shoulder to reveal the top of a breast, Darcy pulled herself up to her knees.

Jim reached down and caught her upper arms. Darcy came to her feet. Circling her small waist with the muscular band of his arm, he smoothed the hair from her face with his other hand. His palm lingered on the gentle curve of her jaw. His mouth felt warm against her temple. Slowly, he enveloped her in his embrace and rested his chin atop her head.

A light breeze whispered across the couple. Defying the surrounding visions of death, they were content to be in each other's arms, their hearts beating in unison.

Chapter 17

In front of the men's quarters, Craig Newley, along with Dave Patterson, observed Jim and Darcy entering the compound.

Patterson inclined his head toward the pair. "They're certainly a couple these days. Boss doesn't go far that she's not behind 'im."

"Like a bitch in 'eat, if you ask me," Craig spat, his gaze riveted upon the riders.

From the corner of his eye he caught Patterson's surprised look. "Don't stand there with your bleedin' mouth open. Everyone knows that's the straight of it."

"I don't reckon you should speak of the doctor that way. She's a nice enough lady. Done right by me."

Newley laughed. "She's just got you fooled, is all. She don't show 'er true self to none of us."

Patterson's lips tightened. "You're wrong. She's been nothing but kind to all of us."

"Not me."

"You've never given 'er a chance."

Newley sneered. "Don't 'ave to. I've seen the likes of 'er before."

"Your trouble, Newley, is you've 'ad your mind in the gutter too much."

"No gutter. Just a page of life."

Craig's expression tightened as Jim dismounted and swept Darcy off the horse, placing a light kiss upon her lips before they entered her house.

Craig ground his teeth. " 'E better enjoy 'er while 'e can."

" 'Ey? What's that?" Patterson asked.

"I reckon she'll leave soon enough." Craig's lip curled in a snarl. "One way or the other."

Patterson's gaze sliced over Newley, but the other man appeared lost in thought, a faraway look in his green eyes.

The next morning, just after breakfast, Jim and Darcy sat by themselves at the kitchen table.

Jim set his cup down, reached over, and covered Darcy's hand with his own. He cherished his moments alone with her, but she'd been distant this morning. Knowing Darcy, he assumed that she probably didn't want to bother him. When would she learn they were in this together?

"I can tell something's bothering you. Is it about us?" he asked.

Darcy regarded their hands, then looked at him and smiled. However, something undefinable lurked behind her gaze. "Funny how in so short a time you've come to know when something's on my mind."

He laughed, in an attempt to lighten her

mood. "How could I not? Most of the time it was me you were thinking about—either good or bad. You might say I had to learn how to read you in order to survive." He squeezed her hand. "Now, tell me."

"I've been thinking about Rosie. As a matter of fact, I haven't been able to stop thinking about her." Darcy's expression darkened. "I'm worried about her. I just feel something's wrong or she would have been back by now."

In the most reassuring tone he could muster, Jim replied, "How do you know she's in trouble? Aborigines don't keep timetables. They come and go as they please."

"But I just can't believe she'd be away from me this long."

He smiled more gently. "You've got to stop torturing yourself. Rosie doesn't belong to you. She's not your child, by law or otherwise."

"She's mine in here." Darcy pointed to her heart.

"But she doesn't want to be yours. Aborigines don't think in terms of family like we do. They're different and you've got to accept that, no matter how much you want to change it. She'll come back when she's ready." He leaned closer. "But, Darcy, Rosie will come back because she wants to, not because you want her to."

"Could you send someone to look for her?" Darcy pleaded.

The lines of Jim's face tightened, and Darcy recognized the regret clouding his countenance. "I can see that you won't."

"Not won't, Darcy. Can't. Not with the bush-rangers roaming about. I can't spare a man. Besides, an Aborigine on walkabout is impossible to find because they don't want to be found. Please understand."

"I'll try."

"I've got to get going. Will you be all right?" Jim asked.

Darcy nodded and smiled once more. "We both have jobs to do. I'll see you out."

They walked to the door and onto the porch.

Jim put his arms about Darcy's waist and pulled her to him. He lowered his head. "I'll give you something to remember me by."

He kissed her slowly, sweetly. There was so much in that kiss that called to Darcy. So much she wanted to answer. But now wasn't the time.

"You're going to distract me from my duties," Darcy said against his mouth.

"Hmmm. So it seems," he whispered back.

Jim held Darcy at arm's length. "I'll be back as soon as I can."

"See that you are," she teased.

Suddenly she tensed as she gazed past his shoulder. "Jim, look!" She pointed toward the compound. "Newley's got Rosie."

Jim spun around.

Newley walked toward them, pushing Rosie in front of him.

Darcy saw the fear pasted on Rosie's face. Her blood flowed faster through her veins, causing her head to pound.

"What's he doing?" she demanded.

"I don't know, but I'm going to find out," Jim replied striding to meet Newley.

Darcy followed. When she and Jim stopped in front of Newley, it was all she could do to keep herself from snatching Rosie away from him. But she knew she had to allow Jim to handle this, and so she stood still.

"Let her go, Newley," Jim said.

"So you've grown fond of 'er, too, mate," Newley spat. "Didn't know you 'ad a liking for nits."

Jim's body seemed to sing with tension. "What I like or don't like is none of your business."

Newley shoved Rosie at Jim. "Well, you can 'ave 'er."

Jim's jaw clenched. "I want an explanation."

Newley hooked his thumbs into the waistband of his trousers. "Nothing to explain. I found 'er while I was riding."

"Why were you out of the compound?"

"Just riding."

"Or meeting with your outlaw brother?" Jim's voice was strident. "You've crossed the line, Newley. I have no use for a man if he's not loyal."

"What are you saying?"

"That you've been seen with your brother, and that can only mean one thing—trouble."

The veins in Newley's neck protruded. "Are you sacking me?"

Anger emanated from every inch of Jim's taut, powerful frame. "You're through on Kopperella. Get out of my sight!"

"I'll go, but not before I 'ave my say. You'd better see to your back, Burleson. Because I'm going to watch your every move. And when you're not looking, I'm going to see you pay for what you've done."

At that moment Tom Rivers walked up.

Jim clenched his teeth. "Rivers, make sure the son of a bitch gets off Kopperella in an hour."

"Yes, boss," Rivers replied.

The next day, Darcy decided to treat Rosie to a picnic. She knew they couldn't leave the compound, so she spread a blanket on the ground in the front yard of her house.

"Look at what I've got for us," she said, taking several dishes of food out of the basket. "I had Kim Loo fix us lots of good things to eat."

Rosie looked bewildered.

Darcy rocked back on her heels and folded her hands in her lap. "Where I come from, this is called a picnic."

Still Rosie seemed confused.

"People do this when they want to have fun with friends," Darcy said.

Eyes crinkling, Rosie smiled. "Fun."

Darcy returned the smile. "Yes. Fun."

Dropping down beside Darcy, Rosie began rummaging through the assorted food. She stuck a finger in the bowl of custard and licked the creamy mixture from her fingertip. Her smile broadened. "Good."

"Very good," Darcy said.

As Rosie made a grab for a piece of meat,

Darcy placed a hand atop the child's. "You must wait until I have everything ready."

"All right."

In minutes Darcy had their small feast laid out on the blanket, and they began eating.

In between bites of fowl, Darcy asked, "Tell me about this walkabout you went on. What did you do?"

Rosie scarcely slowed her chewing. "I walk the country."

"Yes, I know that, but why?"

Rosie stopped and cocked her head to one side. "Why?"

"Yes, why?"

"Because black fella always go walkabout."

Darcy could tell this line of questioning was getting her nowhere. "Do you enjoy it?"

"Yes. See lots of things."

"Such as?"

"Animals, birds."

Darcy wiped her fingers on her napkin. "What do you do with them?"

"Talk."

"You mean you study them."

"No, I talk with them."

Darcy frowned. "How do you do that?"

"Don't know."

"I won't ask you any more questions about it." Darcy laughed. "This is doing neither of us any good."

Rosie smiled and plunged into her food once more. Darcy watched her and felt a keen pain in her heart at the thought of the child leaving again. She had to make her understand that she'd always be there to care for her.

"Rosie, there's something I want to talk to you about."

"What that?"

"I want you to know that as long as you stay with me you'll be safe. I won't let anyone hurt you."

Rosie looked dubious.

"It's true. I promise to do my best to keep you from harm." Darcy pushed back a strand of hair. "Don't you like being with me?"

Rosie put down her half-eaten chicken leg. "I like you much. But you not black fella. I no belong with you."

"You could be with me if you wanted to."

Rosie slowly shook her head. "No. Not stay with you always."

Darcy knew in her heart then that Jim had been right, but it didn't stop the pain.

Several days later, Jim took Darcy to a secluded spot with the intention of teaching her how to protect herself. Newley had gone, most likely to join the bushrangers, and Jim wanted to take no chances with her safety. He had to go on the final muster of the season tomorrow. He knew Darcy would refuse to go because of Rosie. This was his only alternative.

Nervous, Darcy clutched the butt of Jim's pistol with both hands. "I've never handled firearms before."

"There's a first time for everyone." He laughed dryly. "You have to hold the gun firmly. You keep shaking like a leaf, your shot's going to go wild."

"I'm sorry. I'll try harder. It's just that it's so heavy." She could barely hold the gun level; the tip of the barrel wobbled.

"Turn around and face the cans I set up."

She complied. He stood behind her. She smelled the day's accumulation of dirt, sweat, and something else—the masculine scent that was his alone.

She felt the buckle of his belt press intimately into the small of her back. As his chest touched her, the heat of his body penetrated the cotton of her pants and shirt, making her acutely aware of him. His body spoke to her in a language all its own. That made it hard for her to concentrate ... on target practice, anyway.

She heard the measured cadence of his breathing against her ear and felt it as it fell lightly against her neck. Goose bumps of delicious warmth broke out across her skin.

When she shifted her weight, he said softly, "Will you keep still?"

"I'm trying. It's just that ..." She licked her suddenly dry lips. How could she explain what his mere touch did to her?

"Just pay attention."

He draped his right arm like a cloak atop hers as he gripped her wrist and raised her arm, his warmth enveloping her. When his left hand rested lightly on her hip, a tremor raced up her spine. She drew a deep breath to calm her galloping heart.

"Focus on the gunsight. That's how you aim."

His voice was hot and moist against her neck, and he smelled faintly of horseflesh. "Steady. Close one eye and aim."

What she wanted to do was close both eyes and melt into his arms—to have him smother her with kisses. She couldn't be near him without being bombarded with sensual thoughts that had nothing to do with protection, but everything to do with surrender.

As she went through the motions, she asked, "Now what?"

"Brace yourself."

She adjusted her position but heard his amusement. "Not like that. Like this."

He ran his left hand down her hip and to the inside of her thigh, giving a gentle pull, bringing her legs farther apart. Desire tugged at her center. She steadied her breathing.

"Now, squeeze the trigger. Easy."

Swallowing, Darcy pulled her finger back. The gun discharged with a belch of smoke and fire, knocking her into Jim. Just before they hit the ground, Jim locked his arms about Darcy's waist.

Neither moved for several moments.

Darcy lay breathless. She slowly opened her eyes. She was lying atop Jim's hard-knit body, her slender legs tangled familiarly with his muscular ones. He had taken the brunt of the fall.

How right and natural it felt lying on top of him. She had no inclination to move.

Jim rolled over, trapping Darcy beneath him, holding her wrists beside her head. Their bodies seemed to meld into one.

"Woman, you make me forget myself," he groaned.

He caught her face with one callused hand and tilted her chin up so her mouth could meet his.

Oh, God, how his kiss ignited a fire in Darcy's blood that rushed to her head and pounded there!

And, oh, how she loved him.

"Do you have to go tomorrow?" she asked, suddenly not wanting him to leave her.

"You know I do. Especially now that Newley's gone and we're short-handed." He rose and helped her to her feet. "I'll be back as soon as I can. All right?"

She lowered her head. "All right."

With a finger, he tipped her chin upward. "Where's my brave Yank?" he teased.

"She's here. It's just that she'll miss you." But a cold wave of dread broke over her.

His voice flowed like honey—thick, golden, and warm. "Not as much as I'll miss you."

Chapter 18

$\sim\!\!\infty\!\!\sim$

Jim stood at the door, holding it open for Darcy.

Outside, Tom Rivers and Dave Patterson, accompanied by three other drovers, waited with his mount.

Jim's hand rode the small of her back and guided her down the steps and toward the horse that Kim Loo held. Beside his mount, Jim pulled her into his arms and kissed her. It was a kiss crafted by strong sentiment.

Her lips trembled when he released them. She stared into his eyes. "You don't know how much I'll miss you," she said softly for his ears alone.

To Jim, her whispered words were like silk against his face. Innocent, shimmering, and seductive.

He cupped her chin and raised it. "I know only too well. This isn't easy for me, either. But I'll be back as soon as I can."

His touch and his words were like fingers of warm sunshine penetrating her skin, tissue, blood, and bone to take hold of her spirit, never to let go again.

At her nod, Jim swung lithely into the saddle. Darcy stepped beside Kim Loo. Jim reined his horse from her. The drovers followed in his wake. Tom Rivers tugged the brim of his hat at Darcy as he touched a spurred boot to his horse's flank.

Delicate fingers of light heralded the dawn when the six men rode out of the compound to the plain beyond. Darcy watched Jim's retreating figure until he was a speck against the brightening horizon.

With leaden movements, she turned and went inside.

In the whole of her life, Darcy had never been so lonely. Silence throbbed where only moments ago Jim's vitality had charged the atmosphere.

She walked into the bedroom. Draped across the footboard of the bed lay his discarded shift from last night. She picked up the garment, pressed it to her nose, and smelled his scent clinging to the fabric.

Moving to the window, Darcy observed the morning sun's crowning glory rising above the earth's mantle.

Already she missed him as if he'd been gone for days instead of merely moments. If the day passed in weighted chains, how much more torturous would the night be?

Night. . . .

Last night with Jim. . . .

Shivers of remembrance tore at her, as she recalled each delicious, savoring moment.

He had brought her such pleasure. A pleasure so intense that she had felt she had been reborn in body, mind, and spirit. She stroked her lips with her fingers. She felt his lips still.

Lovingly, she folded his shirt across her arm and set about to address the day with a semblance of normality. She retraced her steps to the front room and gave a long, shuddering sigh.

Trembling, Nettie stood inside the door of Craig Newley's room. He lay on the bed, propped up against the headboard, and dragged deeply on his cigar.

She had never been frightened of Edward, but Craig was different. Something was not right about the way he stared at a woman. The way he was staring at her now. Something in his eyes made her stomach twist.

But she had no choice in coming. Craig had paid in advance. And that meant her boss wouldn't interfere with what took place behind closed doors. And if she refused to service Craig, her boss would beat her himself. She swallowed the sick feeling rising in her throat.

The stench from Craig's sweaty, unwashed body hung in the air. It lingered, grew heavy, and mingled with her cheap perfume. Wispy fingers of smoke reached across the distance between them. She gagged, the vile feeling rising again.

Craig Newley was not a man to be crossed. People said he took pleasure in inflicting pain, in inciting pleas for mercy that he never heeded.

Her anxiety deepened when his eyes, hard and glittering like a snake's, slithered over her. He motioned her closer.

Nettie's brain gave a command to her limbs, but her legs wouldn't move. Dread had paralyzed her. Her nostrils flared slightly.

"Come 'ere, you stupid slut," Newley growled.

Swallowing once more, Nettie stepped nearer, offering a quick prayer for protection.

"I didn't pay for a whore to stand there gawking at me. Take your clothes off." Anger laced his low words.

Trembling, Nettie stripped. She squeezed her eyes shut in fear. Her throat threatened to close and deny her breath.

Firelight cast wavering patterns across her pallid skin. Momentarily, Craig grew still—all but his gaze, which slid over her body. Her insides curdled like yesterday's cream. The man was mad. There was no other explanation for the demented gleam in his eyes.

Craig stood. His thoughts were dark. Dark with reprisal, and black with vengeance. His smile was sinister. If he couldn't touch Darcy McCall, he'd think of her, picturing the grimace on her face as he took this one. One whore or another—they were all the same.

There would come a time when he would settle the score with Jim Burleson and his fawning bitch. But for now, he would satisfy himself in other ways. Craig grabbed Nettie's shoulder and held her motionless.

Afraid and breathless, Nettie didn't struggle.

She instinctively knew he would kill her if she did. Sweet Jesus, defend her!

He snarled in her ear, "I intend to get my money's worth."

Darcy stood in the middle of her front room, too stricken to move.

She wanted to cry, but no tears fell, although they burned her eyes and throat. All she could do was stare at the crumpled letter in her clenched hand.

Dismissed! She had been dismissed by the agents in London. Upon the advice and recommendation, they had written, of the station boss, Jim Burleson. So he had done it after all.

How he must have been laughing at her all this time! How easy it had been to lure her into his bed with false words of love, knowing she'd most likely be gone by the time he tired of her.

Fool! she admonished herself. She had taken precautions against becoming pregnant. Why hadn't she guarded her heart? She wasn't some poor, unfortunate young woman who could plead ignorance. She should have known better. But regardless, she was a ruined woman all the same.

The thought had barely crossed her mind when her nipples hardened as she remembered the sheer delight of Jim's touch. Ghostly passion haunted her senses.

Her memory was keen, as sharp as the despair that bit into her heart with icy teeth.

Her head hurt and she suddenly felt exhausted. A choked sob of anguish tumbled past her cold lips to echo in the shadowy room.

Feeling wretched, she made her way to the bed and dropped onto it.

Darcy could no longer withstand the weight of Jim's treachery. She crawled into the center of the bed and brought her knees to her chest. Hugging her calves, she supported her aching forehead with her knees.

She drew a shuddering breath. "Oh, Papa. I wish you were here so you could hold me like you used to when I was a child."

Anguish formed a knot in her throat. She couldn't swallow. She drew upon her reservoir of strength and fought self-pity.

She closed her eyes. Immediately, the face of Jim Burleson filled the dark void behind her lids.

Darcy opened her eyes, determined not to think of him, and of the way he'd used her, until she felt strong enough to figure out what to do.

Edward Newley's eyes widened with disbelief. "Jesus, Craig, what 'ave you done?" He swore at the sight that greeted him.

His stare ricocheted from Nettie's prone, unconscious figure to his brother, who stood near the window. Then it swung back to Nettie. His hands balled into fists at his sides.

Craig faced him. "What do you care? She's just a whore."

Edward's expression tightened with anger. "She may be a whore, but she never done nothing to you."

"Get off my bleedin' back, will you? I'll give 'er more money when she comes to."

Edward moved to the bed where Nettie lay. Her breathing sounded unnatural, gurgling raspily from her lungs.

"If she ever comes around." Edward grabbed Craig by the front of his shirt and slammed him into the wall.

A picture hanging near where Craig's head thudded rattled an ominous warning of what was to come.

Edward's nostrils flared. "I've put up with a fair bit from you only because you're my younger brother. But I won't stand for this. You touch that girl again and, brother or not, I'll break your bleedin' neck."

Craig's eyes widened for a split second, then narrowed. "Touchy, aren't we? I've never known you to be partial to whores."

"Nettie's a good girl—just 'ad a run of bad luck, is all. She can't 'elp what she does for a living, but she doesn't deserve the beating you gave 'er." Edward released his grip on Craig and stepped back.

Craig ignored his brother and strode for the door. "I'm going to 'ave myself a drink."

The breeze stirred the trees and rippled through the grass, keeping flies and mosquitoes away; it freshened and became cooler as the day faded into night.

With his back propped against his upended saddle, Jim stretched his legs out before the campfire, thinking longingly of being in bed with Darcy, her heated skin warming him.

He felt the tightening of his muscles, the razor pain that sliced through him. He had known he would miss Darcy, but he hadn't known to what extent. He wanted her with him, beneath him, crying out softly in hunger and in need.

The fire made a soft hissing sound as the ashes settled, glowing dark red and then yellow as the breeze swept across it. He threw a few more pieces of wood on the fire and watched the flames leap heavenward.

Those flames reminded Jim of Darcy. The crackling intensity of her gaze . . .

The passion firing her spirit . . .

The burning passion for life itself . . .

The room was dark, except for the long slit of moonlight on the floor, as Darcy lay awake in bed, listening.

The silence seemed to throb in her ears. Exhausted, emotionally spent, she closed her eyes and tried to sleep, but her efforts proved futile.

Loneliness and despair broke over Darcy in a crashing wave. Even now the pain of Jim's betrayal hadn't lessened. Rather, it had sharpened.

She wished she could talk to someone, but she knew she would have to bear her shame alone. And possibly all her life. What man would marry her now?

She didn't want a husband, though, she told herself bitterly. Men used women solely for their own pleasure. They disregarded a woman's feelings. She swore that no man would ever treat her that way again. In her whole life Jim was the only man she had wanted to marry. And he had devastated her.

Tears trickled down Darcy's cheeks. She furiously brushed them away. Jim Burleson had made her cry for the last time! When he returned, she would be strong and composed. She was through thinking about him. She only had to wait until her replacement could be found before she could leave and put her life at Kopperella behind her.

The next afternoon, Darcy returned from a horseback ride to find Jim at the paddock. Her emotions whirled and collided. The sight of his handsome face struck a cord of unwelcome memory within her.

She dismounted, forcing strength into her legs, and stood watching him warily.

He moved toward her. His brow furrowed as he stopped in front of her. "I just came from your house. Some of your things are packed. Why?" Jim spoke so softly. Still she felt the sizzling heat and tension behind his words, the energy behind his quiet stance. He was always a force to be reckoned with.

Pain stabbed her anew. How could he stand there and pretend innocence? Her stomach tightened with misery.

She lashed out at him. "As if you didn't know why!"

"Know what? You're not making sense."

Darcy tossed her head back and laughed shortly. "What a liar you are."

The lines on his forehead deepened. "What are you talking about?"

Darcy placed her hands on her hips and regarded him with as cool a look as she could summon. "Spare me." Scorn dripped from her words.

Briefly, she contemplated the wisdom of baiting him when she saw annoyance flash from his blue eyes. But she refused to back down. She glared at him.

He seized her arms. "Talk straight!"

She wanted him to hurt just the way she was hurting. "I'll give it to you—straight to your black heart. You made me believe you cared for me. And all you really wanted was to satisfy yourself at my expense."

He shook her. "What the bloody hell are you saying?"

A dam of emotion burst inside her and all her torment poured out. "That you tricked me into letting you take advantage of me. Then, when my guard was down, you wrote that damned letter you'd threatened me with."

His face darkened. "Letter? I never wrote any letter."

Darcy's lip curled in disdain. How dare he try and act the innocent! "Don't insult my intelligence. The agents said it was you who wrote their office, advising them to dismiss me."

"How could I?"

"I don't know. But you figured it out easily enough."

"I could never do that to you."

"Oh, but you did, you two-faced hypocrite.

You waited until you had me, took what you wanted, then stabbed me in the back."

"You're wrong."

For the briefest second, Darcy thought she saw genuine surprise and regret in his gaze. She steeled herself. No, Jim wasn't capable of feeling those things. He had used her, and she must remember that fact.

"You're the one who's wrong if you think you can fool me again. Never again will I trust you. You've used me and hurt me for the last time."

"I love you."

She ignored the way his words tugged on her heart. The word *love* stung Darcy, even though Jim had spoken it with tender affection. Her pride demanded that she put an end to this mockery.

She pulled free of his hold. "Don't say that."

"What, that I love you? Why not?"

Her tattered dignity cried for action. Heedless of caution, she raised her hand and slapped him.

For a timeless moment, she stared at the angry red mark of her fingers on his face. Her hands grew cold. But no colder than the look in his eyes.

"If you ever do that again, you'll regret it to your dying day," he said slowly, evenly.

"I—" Darcy caught herself before she uttered an apology she only halfheartedly meant.

He would offer no mercy if she weakened.

"You were going to say, Yank?"

She swallowed. Memory rushed through her and left her hot and trembling. How well she knew him. How well she knew the heat of his passion and the chill of his rebuff.

She stared at him for a moment longer, then burst into action, determined to escape him and herself. And those memories.

She took advantage of the distance between them and raced for her horse. Hurt, anger, and fear gave Darcy the strength to scramble into the saddle.

The abrupt movements startled the roan and it reared, its hooves slicing the air, then exploded in a gallop. She never even had a chance to look back.

If she had, she'd have seen Jim frozen in place, his face a mask of shock and pain. After all he'd said and done to her, she doubted him. He had no idea who'd sent the letter about her to London. He'd find out, though, and when he did there'd be hell to pay. In the meantime, he had to follow Darcy—and make her believe that he'd rather die than betray her.

Chapter 19

The sun was sitting on the horizon by the time Jim caught sight of Darcy again, a solitary figure maybe a quarter of a mile in front of him. He spotted a rock formation off to her right and decided to go that way so as to head her off on the far side of the hill.

The bushrangers fell upon him the moment he passed through the monstrous boulders onto the flats beyond.

Suddenly Jim was struck between the shoulder blades. Pain, sharp and near paralyzing, shot down his arms. "What the—" He toppled from his horse and hit the ground.

Disoriented, he raised himself to his knees and held his aching head. Then the inside of his head exploded as a rifle butt struck his skull.

His vision blurred as pain gripped him, then tightened its hold savagely. He groaned. Squinting, he tried to see, but only indistinguishable forms passed before his eyes.

"Well, boys, look who we caught," one of the shifting shadows said in a detached, smooth tone. "I reckoned if I waited long enough, 'e'd fall into my lap."

Jim recognized Craig Newley's voice. He tried to gain his footing, but a boot caught him in the rib cage and his legs crumpled beneath him. He dropped to his knees again.

Jim rocked back on his heels. "Is this your idea of fighting like a man, Craig? Blind jumping a fella?" he rasped.

"Get 'im on 'is feet," came the barked order.

Hands grasped Jim's arms, wrested him to a standing position, and held him fast. His vision sharpened, and the shadows took on the shape of flesh-and-blood men.

The surrounding outlaws watched silently, keen anticipation on their faces.

Jim straightened through sheer willpower and squared his shoulders. Unflinchingly, he returned Craig Newley's glare. It struck him then that he was lucky Newley had found him and not Darcy.

Craig's mouth twisted into a parody of a smile. "Edward, 'and me your stock whip." He thrust his arm out to the side.

His brother laid the handle in Craig's open hand. He flexed his wrist. The long, thin piece of leather coiled across the dusty earth like a serpent.

"I've been waiting a long time to get even with you, Burleson. And I'm going to enjoy every bit of it. You're not boss 'ere. And nothing's going to save you," Craig said.

"You'll never best me. You can beat me, but I'll always be better than you because you're a coward." A muscle flicked in Jim's jaw. "You're hiding behind your mates. Aren't you man enough for a straight-out fight?" His mouth thinned with a cynical twist.

Craig's face convulsed with rage. He struck Jim across the cheek with the whip handle. The blow broke the skin and left a thin trail of blood.

"You'll have to do better than that," came Jim's softly spoken taunt.

"Strip 'is shirt and tie 'im to that tree," Craig commanded.

Jim was jerked sideways and prodded with a rifle in the small of his back toward a large gum. As his shirt was ripped from him, he looked past the bushranger in front of him at the tree that would serve as a whipping post. Involuntarily, Jim shuddered. He'd seen a man die by the whip. It was a slow, living death. If the whip didn't kill you, the sun would. He was forced to embrace the tree trunk when his arms were pulled taut with ropes securing him.

Out of the corner of his eye, Jim saw Craig Newley smacking the whip handle against his palm.

Sweat drenched Jim as the sun rode higher in the sky. His skin crawled as his muscles tightened, and perspiration stung his eyes.

He flinched when Craig spoke in his ear. "You're going to beg for a quick death before I'm through with you."

Jim met the gaze of one of the bushrangers. Warned by the sudden stillness and the man's shifting eyes, Jim clamped his jaws together as he heard the whistling sound of the whip before the leather bit into the skin of his bare shoulders.

The pain was agonizing. Liquid fire spread over his cringing flesh. Before Jim could catch his breath, the biting whip slashed downward again.

His body shuddered. "You son of a bitch," he muttered.

His antagonist heard Jim's choked words and laughed. "Can't take the pain, Burleson?"

Dogged determination, and pride, consumed Jim, obliterating all else. He gritted his teeth and closed his eyes. Splinters embedded themselves in his face and chest as he ground into the tree trunk. Concentrate. The thought pounded inside his head and blurred the nauseating crack of the whip each time it cut him. No one present knew how long Jim Burleson would survive under the merciless onslaught.

Jim was beyond coherent thinking. His body sagged against the tree, supported only by his bound arms. There was a roaring in his ears, and his pulse sent vibrations of pain through his entire frame.

He longed for a peaceful balm for his soul. He fixed his dulling mind on his favorite swimming place, the one where he had taken Darcy. Unconsciousness descended upon him like a thick gray fog.

Finally Craig Newley stopped. He smiled as he viewed his handiwork. Burleson's back was a mass of blood and welts.

"Cut 'im down."

Jim's body slid down the tree trunk and crumpled to the ground.

"We're even now, Burleson. Of course, I'm ahead if you die." Craig laughed shortly. Tossing the stock whip to his brother, he walked to his horse. "I won't be needing that anymore."

"You damned near killed 'im."

"What do you care?" Craig fired in return.

"What you do is your business, but that doesn't mean I've got to like it. That's a cruel thing to do to a man. I don't reckon I know you anymore."

"Shut up and get on your 'orse before someone from Kopperella comes looking for 'im." Craig swung into his saddle and rode his mount near Jim's twisted form.

He cocked his head to the side and spat on his victim's back. "You'll think twice before crossing me again, *mate*." He laughed once more and spurred his horse into a fast run toward the rose-colored plain.

It was Tom Rivers who found Jim. The drover had been in the paddock when Jim's gelding galloped in, and Tom knew right away that it spelled trouble. The frightened animal led him to where his boss lay motionless and bleeding.

Kneeling beside him, Tom swallowed once and grimaced as he took in the fallen man's back. He held his hand to Jim's nose, feeling the faint breath. The boss was lucky to be alive. But Tom didn't know how much longer he would be.

He took him back to Kopperella. Darcy was in

her room when Tom clambered up the steps with Jim on his back. Her ride had calmed her down somewhat, though she'd been surprised to find Jim gone when she returned.

Now she leaped up from her chair and gasped as she saw the two men, all her anger and resentment forgotten.

She tried to keep her voice calm. "Good Lord, what happened?"

"Don't know," Tom said grimly. "This is how I found him." He laid Jim on the examining table as gently as he could while Darcy hurriedly gathered clean linen bandages, ointment, a small bottle of morphine, and a syringe.

For a betraying moment, she could only stare at the bloody mass that had once been Jim's back. Sweet Jesus! Who had done this to him? No human deserved such treatment. Man could be the cruelest animal on earth. Choking back tears, Darcy strengthened her resolve.

"If you don't mind, Tom, I'd rather be alone with him for now," she managed at last.

Rivers' grave regard shifted from his boss to her, then returned to his boss. He nodded, jammed his hat atop his head, and left, the door echoing his departure.

It was only after she'd tended Jim's wounds that Darcy McCall surrendered to tears.

Craig Newley felt a building sense of anger. Somewhere in the twisting corridors of his mind he remembered Burleson's words.

So 'e fancies 'imself above me. Well, I'll show 'im, Craig thought. I'll 'urt 'im where it pains 'im the most. A pain the likes of which 'e'll never get over.

Craig tensed in the saddle and rotated his still aching shoulder and arm. He had never known such satisfaction as that of bringing Jim Burleson to his knees. To inflict pain on others gave Craig a sense of power.

But then his thoughts took another turn. Although hurt, Burleson wouldn't let it keep him down for long. And when Kopperella's foreman was on his feet again, he would come looking for Craig. As far as Craig was concerned, it was all the more reason to finish settling the score as soon as possible.

"Jim? Can you hear me?"

His consciousness pursued that sweet voice like a ship following a beacon of light into a port. The command to open his eyes cut through the swirling fog in his brain. His blurring vision cleared and he saw Darcy. He tried to keep his eyes open, but he couldn't. He surrendered to the velvet darkness.

His next remembrance held more substance. Something thick and cool was being spread across the ripped flesh and quivering muscles of his back. His eyelashes fluttered open, and once more he saw Darcy. Seeing her angelic face was almost medicine enough.

She gently pushed aside a lock of hair that had fallen across his forehead. "You're going to be all right. It's just going to take time."

"I'm not going anywhere." His croaked response rose barely above a whisper.

"Don't talk. You need to save your strength," Darcy advised in a gently soothing tone. "I'm going to give you something for the pain."

Jim felt the brief sting where the needle penetrated his arm.

Darcy's voice rippled across his mind like shimmering heat waves. "You'll sleep now."

He did.

A distant sound woke Jim. His gaze moved across the room to the window. Against the window frame, a loose shutter banged methodically in the wind.

His gaze drifted farther to the left, then found and settled upon Darcy sitting near the fireplace in a silent vigil. She was rocking slowly. Her eyes were closed, and her head rested against the carved wooden back.

The rocking stopped and she passed a weary hand across her brow, then massaged her neck. Her hair hung untidily about her face, and her dress was rumpled. It seemed as if she had slept in that chair. But for how long? He had no conception of time.

He noticed that she held his hat in her hand. She set it in her lap and lingeringly, almost lovingly, traced the crown with a fingertip. She then hugged it next to her heart and rested her chin on her chest.

Darcy must have sensed his regard, because she raised her head and looked toward the bed.

She blinked several times. "I didn't know you were awake," she said in a breathy voice.

Jim realized she had been crying.

She rose and walked to the edge of the bed. "How do you feel?"

He moved slightly and a thousand needles plunged into his back. "I've felt better," he said in a tight voice, swallowing a gasp.

"I wish there were something more I could do to ease your pain."

"All you have to do is tell me you love me, that you don't believe I sent that letter." He attempted a smile. His effort looked more like a grimace.

Darcy studied him silently, then sighed and asked, "Who did this to you?"

Jim didn't want to recall that dark memory until he was strong enough to deal with it. But he couldn't help it. He looked into her eyes. "The same person who's been trying to cause trouble between us. The same person who sent that letter. Newley."

She was too astonished to speak.

"I'll take care of him soon enough," he rasped. "But what's important now is that you believe me."

"How can I?" she cried. Her heart was full of both sympathy for the suffering man before her, and pain.

"By listening to your heart. It'll tell you that I'm speaking the truth."

"You don't know how much I want to believe you. How much I need to believe you. There's nothing I want more."

"If you ever really loved me, you wouldn't give up so easily. You've always been a fighter." His voice strained with emotion. The effect was costing him, but he had to go on. "Don't quit now. Fight for us."

"You make it sound so simple."

"Nothing's been simple since the day I laid eyes on you," he half groaned, half growled.

Darcy became lost in the leaping firelight reflected in his eyes. And in that moment it was as if she had gazed into a crystal ball and had seen the truth of his words.

"Maybe I'm a fool, but I love you more than anything on this earth or in heaven. God help me," she whispered. And then she was kneeling by his side, holding his hand to her cheek and lips.

Chapter 20

During his recovery, Jim and Darcy grew close. She didn't care about their past conflicts or her earlier doubts. She only knew the present and the depth of emotion that she felt for Jim.

Jim, on the other hand, hadn't thought it possible to fall more deeply in love with Darcy, but he had.

"Do you know how beautiful you are?" he asked her one day about a week later as they sat outside on the veranda of Darcy's house.

"Only how beautiful you make me feel," she returned.

Jim smiled at her in a way that took her breath away. Warm and intimate. And knowing.

She noticed the dark smudges of fatigue beneath his eyes. "Why don't you go and lie down for a while?"

"I reckon I will." He stood and came over to her. Leaning down, he tucked a loose strand of hair behind her ear. Softly, he traced her jaw with a fingertip. "I've got to build up my strength for other things."

He kissed her tenderly, then went inside.

Alone, Darcy tried to read a book of poems, but the words kept blurring as her mind drifted to thoughts of marriage. Marriage was never far from her mind these days. Just thinking about it caused a delicious warmth, born of anticipation, to spread through her.

Her quiet time was interrupted when Tom Rivers came up the path, a piece of paper in one hand.

He stepped onto the porch. "Dr. McCall, one of the drovers said a rider gave him this. You're to read it straightaway."

Frowning, Darcy took the message and quickly scanned its contents. Her face drained of color. "It's from Joseph Miller. He says that Mary's been taken ill suddenly. He wants me to come as soon as I can." She stood on trembling legs. "I've got to go. Mary needs me."

She halted at the door at the sound of Tom's voice. "What about the boss? Should I get 'im?"

"No. I don't want to worry him. He needs his rest."

She disappeared into the shadowed interior. Shortly, she reappeared with her medical bag in hand.

Darcy met Tom at the gate, where he waited for her with two saddled horses.

"What do you think you're doing?" she asked.

"I'm going, too. I couldn't rest if I was to let you go to Manalee by yourself. Not after what 'appened when you come back the first time alone."

"Really, it's fine. I don't want to take you away from Kopperella."

"I don't reckon you've got time to argue with me."

She laid a hand on his arm. "I'm glad to have the company."

Hours later, Darcy and Tom were traveling across the land bordering Manalee.

Removing his hat to squint at the sun, Tom smiled at Darcy, his teeth revealed through his gray beard. "Not much further now. I reckon we'll make the Millers by nightfall."

Darcy felt her stomach tighten with dread. "I wish Joseph would have said what was the matter with Mary. I keep imagining all sorts of things."

"I'm not worried. You'll fix 'er up right as rain."

Darcy passed a weary hand across her face. "I didn't think I'd ever hear myself saying this, but I sometimes believe you place too much trust in me."

Tom winked. "The way I see it, it's just the right bit."

"I appreciate your friendship."

"You earned it."

"It took a while, didn't it?" Darcy asked.

"Yeah. But you came around."

Darcy sighed. "Why are men so distrustful of women?"

"They're not, unless women are doing a man's work."

"But why does it have to be that way?

Women are just as capable as men in a lot of areas."

"It's 'ard to teach a man new thinking. Out 'ere in the Outback, the men 'ave always done everything. Women only take care of us."

"That's all I'm trying to do."

"You know what I mean. Doing cooking, 'ousework, and the like."

"I hope that it won't be too long before men look on women as partners instead of servants. I hope there will be more women doctors."

Tom laughed. " 'Eaven 'elp us if there're too many more like you. But I reckon God made only one of you."

"So Jim says."

They had no further time for conversation, for at that moment the report of a pistol split the air. Then someone yelled, "Stop where you are, or the next shot won't be in the air."

Relaxed as they had been and not on guard, Darcy and Tom were taken by surprise. The bushrangers quickly encircled them. Menaced by rifles and pistols, Darcy and Tom halted in their tracks.

Tom studied the outlaws. He was no coward, but he couldn't act without endangering Darcy. Bitter anger and frustration filled him. He had volunteered to accompany Darcy, but instead of seeing her safely to Manalee, he had allowed them to fall into a trap.

To Darcy, the images before her seemed unreal. She prayed this was some horrible nightmare. But they were all too real. Her hopes were crushed when she saw the desperation in the outlaws' faces. What did they want? And worse—what would they do?

Shame-faced at being caught off guard, Tom, tight-lipped, slowly complied with an order to throw down his gun and knife and raise his hands. His hesitation to obey earned him a clubbing with a rifle butt. The blow laid open a bleeding cut on his cheekbone.

Senseless cruelty always angered Darcy. "We have nothing of value. You're wasting your time." Her gaze sliced over the outlaws.

"I never waste my time," came a single response.

Her eyes targeted the man who'd spoken. She heard him laugh, and somehow that sound was familiar.

One of the bushrangers dismounted, seized Darcy's waist, and dragged her from the saddle. Strong fingers twisted in her hair and yanked her backward against the outlaw's chest.

"You'd best keep still," he ordered.

But she wouldn't—couldn't. The danger of the situation clouded her judgment, and she reacted from fear, from the instinct to survive. She struggled furiously against him until his hold upon her hair tightened. The pain racing across her scalp forced her to stop. He shoved her away from him and twisted her arms, forcing her to kneel in the dust. Her chest rose and fell rapidly with pain and defiance.

Suddenly a pistol belched deathly fire and smoke. Tom clutched his chest and fell to the ground.

Darcy struggled to rise and go to him, her

eyes widening with horror at the sight of the gaping hole in his breast.

"No!" she whispered, and then her voice rose to a torment shout. "Tom! Oh, God, no."

The man who held the smoking pistol crowed his satisfaction—an ugly, taunting sound.

Darcy raised her eyes from Tom's body to meet the triumphant, demented gaze of Craig Newley.

Her heart stopped beating for a second, then thudded against her rib cage. Her face twisted with hatred. Never had she know such loathing for another human being as she did for Craig Newley.

He laughed again—this time at her. "Surprised to see me?"

She wanted to spit in his face, yet she refrained. Instead, she spat the word "Bastard."

"I always figured you were no lady." He coolly winked at her. "You can show me just 'ow much you're not one later. You're coming with me."

"I won't go ... I'll fight ... you murdering coward." Darcy was almost incoherent with anger, agitation, and pain.

Craig motioned for the man holding Darcy to move away. He reached down and yanked her to her feet, crushing her to him. His foul breath sickened her, and her stomach rumbled in protest. She thought she was going to vomit on the spot. She had to get away from him and struggled against him.

"I reckon I'm going to enjoy this more than I

'ad thought. It might even take me a while to grow tired of you."

Craig released her and Darcy stumbled back a step. For a split second, her eyes wavered to her dear friend's body lying on the ground. She silently mourned his senseless death.

Craig shoved her toward his horse.

Darcy shot him a disbelieving look over her shoulder. "Aren't you going to bury him?"

"The dingoes can 'ave 'im."

Keeping a grip on her hair, he mounted his horse first, then effortlessly pulled her up onto the animal's rump.

Survive! The word raced along her nerve endings. The thought helped to compose her. She must remain calm in order to think clearly. She'd need her wits about her if she was to escape this madman.

The band of outlaws rode to their camp deep in the Outback.

Once there, Craig took Darcy inside a hut and shoved her down on a rickety cot. He ignored her long enough to start a fire in the fireplace.

Darcy was terrified, but she told herself that she couldn't let Craig Newley know it. She had to be brave. An animal like him must never be allowed to think he had the upper hand. Over and over she told her screaming brain to stop her body from trembling, to make her eyes glare with anger—not fear.

Craig moved away from the fire and squatted beside the cot. His leer was one of satisfaction. "It didn't take much to get you to come out from your hiding place at Kopperella."

Realizing dawned on Darcy. "There never was any message from Joseph Miller. That was you."

"Seems like my plan fooled even Jim Burleson, or 'e'd never 'ave let you leave."

"Don't think you can get away with this. Jim will come looking for me."

"Maybe. But that'll take time. And it won't do you any good."

He reached out and grabbed her left breast.

"Get your hands off me."

"You're not one to give orders." He squeezed her flesh punishingly.

Shamed and degraded, Darcy struggled to escape his grasp.

"If you don't stop fighting me, it'll go the worse for you."

She bit her lip and forced herself to be still. Her eyes delivered a message of undisguised hate and loathing.

"Glad you listened to reason. Isn't that better?" He kneaded the breast. "And it's going to get even better. I've got plans for you."

"The same as you had for Tom Rivers?" She paused long enough to draw a supportive breath. "Only a filthy animal could kill a good man like that. You'll pay for what you've done."

Craig's face turned a mottled shade of red. He sprang forward to twist the fingers of one hand into her hair, yanked her head back painfully as his other hand ripped her bodice, sending buttons flying, and tearing open her chemise.

He gasped his appreciation as the perfectly formed mounds of flesh were bared to his lewd gaze. His fingers closed around one coral nipple, and holding it between grimy nails, he caused it to harden.

"I reckon that means you're wanting it, too."

Darcy felt her skin crawl from revulsion and humiliation at his vulgar touch.

His hands on her shoulders, Craig forced Darcy to lie down on the cot's edge. He bent his head and fastened his wet, greedy lips around the nipple.

But Darcy was ready for him. Acting quickly, she sank her teeth into his ear and locked her jaw much like a dog with a bone.

"Goddamn you, bitch!" He jerked his head up, swinging his hand at the same time to strike her across her face. The force of the blow broke her grip and she fell to the floor.

Lying stunned at his feet, she shook her head to clear her reeling senses.

He was up on his feet, blood trickling from his ear. "I'm going to teach you a lesson you won't forget. I reckon to ride you like I do any other bucking horse by putting my spurs to you. You won't be able to throw me off."

He knelt and wrenched her legs apart, fumbling with his pants.

Summoning her strength, Darcy lashed out with her heel, landing a solid blow squarely on his groin. Howling in pain, Craig grabbed himself and rolled to the side, away from Darcy.

Wasting not a precious moment, she leaped to her feet and raced for the door. It didn't matter that she had no plan for escape, or that she wouldn't make it past the outlaws outside. All she knew was the driving desperation to flee Craig Newley.

"Bitch!" Craig moaned. "I'll get you."

He caught her by the shoulders and whirled her around to face him. Snarling, he struck her a second time across the face, then threw her to the floor. His oppressive body weight kept her there, and it seemed his hands were everywhere—groping, pinching, punishing. Every inch of her skin felt on fire from revulsion and pain.

She prayed for God to be merciful. Take my soul, Lord, her mind desperately cried. Every fiber of her being concentrated on the urgent entreaty to her Maker. There was no one to save her.

She squeezed her eyes shut and swallowed convulsively while she lay beneath Newley as his hands swarmed over her like angry wasps.

Suddenly she went still when the cold steel of a knife blade was pressed to her throat.

"Stop, bitch, or I'm going to slit you open like a bleedin' pig."

The breath caught in her throat as she felt the razor-sharp knife press harder against her throat.

Her nerves screamed in anticipation. Seconds stretched into eternity.

At last she heard his voice. "That's better."

Newley stood and jerked Darcy to her feet. She grimaced as his fingers tightened around her upper arm. With his free hand, he felt the silky texture of her hair by rubbing a strand between his thumb and forefinger. He released the velvet skein and it fell softly across her shoulder, curling at her waist.

He smiled, the lines around his eyes deepening, but Darcy knew it boded ill for her. However, instead of cowering before him, she cocked her chin and regarded him with a display of composure she little felt. If she was going to be raped and killed, she would maintain her pride to the end. She refused to beg for either her life or her virtue.

Meanwhile, Newley scrutinized his captive. Her manner rankled him. Others would have groveled at his feet and pleaded for mercy. But not this woman.

His lip curled back in a feral growl. He would teach her fear. He reached for her.

Out of the stillness came an authoritative voice. "You're not going to do to 'er what you did to Nettie." Edward Newley leveled a steady look at his brother. "You're to leave 'er alone."

"And who's to make me?"

"I am." His words brooked no challenge.

The two brothers regarded each other beneath hooded stares.

"I 'ave as much right 'ere as you do."

"That's where you're wrong, little brother. I'm in charge 'ere. And don't you forget it."

Craig grimaced when he stood. "For now. But when I get ready to 'ave 'er, Edward, nothing will stop me. Not even you," he spat, then staggered out of the shack.

Breathing heavily, Darcy faced Edward, wary and on guard, not knowing what to expect from this man.

His shuttered green eyes slid to her exposed breasts. Immediately, Darcy crossed her arms against her chest to cover herself.

"You've got no worries from me. I don't 'ave a taste for women who aren't willing." With that, he pivoted and left.

Darcy leaned against the wall near the door. Her knees buckled and she slowly slid down the wall to the floor to console herself.

Chapter 21

That evening, Darcy sat in front of the fireplace. The crackling of the flames matched her own nervous tension.

Since late that afternoon, the bushrangers had come and gone, staying long enough to talk, then disappearing again. They were planning something. Darcy felt it in her bones.

At that moment, Craig and Edward Newley entered, followed by a third man. As all three crossed the room, they glared her way. Outwardly, she coolly returned their looks. Inwardly, she seethed with anger.

They sat at the table at the opposite side of the room, away from the fireplace, seemingly dismissing her. Relieved, Darcy released the pent-up air in her lungs.

Soon they were engaged in earnest conversation, keeping their voices low. Darcy was glad she couldn't hear them. She didn't want to know what terrible things they planned.

Short minutes later, the third bushranger rose from the table. Craig accompanied him outside. Voices filtered through the closed door, but the words were unintelligible. Soon Craig reentered and sat back down at the table with Edward. Another conversation began. Although she couldn't make out what they said, Darcy caught a note of dissension and disapproval in Edward's voice. That meant that whatever plans were being laid were masterminded by Craig. Her stomach dropped with a sick feeling.

The two men lapsed into silence. Only the crackling of the fire was heard.

Thundering hooves echoed across the hard-packed earth, followed by a spate of heated curses.

Edward and Craig leaped from their seats and rushed outside. Curiosity caused Darcy to follow safely behind.

From the porch, she observed the chaos around her. Hope of rescue flared within her.

Three riders, bathed in brilliant moonlight, barreled into camp. When she realized that they weren't from Kopperella, her heart sank.

Two rode abreast. A third trailed behind. The third man was slumped in his saddle, one leg dangling from the stirrup. A large spot darkened his light-colored pants. Blood.

Before she could ponder the situation further, Craig Newley grabbed her arm

"Get inside. Charlie's shot. You've got to help him." His eyes were wide, angry. "Three of our gang are dead. And we're not losing another." He gave her a hard shove through the door.

She stumbled on the hem of her dirty, torn dress, but caught the back of a chair and steadied herself.

Two men, one supporting the wounded man beneath his armpits, the other carrying his legs, brought Charlie inside.

"Get 'im on the table," Craig ordered. "Go fetch the doctor's bag," he shouted to another beyond the door.

The two outlaws followed instructions and placed Charlie's limp form on the table.

Darcy whirled on Craig. "What makes you think I'm going to help?"

"You're a doctor. Aren't you sworn to?" he said with a sneer. "And because I've killed before. One more time isn't going to worry me none."

A man thrust her bag at her.

"My mate's bleeding to death like a stuck boar while you stand there and gawk. Get busy." Craig prodded Darcy from behind.

Charlie cried out in agony, and Edward Newley lifted a cup of rum to his lips. The wounded man gulped, coughed, then dropped his head back. His eyes closed. For the moment, his misery abated.

"You'd best make sure that 'e comes out of this, or you're going to be dead alongside 'im," Craig growled near her ear.

"Bring me that smaller table and place it beside me here, near this man's head."

Her instructions were carried out without delay. Darcy set her bag atop the table and opened it. She withdrew a pair of sharp scissors.

Bending over her patient, she cut away his pant leg with deft, practiced movements, tossing the blood-soaked cloth aside. She rolled up her sleeves and washed her hands. Carefully, she probed the wound. She found that the bullet was lodged in the man's kneecap. The joint had been splintered. With grim certainty, Darcy knew the man would have to lose his leg if he wanted a fighting chance of survival.

"Can you save 'im?" asked an anxious Edward Newley.

"Not without removing his leg," she answered quietly. "There's been too much blood loss, and his kneecap is shattered."

A hush fell over the other outlaws. They seemed frozen to the spot where they stood, their gazes locked on Darcy.

"You saying you're going to take 'is leg off?" Craig ground out the words.

"That's exactly what I'm saying. There's no other choice. Not if you want him to live. A man alive, even if he's only got one leg, is better than a dead one," Darcy said matter-of-factly.

Edward looked down at his wounded partner. He swallowed. "Just do what's got to be done."

In the meantime, Craig picked up a bottle of rum and lifted it to his lips, liquor dribbling down his chest. "You 'eard my brother. You're wasting time."

"Have any of you men ever seen this kind of operation before?" Darcy inquired.

They all shook their heads, their faces a chalky color.

"I must warn you, it's not pretty. You're going to have to hold him down. I don't have anything for the pain. You'll have to give him some of that liquor."

Edward lifted Charlie's head and trickled rum down his throat.

"I need that pot of boiling water on the fire, and bring me that pan from over there," Darcy said, pointing to a washbasin.

She arranged her instruments in the basin and poured scalding water over them to disinfect them.

"You sure this is the only way?" Edward asked.

Darcy spoke with bleak finality. "Yes."

Edward nodded for her to begin the operation.

"I'll need some more light. It's too dark in here," she said.

A rope suspended a lantern above Darcy's head. The light cast monstrous, deformed shadows across the walls.

For the briefest of moments, Darcy stared at the unconscious man. The pain would be excruciating, but she could do nothing. She had no chloroform with her. Sympathetically, she laid a cool hand on Charlie's fevered brow.

Darcy then set about her somber task. She placed a tourniquet on his thigh to prevent hemorrhaging. She paused so the tourniquet could dull the nerves. Her fingers closed around the handle of her scalpel, situated atop her makeshift tray.

Craig's hand snaked around hers. The basin of instruments rattled ominously. "Just don't try anything. I'll be watching your every move. Understand?"

Through gritted teeth, Darcy replied, "He's

going to die before I have a chance to operate it you don't let go of my hand."

She had never performed an amputation before without anesthesia, and she prayed this would be her last. As she began, Charlie's body twitched violently and he howled in agony. His eyes snapped open in painful horror.

"Whatever happens, don't let go," Darcy cautioned the men holding their comrade down.

Charlie must have sensed her intent, because he screamed, "No! No! I can't stand the pain. Don't cut. Don't cut!"

His agonized cries swept over her. She paused for a moment, then proceeded.

Later, exhausted and feeling shaky, Darcy asked Edward Newley if she could lie down. He assured her that she wouldn't be bothered. Somehow, she believed him. She had seen the respect in his eyes for the job she had done.

After she had rested, Darcy checked on her patient. She was satisfied that, with proper treatment and rest, he had a good chance of pulling through—if he wasn't moved. She'd done all she could. It was up to heavenly hands now.

As the sun peeked above the horizon, Darcy sat up and peered across the room at Craig Newley's prone form. She had waited, holding her breath, until she had decided he was asleep.

After an interminably long time, she rose. She hit a chair with her elbow. She froze, waiting to hear something. He didn't rouse.

With her shoes in one hand, Darcy padded

barefoot to the cot where he slept on his back. She stared down at him. His features were dampened with perspiration and twisted with pain as he drew one labored, raspy breath after another. He had a fever. Darcy shuddered.

She reached out slowly for the pistol beside the wadded blanket serving as his pillow. Her fingers grazed the gun, feeling the ridges of the cartridge chamber, the sharp, crooked hammer, the butt, the barrel. She shivered. Go slowly, she warned herself. Be patient.

The fire had longed ago died out and the air in the hut had grown chilly. Her muscles cramped as she kept her hand extended, waiting for him to move his head so she could grab his gun. She longed desperately to stretch her aching, burning limb, but she didn't dare.

Darcy recoiled in fear when Craig coughed and rolled onto his side, away from the gun. Now was her chance. She'd grab the pistol and run. She'd shoot any man who tried to follow.

Wrapping her fingers around the smooth wooden butt, she picked up the weapon. It was heavy. She nearly dropped it, and had to clasp it with both hands, the metal barrel cold against her skin. She was almost giddy with relief.

Newley's chest rattled when he coughed, trying to clear the building fluid in his lungs. However, even sick, he was a formidable foe, and she cautioned herself not to grow careless now. She shuddered at the thought of getting caught. Patience. Have patience.

With the gun in one hand and her shoes in the other, Darcy poised for flight. Her eyes never left Craig Newley. Soundlessly, she inched toward the door.

She reached it and straightened. Turning toward the door, Darcy sighed with relief. Suddenly her wrist was seized in a bone-crushing grip from behind, and she was shoved against the wall.

With one forearm pressed against her windpipe, Newley wrested the gun from her. "Where do you think you're off to?"

Darcy gasped, unable to breathe from the pressure on her throat. She clawed at his arm.

Newley's eyes were unnaturally bright. "Don't worry, I'm not going to kill you. Not for a while anyway." He retreated.

Darcy stepped forward and away from the wall.

Suddenly Craig trembled violently and vomited. He pitched forward, knocking her back into the wall. She staggered beneath his weight. His chin hit her shoulder, and he feebly tried to right himself. He dropped to the floor in a heap, pulling Darcy down with him. She struggled to get out from beneath him.

Darcy then knelt beside him and felt his forehead. He was burning up with fever.

At that moment she heard the sound of approaching horses. Edward Newley and his outlaws had returned. With their arrival, any hope of escape vanished.

Edward entered the shack. He paused inside the doorway and looked at his brother's crumpled body. His accusing gaze swung to Darcy.

"I haven't done anything to him. He's sick," she said.

Edward's eyes widened. "Fever? 'E'll give it to the rest of us if nothing's done."

"And whose fault is that? He wouldn't let me have my medical bag, thinking I'd use my instruments as weapons against him."

Edward had no reply.

"Help me get him to the bed. He can't stay on this cold floor."

Edward held his ground. "Look, I want you to take 'im with you. I'll send a man with you as far as Kopperella."

"You'd send your own brother away, knowing he was ill?"

"I can't 'ave 'im 'ere. 'E'll be the death of us if 'e stays. You've got to take 'im with you. I'm letting you go. Besides, I saved you. I reckon that ought to be worth something to you."

Darcy paused, and shuddered when she considered what her fate could have been. Edward was right. He had saved her.

As much as she hated him, Craig Newley was a human being, and she couldn't just let him die. Yet, equally important, she wasn't going to allow freedom to slip through her fingers.

"All right. But we've got to hurry."

Edward turned his head and bellowed over his shoulder. "Jake, get in 'ere."

Jim stirred from his sleep and a twinge of pain flared across his back as he sat up on the edge of the bed.

Kim Loo appeared in the doorway. "Boss?"

"What is it?"

The cook came to stand in front of Jim. He saw how strained and weary Kim Loo's face looked.

"Missy get message. Tom Rivers go with her to Manalee. But I worry. Something wrong." He pointed to his stomach. "Inside, I know this."

Jim swore. Kim Loo had the uncanny ability at times to know things before they happened. Now was not the time for him to start doubting the Chinaman's abilities. "How long have they been gone?"

"Since yesterday."

"Damn. How is it possible I've slept so long? She must have given me something and I didn't know it." Jim's gaze swung to the front room. "Go fetch me some bandages and a roll of gauze."

Kim Loo brought the requested items from Darcy's supply cupboard, but he looked skeptical. "What you do, boss?"

"First, it's what you're going to do. You're going to wrap my back with a thick layer of bandages. I've got to be able to ride without the skin on my back breaking open."

Kim Loo paled. "Boss—"

"I give the orders here. Just get on with it."

Jim raised his arms and Kim Loo began to wrap his back.

When Kim Loo had finished, Jim gave him another order. "Have my horse brought out front."

Jim then slowly dressed himself.

Determined, grim with pain, he mounted his horse and set out to find Darcy.

The man Edward Newley had sent with them had deposited Darcy and Craig near the boundary of Kopperella. Then he'd turned his horse and ridden away, leaving the two of them to proceed as best they could through the heat of the day.

Darcy was past feeling and thinking by this point, concentrating only on getting her charge to safety—not to mention herself. Occasionally she looked back at Newley, who was slumped forward in his saddle. She knew he was very ill indeed, but lacking the ability to make a complete examination of him, she could only guess about his ailment. When she got him back to the station, she'd attend to him more thoroughly, she told herself.

She heard him groan and checked him again. Suddenly he swayed in the saddle, clinging to the wiry mane of his horse before sliding to the ground. His legs buckled beneath him and he dropped to a sitting position. A breeze blew across him and licked at his hot, moist skin. Violent tremors seized him, rattling his whole frame.

Darcy dismounted and grabbed the water bottle that hung from her saddle, took it over to Newley, and held the back of his head so he could drink. She hated to touch him. But then she reminded herself sternly that she was a doctor who'd taken the Hippocratic oath. It was her duty to tend those who needed it—be they friend or foe.

For a minute it looked as if the drink would revive Newley. But when he tried to get up, he collapsed again. Darcy could see now that it was no use going on. She almost screamed her frustration. How she'd have loved to get on her horse and ride away from the awful man. But she could not do it.

She looked around for some shelter from the sun and found a gum tree not too far away. Summoning up her last bit of strength, she dragged him over to it, positioned him as comfortably as possible, and bathed his face with a moistened handkerchief. After that she leaned back against the trunk. She intended to watch over her patient. She didn't want the dingoes to mistake them both for dead. But her struggles and travails during the last twenty-four hours had been so intense that she was exhausted, and before she knew it, she closed her eyes and slept.

Feeling desperate, Jim ignored his throbbing back, pushing his horse unmercifully. As he rode, disjointed thoughts assembled into words of prayer.

He had never felt the urge to pray until Darcy had become lost on her return from the Millers and had nearly perished in a sandstorm. A single word—*please*—had been all he could manage. Now was different. Now he'd come to believe that God wasn't short on performing miracles. He had led Jim to Darcy when anything short of a miracle wouldn't have saved her.

Desperately, Jim Burleson clung to that thought. God would lead him to Darcy again.

The sudden appearance of a pair of figures on the horizon drew his stomach into a knot.

Jim was afraid to hope, afraid to believe. His pulse raced as he drew near them. He found Darcy and her patient resting beneath the shade of a solitary tree.

Jim sawed on the bridle and caused his horse to slide to a halt on its hind legs. Instantly, he was off the animal and striding toward Darcy.

Wordlessly, he took in her torn and tied-together bodice, then gathered her into his arms and held her.

Against the top of her head, he murmured, "Darcy, Darcy. You don't know what hell I've been through since Kim Loo told me that you had left."

Jim broke contact and looked at her again, as if to reassure himself that she was indeed real, and in his arms again.

Darcy placed a hand over his chest. The frantic thumping of his heart invigorated her weary, aching body. Love swept through her veins and rejuvenated her lagging spirits.

She cradled his lean cheek in her palm, her eyes lit from within by an unearthly radiance. "Somehow I knew you'd find me," she said weakly. "It was the one thought that kept me going."

Jim's heart lurched with happiness and relief.

He lowered his head and kissed her urgently, checking his passion when she winced.

He drew away, his eyes promising more.

And soon.

Darcy's changed expression made him uneasy on some deep, intuitive level. "What is it? Where's Tom Rivers?"

Darcy looked at him. Fatigue etched his face, tinted his voice, and clouded the blue eyes trained expectantly on her. She didn't want to add to his burden.

"What happened?" he persisted.

Her immeasurable joy at seeing him wilted under his intense regard, and guilt overwhelmed her. Tears blurred her vision.

"Craig Newley sent a false message that I was needed at Manalee, that Mary was ill. Tom wouldn't let me go by myself." Her voice thickened with emotion. "We never knew the bushrangers were there until they jumped us. There was a fight and Tom was shot." She choked on the last word.

"It was Newley, wasn't it?"

"Does it matter? Does it help to know who his murderer is? Will it bring Tom back? Let it go. I'm tired of all the violence and killing."

"I can't let it go. I've got to know. You've got to tell me who it was." Each word rang with bitter fury.

Darcy looked behind her at Craig Newley's unconscious form, then back at Jim.

Finally Jim took in the fact that the crumpled body was none other than Craig Newley himself.

Menace outlined his facial lines and muscles. "Craig?" he asked in a savagely angry voice that sounded as if it were strangling in his throat.

Darcy's raw nerves throbbed, then simply snapped. It had all been too much. She leaned into Jim's chest and sobbed. His arms went around her, strong and comforting. He stroked her hair as gently as if she were a child.

She struggled to explain. "I ... He tried to rape me. ... He ..."

Jim cursed viciously, but he kept cradling her. "Hush now. Don't try to talk. You've been through too much."

"But he's sick. And they made me take care of him." Her words came out in a whisper of pain.

Jim carefully disentangled himself from her and went over to Newley. He leaned over and looked at him for a moment, then rose. He took off his hat and wiped the sweat from his brow. "Newley's past sick now, Darcy. He's dead."

"Darcy?"

She sat up in bed with a start and opened her eyes. Jim stood over her, his face gaunt in the early morning light.

"What's wrong?" she asked.

He shook his head. "Nothing. I just wanted to see how you were." He sat on the edge of the bed and rested his head in his hands in a weary gesture.

"I don't remember coming to bed. How'd I get here?"

"I carried you. You insisted you were all right when we got back here, even went to get something to eat. But then you fell asleep in the middle of dinner."

She sighed. "We're lucky to have each other."

"We're lucky to be alive."

Her throat worked and she lowered her eyes to hide the tears glistening there. "I shouldn't have bothered with Newley."

Jim caught her face in both hands and forced her to look at him. "Stop blaming yourself, Darcy. You're a doctor, remember? And doctors save lives; they don't disregard them."

"And Tom? What about him? Somehow I feel responsible for his death," Darcy replied, her lower lip quivering.

His mouth hovered near hers. "You're responsible for no one but yourself."

He kissed her softly, tenderly.

His kiss promised sweet, blessed forgetfulness in his arms.

Chapter 22

Darcy was humming as she went about straightening her house. Jim stood unnoticed inside the doorway, looking at her. Even with her hair tucked up, ends trailing down her neck and the sides of her face, with dust sprinkled on her cleaning clothes, Darcy was beautiful. And he loved her more than ever.

He crept up behind her and playfully swatted her bottom.

Gasping, she whirled and stuck a feather duster in his face.

"En garde," she squealed, making several playful swipes across his face and chest.

Jim reached out and grabbed the end of her apron, flicking it across her nose. "The same to you."

Infectious laughter rose and swelled to fill every nook and cranny of the house.

He took the feather duster from her hand and tossed it aside. "Enough."

Darcy leaned into him and gave him a peck on the cheek. "That's the first time you've told me enough. Usually you can't get enough."

He kissed her full on the mouth. "Hmm. You're usually right."

"Usually or always?" Darcy giggled in his ear, rubbing her cheek against his.

Jim placed her at arm's length. "Be serious for a moment."

"Why?"

"Because I have something for you," he said soberly, although his eyes danced with merriment.

Gaiety surged into Darcy's throat and escaped. "You do?" She felt like a child at Christmas, eagerly awaiting her treat.

Jim sat down in a chair and pulled her across his lap. He kissed her soundly on the mouth once more.

His smile was sunshine itself. "That's just to let you know how much I love you." He tapped the end of her upturned nose with his index finger. "Now I want you to close your eyes. No peeking, understand?"

She obeyed. She felt him drop a small box into her palm, and her fingers closed around it.

"You can look."

Her eyes snapped open in fascination. A carousel of colorful, delightful emotions turned inside her, her curiosity unbearable.

She wiggled in his lap, unable to stand the suspense any longer. "What is it?"

Jim looked very pleased with himself. "You'll just have to open it and find out, won't you?" he teased.

With trembling fingers, she did so. Nestled in the brown paper was a diamond ring.

Darcy was speechless, her throat closed with emotion. It was the loveliest thing she had ever seen, much less been given. It was a shining testament of Jim's love and devotion.

Sparkling tears competed in brilliance with the gem that Darcy held in her hand. "Oh, Jim. It's lovely."

"No lovelier than you."

"Where did you get it?"

"It was my mom's. I think she would have wanted you to have the ring. It was her dying wish that her wedding band not be buried with her, but rather, when I found my future bride, it was to be a gift to her."

Darcy was speechless. Her lips moved, but no sound came out.

"I reckon what I'm wanting to know is when do you want to get married, Yank?"

With a joyful cry, Darcy flung her arms around his neck and whispered against his mouth, "Soon! Very soon!" Instantly, she sobered. "But what about Kopperella? I've been dismissed, remember?"

"Then there's nothing for me to do except buy that section of land near Manalee that I've had my eye on. I reckon it's a good a place as any for a doctor's office. People could come from all over the district."

Darcy gave a small cry. "Oh, Jim. You're so good to me." She trailed tiny kisses across his lips, his cheek, his eyes, his forehead.

"Hey, slow down," he teased.

At that moment Darcy shifted her weight in his lap and set Jim off-balance, and the chair teetered backward. Giggling, they crashed to the floor, locked in each other's arms.

To Darcy, Jim was the soul of the Outback.

To Jim, Darcy was the heart that gave life to that soul.

Avon Romances—
the best in exceptional authors and unforgettable novels!

LORD OF MY HEART   Jo Beverley
76784-8/$4.50 US/$5.50 Can

BLUE MOON BAYOU   Katherine Compton
76412-1/$4.50 US/$5.50 Can

SILVER FLAME   Hannah Howell
76504-7/$4.50 US/$5.50 Can

TAMING KATE   Eugenia Riley
76475-X/$4.50 US/$5.50 Can

THE LION'S DAUGHTER   Loretta Chase
76647-7/$4.50 US/$5.50 Can

CAPTAIN OF MY HEART   Danelle Harmon
76676-0/$4.50 US/$5.50 Can

BELOVED INTRUDER   Joan Van Nuys
76476-8/$4.50 US/$5.50 Can

SURRENDER TO THE FURY   Cara Miles
76452-0/$4.50 US/$5.50 Can

Coming Soon

SCARLET KISSES   Patricia Camden
76825-9/$4.50 US/$5.50 Can

WILDSTAR   Nicole Jordan
76622-1/$4.50 US/$5.50 Can

America Loves Lindsey!

The Timeless Romances
of #1 Bestselling Author
Johanna Lindsey

Avon Romantic Treasures

*Unforgettable, enthralling love stories,
sparkling with passion and adventure
from Romance's bestselling authors*

ONLY IN YOUR ARMS *by Lisa Kleypas*
76150-5/$4.50 US/$5.50 Can

LADY LEGEND *by Deborah Camp*
76735-X/$4.50 US/$5.50 Can

RAINBOWS AND RAPTURE *by Rebecca Paisley*
76565-9/$4.50 US/$5.50 Can

AWAKEN MY FIRE *by Jennifer Horsman*
76701-5/$4.50 US/$5.50 Can

ONLY BY YOUR TOUCH *by Stella Cameron*
76606-X/$4.50 US/$5.50 Can

FIRE AT MIDNIGHT *by Barbara Dawson Smith*
76275-7/$4.50 US/$5.50 Can

ONLY WITH YOUR LOVE *by Lisa Kleypas*
76151-3/$4.50 US/$5.50 Can

MY WILD ROSE *by Deborah Camp*
76738-4/$4.50 US/$5.50 Can

1 Out Of 5 Women Can't Read.

1 Out Of 5 Women Can't Read.

1 Out Of 5 Women Can't Read.

1 Xvz Xv 5 Xwywv Xvy'z Xvyz.

1 Out Of 5 Women Can't Read.

*As painful as it is to believe, it's true. And it's
time we all did something to help. Coors has committed $40
million to fight illiteracy in America. We hope
you'll join our efforts by volunteering your time. Giving just a
few hours a week to your local literacy center can
help teach a woman to read. For more information on literacy
volunteering, call **1-800-626-4601**.*

LITERACY. PASS IT ON.

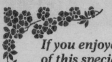

*If you enjoyed this book, take advantage
of this special offer. Subscribe now and . . .*

GET A *FREE*
HISTORICAL ROMANCE
—— NO OBLIGATION(a $3.95 value) ——

Each month the editors of True Value will select the four best historical romance novels from America's leading publishers. Preview them in your home Free for 10 days. And we'll send you a FREE book as our introductory gift. No obligation. If for any reason you decide not to keep them, just return them and owe nothing. But if you like them you'll pay *just* $3.50 each and save at least $.45 each off the cover price. (Your savings are a minimum of $1.80 a month.) There is no shipping and handling or other hidden charges. There are no minimum number of books to buy and you may cancel at any time.

send in the coupon below

Mail to:
True Value Home Subscription Services, Inc.
P.O. Box 5235
120 Brighton Road
Clifton, New Jersey 07015-1234

YES! I want to start previewing the very best historical romances being published today. Send me my FREE book along with the first month's selections. I understand that I may look them over FREE for 10 days. If I'm not absolutely delighted I may return them and owe nothing. Otherwise I will pay the low price of just $3.50 each; a total of $14.00 (at least a $15.80 value) and save at least $1.80. Then each month I will receive four brand new novels to preview as soon as they are published for the same low price. I can always return a shipment and I may cancel this subscription at any time with no obligation to buy even a single book. In any event the FREE book is mine to keep regardless.

Name _____

Address _____ Apt. _____

City _____ State _____ Zip _____

Signature _____
                (if under 18 parent or guardian must sign)
Terms and prices subject to change.